THE ROSE

The Rose

BRONWEN WRITE

Bronwen Write

For Emma, who puts up with me and continues to be the source of stability this flighty creature needs.

CONTENT WARNING

Please be aware, in this book you will find:

- Violence and some gore

- Mentions of domestic violence and abuse

- Mind control

- Mind control during sex

- Medium Heat Level, no graphic scenes

- Depictions of anxiety and depression

- Mentions of war and genocide

- Swearing

~ One ~

There was always a temptation for Kyra to lose herself in the gentle ticking of the clock marking the trailing seconds. Nestled in the soft leather of her chair, the mechanical march of time soothed her nerves. Eyes slipped closed in a moment of self-indulgent pleasure, she could almost forget she wasn't alone in the silence of her office.

A creak of wood, the whisper of fabric, pushed at the edge of her carefully distant thoughts. Frustration was quick on its heels, but Kyra ignored it. Opening her eyes slowly, she tilted her chin down to examine her prisoner through dark lashes. She had wanted to keep ignoring him and the dark directions he pulled her thoughts in.

He watched her warily. Thickly muscled arms rested against the wood of his chair, strong fingers wrapped around the edges to keep him anchored in reality.

"I won't tell you anything," he spat. "You won't get anything from me."

Kyra held her silence, lazily running a hand up her other arm. Long nails painted midnight black were a sharp contrast against the paleness of her skin. She watched the vivid blue of his eyes follow the movement, no doubt imagining how soft her flesh would be. Leading his gaze to her mouth, she tapped a finger against her lush lower lip. His own lips parted to suck air through clenched teeth, creating a faint whistle in the motionless air of the office.

"I can't be broken." The wood creaked again under his grip though he made no move to rise. Her fingers drew his gaze down and away from her mouth as they skimmed over her neck before dropping to play at her clavicle. "I won't betray them." His words were weakening with his resolve.

Pulling herself up by the arms of her imposing seat, Kyra ensured the curve of her body displayed every line in sharp relief. The dry click of his throat warmed her. She trailed her fingers along the cool mahogany of her desk, the calculated sashay of her hips drawing his focus. She was close enough to feel the heat of his lust now, to taste it.

"Do your worst, demon."

Kyra laughed. It was dark and sultry, tinged with a bitterness he wouldn't hear. Her fingers tightened briefly, nails digging into the soft flesh of her palms. The stab of pain was grounding, pulling her away from the flash of rage that threatened to distract her entirely.

"I was rather thinking..." Catching her bottom lip between perfect teeth, Kyra watched his eyes dart down as she leaned forward. "I'd do my best." Her breath whispered across the shell of his ear; the weight of promise carried in the warm, wet air. His hands spasmed against the chair, releasing the wood from his crushing grip.

Reaching out with magic that sung with the cloying tune of his lust, Kyra brushed his mind with a lover's touch. It burned under her skin, screaming to engulf him. A lick of power here to dull his panic, a brush of magic there to enhance his senses, a mental flick of her wrist, and his mind was clouded with her.

She steadied herself with one hand on the chair; the other rested lazily on his thigh to heat his flesh through the denim of his jeans. His chest heaved with each breath, near panting in his fight for control. Her fingers splayed until they brushed the inseam of his jeans. His hips jerked back, but that just wouldn't do.

Kyra ducked her head, mouth hovering over the racing pulse in his neck. She could feel the warmth of his blood and lust on her lips, barely contained under the fragile hold of skin. She drank in the intoxicating taste of desire.

With practiced ease, Kyra drew a deep breath that threatened to free her breasts from the precarious hold of her blouse. The sudden weight of his hands on her waist was a pleasant surprise, fingers tightened to a punishing grip.

Her lips brushed barely-there kisses up his neck, and his fingers spasmed against her flesh with every press of her mouth. Lust and magic filled his senses even as Kyra filled his vision. Their breath mingled in the space between them, heavy with the sickly-sweet taste of his hunger.

As though approaching a wild animal, Kyra lifted her arm slowly from his chair to rest on the corded muscles of his forearm. Focused entirely on him, the heat of skin under one hand and denim-clad flesh under the other, the smell of his skin and taste of his lust, Kyra played his senses expertly. Matching his breaths, she could almost feel his heart racing as his eyes locked with hers. There was panic in his gaze, but a push of magic and squeeze of his thigh drowned it in lust.

A strangled groan was all the warning Kyra had before her mouth was plundered, the Hunter pushing her back in his lunge forward. One hand remained on her hip, holding her close against the hard planes of his body and still against the edge of her desk. The other wrapped itself in her hair, tangling fingers in auburn waves not to cradle her skull but to force her at an angle that pleased him best.

His desire demanded she go limp, become pliant under the crashing waves of his need. Resting a hand on his arm, she kept it light, weak from his attentions. Lips tore away from her mouth, panting breaths hot on her skin. The hand in her hair tangled deeper, using the anchor to pull her head back sharply.

Teeth pressed against the skin of her neck. She arched her back against the pain, reading the movement in the dark recesses of his mind. Caught in the fog of passion, he didn't notice her clothes melt away. Instead, he busied himself with the fly of his pants, releasing Kyra's hair with a final tug that would no doubt result in a headache. While he was distracted by getting naked and the heat of her magic singing in his blood, she lifted her hands to press splayed against his cheeks. The tips of her fingers brushed his hairline, stretching to touch both temple and blocky jaw.

Air rushed from his lungs in a broken sound. His eyes glazed and hands fell away from half-open pants, his body knocked limp. Kyra lowered him awkwardly back into the chair, struggling to manoeuvre his dead weight. Huffing her own breath, the ticking of her clock was deafening in the sudden silence. The Hunter's lust continued to sing in her veins, the taste still thick on her tongue, but it was easier to ignore, locked in the back of her mind.

He was virile despite his age, the strength of his body matched by the strength of his will, of his mind. Kyra's magic, flowing steadily through the points of physical connection around his face, delved into his depths. Riding the waves of his blood, propelled by the hard thumping of his heart, it entered every crevice to taste him. Her magic gathered power, swirling along veins to pool in his centre.

Twin Hunters groaned, Kyra's magic fuelling his fantasy as he imagined spearing her. The sensations, the warmth of her skin, the smell of sex in the air, all rendered with painstaking detail. His thrusts were rough and primal, dragging her desk across the floor with a squeal barely heard over the sounds of flesh and moans he tore from her lips.

In reality, Kyra was settling back against her desk with clothes back in place and her hands cupping his face. The touches playing out between their minds were far from gentle. The sensations were muted, happening beyond her body, the barest hint of a near-forgotten memory. She closed her eyes against the memories of others, the taste of their lust, a parade of meals she'd rather forget.

Heat radiated from her mind, from her fingers, bathing him in fire. Animalistic moans faded into wounded whimpers with each wave of pleasure Kyra fed him. In the darkness of his mind, he took from her. In the non-reality she created for him, he ravaged her with punishing movements, bared teeth and bites that drew blood.

Every movement, every sensation, Kyra carefully crafted them all and wrapped him in them.

He reached the pinnacle of pleasure, and she pushed him further. Within the confines of his mind, trapped by Kyra's will, he shuddered through his release. She took him to the peak and held him at the edge before throwing him into the abyss.

Kyra wielded her magic nimbly, honing it into a blade designed to slice and carve his mind. First gently, the barest hint of sharpness, she pressed it to his edges and carved slivers of power from him. With inexorable pressure, she cut into him with his own pleasure. The scene between them didn't fade, didn't falter; he found himself unable to stop. His release wasn't the end, not even worth pausing for. Kyra's magic demanded more.

Whimpers turned back to moans, now edged in pain. Kyra watched his strong face, so wide and plain, twist and contort into a mask of torturous rapture. His body jerked feebly in the sturdy wooden chair, a weak shadow of the rage Kyra cultivated in his fantasy. Cutting deeper with a thought, he choked against the sensation.

His mouth fell open, wide and gasping. Breath rattled hollowly, trying to fill his lungs. Finally, too full of air to take in more, he let it out in a ringing scream.

Kyra's lips curled into a smile, her blood thrumming with the rush of power. His lust was drawn out with practiced ease. And she drank it in, wrapped it in her magic, shaped it to her needs, and fed it back to him. The anchor of her fingers on his face held the ever-growing loop of lust and pleasure, each cycle through their bodies stronger than the last.

Her nerves danced to the music of his pained pleasure, a hedonistic roiling that lit up every inch of her skin. The room felt bathed in red light, her head pounding with blood and concentration. Another press of the blade and his screams reached a crescendo. The Hunter in their minds bellowed. His body seized and muscles cramped with rapture beyond comprehension.

The Hunter in Kyra's office gave a similar sound, back bowed, every line of his body screaming in ecstasy and pain before falling silent.

Twisting her lips in disdain, Kyra pulled her fingers away from his face. There were no more thoughts to share, no more lust to taste, and no more desires to play with. She wiped her fingers on the cotton of his t-shirt, though the feeling of filth wouldn't be so easily removed. Her stomach clenched around nothing, the dead flow of magic demanding a meal she had refused to consume.

"I'm not just a demon," Kyra spoke into the quiet, unable to look at the corpse. Something too close to regret filled her. "I'm a succubus, older and more powerful than you could ever imagine. I am death to men like you."

~ Two ~

The body had cooled considerably in the time it took Kyra to calm her stomach and her nerves. He was hardly her first Hunter or kill, but his open disgust had found a crack in her armour. A flaw she hadn't known was there but would seal nonetheless.

Weakness was unacceptable.

Her heels clicked sharply on the hard wood of the floorboards, their dark grain soaking in and softly reflecting the fading afternoon sun. Crossing the space between her office door and Wendy's desk at reception, Kyra ensured her careful mask of calm was firmly back in place.

Cool air brought the taste of autumn through the large open foyer, brushing walls of muted cream as Kyra's footsteps echoed slightly. The clean smell of flowers hung in the air, not so thick to be cloying but enough to cover the less pleasant aspects of their business. There was nothing dark or dingy about The Rose, no back-alley entrance guarded by a wall of muscle clad in black. It was airy and open, full of soft lighting and smiling beauties of every shape and colour.

Kyra was warmed by pride every time she crossed the hard-wood floors, listening to the weight of her footfalls. The sound was solid and strong, like the walls around her. The Rose was a place of sanctuary and safety, not just pleasure.

Safely behind the barricade of her curved desk, Wendy made no motion to show she heard Kyra's approach. Not even when Kyra cleared her throat in a rather unladylike fashion. Or when Kyra moved into her field of vision, arms crossed and hip resting against the corner of the desk. Unrepentantly absorbed in her game of solitaire, the young blond didn't even bother to flash her baby blues at Kyra. As though it would have worked. As though Kyra hadn't paid for them in the first place.

"Damian isn't back yet," Wendy spoke a fraction of a second before Kyra finished opening her mouth. If the click of Kyra's teeth closing gave Wendy any joy, she knew better than to show it. "There's also another Hunter."

"A second one?" Kyra's frustration evaporated in an instant. "Are they working in teams now?"

Wendy shrugged elegantly, her slim frame so at odds with her gruff attitude. "I guess?" A click of the mouse, and the queen of hearts dropped on the king of spades.

"Where is he?" Pushing herself from the desk, Kyra tried to ignore the sudden tension across her shoulders. It wouldn't take long for the pain to radiate down her back and up into her skull.

"She's in the shed." Wendy's voice was flat, calm to the point of apathy, yet Kyra stiffened. The swoop of her stomach did little for the growing pain behind her left eye. Blood throbbed in her temples. This was not good.

"Shall we go for a walk?" Her tone missed light and airy completely, but Wendy was kind enough to pretend to ignore it.

Wordlessly, Wendy closed her game and pressed the off button on her monitor. Kyra turned to the short hall that led to the back rooms, refusing to breathe a sigh of relief when Wendy's footfalls joined hers. They beat a sharp rhythm striding into the relative darkness of the unlit hall.

The cadence of their footfalls changed from wood to tile, marking the transition to the brightness of The Rose's large kitchen. Murmured conversations fell away, and curious eyes tracked their procession through the room. If the hard line of Wendy's mouth or tension in Kyra's frame caused concern, it was held silent until the heavy back door slammed behind them. Voices followed them into the fading light, though Kyra's mind raced too fast to catch their words.

A woman.

A small scrap of grass, barely large enough to earn the title of yard, broke the concrete between the main building and the shed. Less an oversized tin can used to store tools than a hulking bunker of solid unadorned brick, the shed had once been a place of pleasure laced pain, willingly spilt blood, and cries of anguish. Modern soundproofing and a handful of expensive charms had made it obsolete, though Wendy had insisted on maintaining the aesthetic.

Wendy darted forward, managing to make the movement appear lazy and apathetic in a twist of perception that only added to Kyra's headache. The steel door proved no trouble for the petite woman, though Kyra knew from experience it was heavier than it looked. Nodding resolutely to indicate she would be fine proceeding alone, Kyra wasn't sure if she was trying to reassure Wendy or convince herself. It made no difference; the harsh white glow of humming fluorescence lights would wait for no one, and she had a job to do.

The chill of the air seeped into the room, wrapping it in a blanket of cold only heightened by the metal adorning the walls and hanging from the ceiling. Chains decorated the otherwise bare space broken only by black leather designed to hurt in ways that healed. The only furniture was two chairs, one of hardwood devoid of comfort and the other cushioned in resplendent purples. Wendy understood the importance of psychology in torture, and in this room, she was queen.

Kyra took Wendy's throne with more confidence than she felt, eyeing the bound woman before her with what she hoped was haughtiness. Trembling fingers were stilled in her lap, regally folded atop her crossed knee. In contrast, the Hunter across from her was calm. There was no wide-eyed fear, no fruitless pulling on bonds, not even snarled threats. The Hunter's stoic acceptance did nothing for Kyra's own disquiet, a sense of foreboding settling an additional weight across the band already tightening around her skull.

"Welcome to The Rose." Kyra spread her arms in welcome. "I am her humble proprietor." Making a show of running her gaze over the bound form of the Hunter, only a small part of Kyra's mind was able to catalogue useful details beyond the girl's striking youth and the painful innocence of her eyes. Completely guileless, they regarded her with an unwavering intensity that was offputting.

"I know who you are." Her voice was surprisingly deep for her lithe frame. Paired with a strong jaw, aquiline nose, and thin lips, there was an undeniable androgyny about her made all the worse by a severe ponytail, her honey blond hair pulled tight against her skull.

"So you have me at a disadvantage." The words were stiff, formal, despite being part of a game Kyra had played countless times before. The fire in the hazel eyes across from her was distracting.

"Leah," she said, head tilting to the side, listening to a voice over her shoulder.

Silence stretched between them, Kyra fighting for an equilibrium that didn't seem to exist. The Hunter watched her with eyes that weighed and measured, seeing more than they should. The quiet intensity of her stare didn't diminish, and the soft fire of her green flecked eyes warmed Kyra's skin in a flush that swept up her cheeks. Blushing like a child. Waves of cold cut through the heat.

"And what can I do for you, Leah?" They weren't the right words; the tone was wrong. The bitter taste at the back of her mouth trickled down her throat.

Pale eyebrows furrowed in the first real expression Kyra had seen. "I don't know."

Kyra snorted, the harsh sound caught between disbelieving and a laugh. "Sorry, most people just say something cheesy like 'die.'" Wiping at imagined tears and dabbing at non-existent makeup, Kyra felt the situation rapidly slipping out of her control. There should have been panic at that, but the soft smile on Leah's lips eased the tension in her stomach.

"I can't really expect to kill you when I'm tied up." She lifted her arms in a movement that barely tested the strength of the ropes woven between the slats of the chair back and held her tight against the wood. It wasn't a sign of struggle, but it was enough to burst the buoyancy Leah had created in Kyra's middle. She was a young Hunter, a captive under Kyra's will.

"No, I guess not." Clearing her throat against the sudden realisation that she was on the verge of flirting with the Hunter, Kyra searched for the right words, something to get her out of this. Leah was here to kill her, here to destroy The Rose.

"Where's Michael?"

"Who?" The word was out before Kyra could even process the question.

"Michael?" There was no fear in her voice, no desperation. Not even resignation that her partner might be dead. Only calm curiosity and a reversal of the tilt of her head. Rather than disquieting, Kyra found the movement charming. "Where are you keeping him?"

"You don't seem overly concerned." It was easier to tease, to speak in a lazy drawl while rearranging her limbs in a carefully placed artless sprawl than admit she was thankful for the distraction. Focusing on the angle of her legs, slanted to the side to show the full length of smooth skin while pointed to her prisoner to show her interest, was simpler than dissecting the way her stomach was churning. Even the guilt at having destroyed the Hunter, for the pain it would no doubt cause Leah to hear his fate, could be buried when Kyra trained her mind on seduction. "Or yourself, for that matter." If only her powers extended beyond men.

"Should I be?" This was not how this was meant to go. The ageless demon was meant to be the calm one, not the bound Hunter. It wasn't the false bravado of the young men Kyra had faced previously or the quiet confidence of the well-trained and battle-hardened. It was something akin to cool calculation but without the murderous intent. Leah seemed to be ignoring that her life was hanging in the balance in favour of gaining information. All Kyra could read in her harsh features was curiosity.

"You are here to kill me." Somewhere between a question and a statement, Kyra raised a perfectly sculpted eyebrow in challenge.

"Yes." A small smile played at the corner of Leah's mouth, twitching in a fight to keep a straight face. Did she find the situation ridiculous too? Was it for the same reasons?

"And I have you captured. You're bound and at my mercy." Flirting with a male Hunter was a matter of course. Flirting with a woman was suicide, yet Kyra lent forward to highlight the ample expanse of flesh on display. Her heart fluttered, caught between racing and grinding to a halt, her whole body tingling with height-ened sensations. "Doesn't that worry you?"

Her head tilted back to the other side. "Not really. Should it?"

Kyra couldn't hold back her bark of a laugh, a harsh, honking sound so at odds with the graceful beauty she wore. For a moment, she regretted the sound, if not for Leah's shy smile.

"I can't tell if you're incredibly brave or incredibly stupid."

Something flashed in Leah's eyes, her shoulders tensing momen-tarily. The light, flirty air between them evaporated. Kyra's stom-ach clenched, making her wince against the pain.

"Does it matter?" The low purr of Leah's voice sent a shiver down Kyra's spine, the small hairs at the back of her neck standing painfully to attention at the dark calmness of Leah's words. "Why are you delaying the inevitable?"

There was no resignation to the question, no sense of defeat. Curiosity was the only emotion Kyra could see in Leah's gaze, and it chilled her. She felt flayed open, skin pulled back to reveal the inner working of her organs. Too wide eyes counted the struggling contractions of her heart, tracing the icy blood fighting to fill her cheeks, rushing to her extremities, screaming for her to run while it solidified into weights in her legs.

"Are you so ready to die?" The words cracked from her dry throat. To Kyra, they were weak and frail. A pathetic attempt at pretending she was in charge, in control of the situation. A bluff easily called.

"You won't kill me."

"You were sent here to assassinate me." Kyra folded her arms across her chest and forced herself to lean back in the chair, the picture of arrogance. Inside, her stomach had finally succeeded in dropping far enough to leave her body completely. Muscles cramped around the empty space as acid burned up into her lungs. Everything hurt, but she refused to allow it to show no matter how clear it felt painted across her face. "Why wouldn't I kill you?"

"I don't know, but I don't think you will." All previous signs of flirtation, of laughter, were gone from Leah's face. The Hunter's mood was quicksilver, but it wasn't arrogance in her eyes. Even she looked confused as to how she'd come to the conclusion.

It was preposterous, of course. It was ludicrous; it was laughable and unthinkable. It was a hundred things before it could be true. In the silence following the statement, during which Kyra eyed the Hunter, the tension within her bled away. The girl across from her watched with wide, patient eyes.

The alternating chill of her insides and warmth of her skin finally found balance. A tingle washed over her, muscles loosened, and the suffocating sense of dread lifted from her mind. In a moment of perfect clarity and peace, Kyra decided she wouldn't kill Leah. She should, but she wouldn't.

"If it makes you feel any better, I don't think I'll kill you either."

Leah's words snapped Kyra from the momentary calm. Spurned into motion, Kyra launched to her feet. The Hunter jerked back at the sharp sound of chair legs against concrete but didn't speak. Leah only watched as Kyra spun and strode to the door, wrenching it open with more force than necessary.

The heavy metal door bounced off the wall, momentum bringing it back to slap solidly into Kyra's waiting palm. Wendy flinched back, the small movement her only outward sign of shock.

"Take her inside." Kyra was quick to hide her disquiet, keeping her eyes focused on Wendy as though not looking at Leah would simply make her disappear. "Put her in one of the rooms."

"To work?" The words were carefully flat, the slight lifting of an eyebrow the only sign of Wendy's judgement.

The sound of wood scraping against the floor interrupted Kyra before she could even begin forming her indignant response. Still refusing to acknowledge the Hunter, Kyra couldn't help but picture her struggles anyway. How quickly would her skin redden, pulled taut against the rope? It would bite, the thick coils pressed tight against pale flesh until red welts formed under punished skin. The image shouldn't have been tantalising. Guilt joined the roiling confusion in Kyra's gut.

"Just put her in one of the rooms." Keeping her voice even was a struggle, but Wendy read Kyra's mood easily enough.

"You won't break me."

Leah's voice chased Kyra into the darkness of twilight. A cool dark, a symbolic return to her natural habitat as the creature of evil the Hunter sought.

Taking long strides, it was impossible to hide that she was running away. If anyone was there to witness her shame, Kyra didn't see them. The racing of her heart and pounding of blood in her ears was all she knew. There was nothing beyond the tangle of guilt, dread, and elation in her middle, her mind dancing from the image of Leah's smile and the fear in her voice.

"Kyra?" The voice jolted her into awareness. Kyra didn't remember climbing the stairs to the top floor or walking the softly lit corridors to her door, yet the handle was under her fingers.

Turning to Bell, she hoped her smile wasn't sickly. Calm, calm and in control, that's what Bell expected, what she needed, and that's what Kyra was. Calm and in control.

"Yes?"

"Do you have a moment? I..." The younger woman faltered, looking down and away. Long dark hair fell into her face to obscure soft features.

Kyra looked longingly to her door before she could catch herself. Waiting for the movement, for any sign of disturbance, Bell jumped on it. "Never mind. You're busy. It's fine."

"No, I always have time for you." Kyra pulled the partially open door closed again, placing her back to it. "We can go down to my office if you'd like?"

"No, it's okay. My shift is starting soon anyway."

Bell disappeared back around the corner before Kyra could form the words to call her back. It seemed on form for her night, just another way she wasn't in control. Just another way she was failing.

Pulling her dark thoughts in, Kyra wrapped them tight like a blanket. Rather than warm her, they chilled the corners of her mind, searching for allies in painful memories and dejected musings of the future.

A warmth, a small flame that tickled at her middle, blossomed against the cold. Shaped by the gentle curl of Leah's smile, it somehow managed to beckon and battle all at once.

~ Three ~

A new dawn, a new day. The mocking voice at the back of Kyra's mind was unbearably cheery and far too awake to truly belong to her. Dried sleep crumbled under slender fingers that rubbed painful points of light into her eyes. The dull afterimage did nothing to darken the spear of dawn creeping towards her head.

Time to check in with Wendy, see if Damian had returned, and follow up with Bell. Running through her mental checklist, Kyra tried to ignore the sunshine that had now angled itself into her eyes. Moving was outside the current realm of possibility.

There was paperwork on her desk from last night, abandoned in the wake of Hunters and calls to make. Erik shifted to the top of her list. Light pounded against her eyelids, pressed closed in a vain attempt to ignore the world, radiating from brilliant white through the lilac of her skin before darkening to midnight at the edges of her sockets. Sounds from outside were beginning to filter through the window, the rumble of traffic and blasting of car horns, the world moving ever onwards regardless of her own ability to rise. Kyra pushed the noise from her mind, and it went easily. Unlike a pair of striking eyes trained with laser focus from a head tilted at the barest angle.

The young Hunter nestled in the corner of Kyra's mind, waiting patiently while Kyra's thoughts skidded around her. Leah seemed to be every second point of her mental checklist. A problem and a temptation.

She was a threat simply by existing, simply by sharing the space of so many demons. And yet Kyra risked it. For what? Lying in the centre of her bed, bathed in the harsh light of day, there was no way to fool herself into thinking this could work. But the Hunter enchanted Kyra.

Pulling herself from her bed, Kyra shook her head to dislodge the unwelcome thoughts. Her thumping footfalls, made heavy with indulgent frustration, rolled hollowly across the nearly empty room. They echoed back to Kyra, stopping only with the slamming of her bathroom door.

Like every room of The Rose, Kyra's was sparsely furnished yet opulent. The bed was large and plush, the attached bathroom spacious and inviting. Stepping into the modern shower, easily big enough for three, Kyra set the water to near burning. Unlike the other rooms of The Rose, Kyra's bathroom lacked the gaudy spa bath, and her room held no furnishings beyond the bed and desk. There was no need to keep up appearances here.

Once bathed but no less frustrated at having to face the problems she had so readily created for herself, Kyra towelled herself perfunctorily. Dry enough despite the sheen of water on her skin, slipping into a glamour felt grounding. The wash of magic over her skin, the well-worn mask of humanity, had her almost feeling in control again.

The walk from bedroom to kitchen was blessedly empty, the late shift long abed and early shift not required for another few hours. Coffee was still warm in the pot, fresh enough to soothe her nerves yet old enough to be enjoyed alone. The calm quiet of the kitchen was comforting despite the harsh lines of metal and monochromatic decor. Some called it cold, but for Kyra, the clean lines and sharp angles gave a sense of purpose and control so rarely found around humans.

The calm, morphing slowly into warm contentment, was shattered once Kyra entered her office and caught sight of Damian's back. It was too late to turn back and pretend she wasn't there; even if he hadn't heard her coming, he would have picked up her scent immediately. Her own nose, still full of coffee fumes, had found his a second too late. But even if she had known he was there, fleeing would never have been an option. Not with Wendy perched behind her own desk at reception, knowing eyes tracking every movement.

"So, you're back." Keeping her head high and pace even, Kyra pretended the gnawing at her gut didn't exist. This was her office, her dominion, her sanctuary. Everything about the room was designed to reflect her power and presence.

"Why is there a Hunter on the top floor?"

Walking around his looming form, his back straight and arms firmly crossed, Kyra was proud of herself for not faltering at the cold anger in his voice. Maintaining her calm was difficult, with her heart pounding in her chest and pulse fluttering in her neck. Could he see it? It felt too strong to not be visible.

She arranged herself carefully in her high-backed chair, pretending for all the world that she was alone. Nestled in the worn leather of her throne, Kyra let the silence stretch. Meeting his eyes was more difficult, today an icy grey in a face of hard lines and chiselled features. Not even barely concealed rage could dampen his beauty.

"Because I put her there."

The visible twitch of jaw muscles would have been sweet vindication any other day. Instead, her eyes darted to the ripple of muscles as his arms tensed. Years of experience saw it as a warning sign. Too many old wounds, some still too fresh to risk it.

"I thought I could-"

"Could what?" He slammed his hands against the desk, using his impressive height to tower over her seated form. Kyra didn't flinch, only raised a cool eyebrow of distaste. "Could take her to bed? Could risk everything we've built for a quick fuck?"

"Everything *I've* built." She kept her tone soft and even, no matter how his words stung. "And I have no illusions or desire to sleep with a Hunter."

"Why isn't she dead?"

"She could be useful."

"Useful?" He shoved away from the desk, needing to put space between them. Kyra could read the urge to lash out, to hit her, in the stiff lines of his shoulder. She had seen that same look directed at others but never at herself. His hand groped momentarily for the chair beside him before pulling it out to drop into an artless sprawl. The wood groaned under the sudden weight. "She was sent here to kill you."

"And she didn't." Kyra's skin itched; she wanted to rise, to pace. She wanted to be in control. Refolding her hands in her lap, her fingers tightened around each other, the only concession to the restless energy building within her.

"Because Wendy caught her first." He sighed, running a tired hand through thick, dark hair. It flopped across his forehead with the same listlessness as his hand landing back in his lap. "You know this is insane. We kill Hunters for a reason."

"Not this one."

"When Buddug finds out—"

"She won't." Heat entered Kyra's voice, sharpening it. Fighting down the urge to vomit, forcing her tone to even out, Kyra continued, "This doesn't need to concern her. She has enough to worry about."

"You've brought a Hunter into a building full of demons, and you don't think that's something to worry about?"

"It's nothing for Buddug to worry about."

"Kyra..." His tone and eyes went soft. Kyra flinched back from it before she could stop herself; it cut deeper than the rage. "You'd don't exactly have a great track record with..." he trailed off, shrugging awkwardly over the unspoken words.

"With relationships? With women?" Claw-like nails dug into her palms, fingers curling into tight fists. She scrambled for control, thoughts of deep breaths and slowing heartbeats skidding over the otherwise rolling expanse of her mind. The rational voice was swallowed by the rising pain, the twist in her gut, and the hot rage at the unnecessary truth of his words. "This isn't about that."

"Then what is it about? If this isn't a pathetic attempt to fill some void you think is there, please educate me because I have no idea what else it could be." Damian lunged to his feet, the chair scraping back before settling to the ground with a thump. Turning abruptly on his heel, he strode to one book-lined wall before spinning and crossing to the one opposite. "What could this possibly be about? Give me one good reason why she should be here. Why the hell shouldn't I be killing her right now? You've kidnapped a damn Hunter and expect nothing bad to happen." His steps were as sharp as his words, the movement jerky with frustrated energy. "What if she tries to run? What if she manages to kill you? Can't you see how stupid this is?"

"We could learn from her."

Snorting, Damian didn't slow his staccato laps of her office. "Yes, the finer points of demon killing."

"No." The word was sharp, mouth running quicker than her thoughts. This was her plan; this was all intended. If she could convince him, she could convince herself. "We could find out what they know about us. Get a better understanding of their knowledge, their techniques." The reasoning was flimsy at best, but Kyra delivered it with confidence. "With an understanding of their training, we can better identify their weaknesses."

"You've never shown an interest in intel gathering before." Damian paused before her desk, assuming his original stance of ramrod straight back and tightly crossed arms. "Are you finally ready to concede?"

"Just because I want to understand the people trying to kill us doesn't mean I'm looking to join Buddug's war."

"No, of course not. That would involve not running from your problems." Damian's tone was dry. His lips twisted bitterly, caught between a frown and sneer. There had been a flicker of hope, but neither of them acknowledged it, no matter how it stabbed at Kyra's heart.

"The Hunter stays," she said. The fight drained from her, leaving her empty. Exhaustion tightened a band across her temples. "Alive."

A muscle in Damian's jaw twitched, holding fast against words that shouldn't be said, words that couldn't be taken back once uttered. They watched each other, silently, reading thoughts and emotions that would remain unsaid in eyes that refused to look away. Decades of friendship made reading each other a second nature. Left unspoken, the hurt and anger could be ignored; they could pretend it wasn't there at all.

He huffed into the quiet of the room, the sound barely audible over the ticking of the clock. Shaking his head with the ghost of a defeated smile on his lips, Damian turned his back to Kyra. She didn't have the words to stop him.

The echoing silence Damian left behind with the sharp sound of the door closing behind him beat at Kyra's senses. Her eyes stung. Forcing her breathing back to a normal rhythm, she pulled air in through her nose and held it long enough to burn before letting it go in a rush between her teeth. It helped; the sting in her eyes faded, but her stomach refused to move from where it had fallen.

There were still things to do—paperwork to finish, bills to pay, people to call. The day didn't stop because of a fight with a friend. It never had before and wouldn't be nice enough to start now.

Lifting the receiver of the sleek phone on her desk, Kyra barely waited for the click of the answered line before speaking. "Get me Erik once he's done."

Wendy didn't answer. She didn't need to. The line went dead, and Kyra dropped the phone back in place. There was too much to do. Always too much to do.

The band of tension around Kyra's head seemed to throb in time with her pulse, each lap of blood pulling it tighter. Her fingers twitched against the cool keys of her laptop. The urge to press them to her temples, dig deep in the flesh there and pull the pain from her skull, was hard to ignore.

Rustling fabric drew her attention to Erik, still sat in the chair across her desk. Even seated, he was huddled, curled over himself in a bid to protect internal organs. Oily in countenance and weaselly in appearance, the small man was a cowering rat before a cat.

Bile roiled in Kyra's gut and rose to coat the back of her throat in bitter film. Erik had his uses, and she her obligations, but dealing with him left her feeling dirty.

"If that is all?" The first dismissal had been clear. This one carried bite.

"Well..." The baritone of his voice always managed to surprise her, so at odds with his stature. Like a lion's roar from a mouse. "There's been rumours of a fledgling."

A burst of rapid-fire typing drowned the end of his sentence, Kyra's pale finger flashing in the late afternoon light. She shifted in her seat, muscles protesting the movement, frozen in place by long hours. Another email danced off into the electrical ether.

"Deal with it."

"I was hoping-"

"Just deal with it." Snarling fangs momentarily broke free of her glamour, needlepoint tips pressed into lips the colour of freshly spilt blood.

Erik shied away, bending further into himself. Placating hands rose in the air, half to calm Kyra, half to shield himself from her wrath. When Kyra made no further movement to attack or other-wise, Erik slid from the chair and scurried from the room.

Leaning her head back, Kyra focused on her breathing while silently berating herself. Small thuds filled the room in quick succession, Kyra's head connecting solidly with the back of her chair. The soft, padded leather gave little satisfaction.

Opening a new email with a click, her fingers danced across the keys once more. A simple message, barely a line long. Wendy would see to smoothing any ruffled feathers.

For the fifth time that hour, Kyra opened her calendar. Backlit pixels obediently stated the day and date, refusing to lie. Gnawing on the inside of her cheek, the spot already raw and tender from days of abuse, Kyra counted backward through those little white boxes. The number didn't change, and neither did the way it made her stomach churn.

Thirty days. In an hour, it will have been thirty days since Damian last fed. The knowledge, held at the back of her mind for the past week, was little comfort. He had been gone a fortnight before Leah arrived and had disappeared again following their argument this morning.

A tooth slipped, catching flesh awkwardly and slicing deep enough to draw blood. Cupping her cheek with a wince, Kyra pressed her tongue against the spot hard. The metallic taste of blood, diluted with saliva, did nothing to ease the churning of her stomach. The chance that he would go to someone else was minuscule, though the thought was almost as nauseating as him suffering starvation.

Reaching for her phone, Kyra continued to poke her tender flesh with a curious tongue. "Apologise to Erik. I'm going to visit the Hunter. Call me when Damian gets in." Her clipped orders were met with equally curt grunts of agreement. The handset fell back in place with a clatter, quickly forgotten as Kyra pushed herself from her chair and strode from the room.

~ Four ~

There was a temptation to take the elevator to the third floor, to break her own personal rule. If it had been earlier in the day, if she could ensure there would be no clients, maybe. Instead, Kyra slipped down the hall to cut through the kitchen to the back stairs. Despite the purpose of her stride and stiff set of her shoulders, her steps barely echoed.

Rather than sharp stilettos, slippers whispered against the wood and tiles as she traversed through the building. The change had been subconscious, creating a strange contrast with her expertly fitted power suit of clinging pencil skirt and pale blouse. The slippers, fluffy pink monstrosities, muted Kyra's hurried strides.

Her mind whirled with thoughts, her hands restless at her sides. Fingers curled into fists before forcing themselves flat, running over hips to smooth fabric that didn't need it only to curl back into fists. Like the slippers, the movement wasn't intended but inescapable. The band of tension around her skull tightened with every step she climbed.

At the top landing, partially hidden in the doorway leading to the stairwell, Kyra ran a critical eye over herself.

"Shit," she breathed, brushing a hand down her body in a sweeping movement from shoulder to knee. Her glamour rippled in the wake of her hand, the silken blouse shifting into a plain cotton t-shirt. The black pencil skirt became faded blue jeans, still tailored to her form but well-worn with relaxed comfort.

The slippers resisted. Kyra frowned at her feet, eyebrows drawing down. Fighting past the throbbing in her temples, the slippers conceded slowly. The simple black sneakers that replaced them were equally silent as she crossed to her destination.

Leah's room was only a few doors down from her own. There was nothing to mark it as different from the identical doors lining the hall. Nothing to distinguish it from any other door in the building. Standing in front of the plainly painted wood, Kyra's arms felt too heavy to lift. There was no moisture in her mouth, her breath rattling in a throat gone dry.

Frozen in the hall, eyes trained on the doorway, she desperately tried to picture what she would find on the other side. Would Leah be sleeping? Curled in on herself, pale eyelashes fluttering on her cheeks as her eyes danced behind their lids. The image, painted in painstaking detail by her mind, was enchanting, breathtaking.

It shattered with a rough shake of her head. Kyra straightened her shoulders with a deep breath, forcing her hands and mind into stillness. She took the handle of the door and pushed it open resolutely before she could change her mind.

The deep darkness of the room was shocking, her eyes unprepared for the thick shadows. The air was warm and smelled slightly stale, musty with the scent of human. It coated Kyra's tongue, drawing out the little moisture left in her mouth.

Thin lines of pink and orange light peeked through the gaps in the heavy curtains, but they weren't enough to ease the dark. Kyra's hand groped for the light switch, eyes straining to identify any movement as they adjusted.

The sudden bloom of light, bright and warmly yellow, had Kyra blinking back spots. Maintaining outward composure, her gaze honed in on Leah immediately.

Curled in the middle of the still made bed, the covers rumpled but otherwise undisturbed, Leah held her knees tight to her chest. Slender arms were wrapped around her legs, her forehead resting on top of her knees. Kyra thought the Hunter asleep at first, strands of golden hair creating a halo around her head, the unruly fuzz glowing in the artificial light.

"I told you, I won't eat it." Her voice was strikingly deep, even muffled by her legs. "I won't let you poison me."

The accusation twisted a knot in her stomach. Kyra tried to ignore it as she drifted further into the room. Plain, like her own, it boasted an additional wardrobe and a bare nightstand. An errant thought drifted through her mind, whether the lamp that should have been on the nightstand had been removed in one piece.

Pulling the wooden chair away from the desk and into the centre of the room, Kyra arranged herself carefully on the hard surface. Positioned equal distance from the door and the bed, she considered shifting closer. Survival instincts, honed over decades of danger and fleeting pools of peace, screamed that was a bad idea. The hairs on her arms stood stiff from tightened skin, her glamour reflecting more of her emotions than her control.

Kyra eventually broke the silence. "I'm not here to poison you." Leah had remained wary and still as Kyra had moved around the room. Though the Hunter hadn't raised her head, Kyra felt her focus like the sun on her skin, the warmth a touch too harsh to be comfortable.

A dry chuckle was the only answer Kyra received, still muffled by the knees held against her chest.

"I'm not here to poison you," she repeated firmly, wishing it didn't sound as though she was trying to convince herself.

"Then why?" Leah raised her head sharply, the movement knocking the breath from Kyra's lungs.

Pale skin was drawn taut against her cheeks, her wan colour made all the more striking by the dark circles beneath her tight eyes. Her lips, pulled into a harsh line, were dried at the edges and caked with saliva gone gummy and foul. Her clothes were rumpled, the same simple garb she had arrived in. A neat pile of Wendy's own clothes sat on the floor beside the doorway to the bathroom, forgotten or ignored.

"I'm not here to hurt you." It didn't answer the question, but Kyra wasn't sure she could.

"Then why?"

Long legs stretched from her body, the movement slow but jerky. How long had she been sat like that? Her face contorted in a flash of pain, blood rushing through muscles and veins bent and bunched for too long. Shifting herself against the wooden headboard of the bed, Leah stretched her legs and cocked her head to the side, the curiosity of the night before returning in full force.

"If you're not here to hurt me, then why?"

"I thought we could talk." The idea sounded ludicrous, even to herself.

"About what?"

"About why you're here." The women sat mirrored, Leah with her legs stretched and head tilted to the side, Kyra with her ankles crossed and hands folded in her lap, knees angled towards the bed. They were both open, unguarded. It wasn't right, wasn't natural. Kyra felt less like a half-feral cat faced with an intruder and more like a puppy rolling over for its master. It would have rankled if Leah didn't reflect the same openness. "You said you wouldn't kill me, so why are you here?"

"I don't know." She shrugged. "You're the one keeping me alive."

"That's true." Kyra couldn't help but chuckle. Their words slipped so easily back into soft teasing with an edge of flirting. Even unbound, Kyra feared Leah's tongue more than her fists.

"So, why are you here?" Leah shifted against the headboard, unblinking eyes watching for any sign of reaction from Kyra. The demon remained carefully still, refusing to show any sign of fear when the Hunter moved to tuck her legs in beside herself and leaned forward slightly, one arm keeping her propped up while the other curled around her lap. She became a flowing line, a soft curve of flesh lazing on a bed more than large enough to accommodate them both. If she patted the space beside her, silently invited Kyra to join her, would she resist? Would she give in?

"I think we have a lot to discuss." The words, carefully flippant, cracked in her arid throat. "To learn from each other."

"I won't betray the Church." Steel coated Leah's voice, the razor edge cutting the careful warmth Kyra had been building. "I won't tell their secrets."

"I have no interest in the secrets of the Church."

"No," Leah agreed, "I don't think you do." The Hunter reversed the angle of her head, the movement unnerving and enchanting.

Kyra scoffed. As if a Hunter, a stranger, could know her mind better than herself. "Then why am I here?"

"Because we are alike, I think." Hazel eyes shone with curiosity and something akin to mischief. "You want to see where this will take us badly as I do. You wear a mask of calmness, but I don't think that's really you. I think you're missing something, but you don't know what. I think you're unsure."

The pounding of blood in her ears wasn't enough to drown out the words of the Hunter, the girl seeing through to fears she had no right to voice. Kyra's stomach twisted and boiled with rage. It dropped to her feet and froze in fear.

"I think I'm starting to see how you ended up at my door," Kyra drawled, stopping Leah from continuing. Observations with such clarity were rarely welcomed. "So, we've established we won't kill each other." Kyra stood, locking knees that threatened to tremble. Pulling an air of calm confidence around her, blanketing herself in it, Kyra tried for a haughty stare as Leah's smile slipped at the sudden movement. There was still no fear in the Hunter's eyes, though the angle of her head shifted as she tried to read Kyra.

"But?"

"You'll stay in this room until I can decide what to do with you."

Leah sighed, unfurling her body to rest against the headboard once more, legs crossed loosely before her. "Can I at least have a book to pass the time?" The question followed Kyra out the door.

Her heart jackhammered in her chest, something far too close to fear thrumming through her veins. Pressed against the door, handle still in her clammy palm, Kyra fought to get her breathing under control, thoughts and control spiralling away from her at dizzying speeds.

~ Five ~

Ensconced in her office, Kyra was able to finally bring her thoughts and breathing under control. Her legs twitched restlessly, right knee bouncing alarmingly close to the underside of her desk in short movements that were nowhere near enough to ease the energy pulsing through her.

Damian was right: the Hunter was too dangerous to keep alive. Unfortunately, Leah was right too; Kyra couldn't kill her. Logic and decades of experience with humans screamed that Leah had to die, but Kyra knew she couldn't do it. The same way she knew Damian would never betray her and Buddug would destroy the entire building if she so much as suspected a Hunter was inside. The same way Kyra knew breathing was vital for living.

Groaning into the quiet of the room, Kyra let her head fall into her hands, elbows dug into the solid weight of her desk. She indulged for a long moment, carefully not thinking in favour of simply suffering in the situation she had created for herself. Fingers threaded through her hair, pressing hard against her scalp, trying to force out an answer or simply squeeze hard enough to crush her brain. Even in the safety of her own mind, Kyra huffed a laugh at her melodramatics, wondering vaguely what Damian would say.

He would tell her to kill the Hunter.

Kyra dropped her hands to the desk, head falling backwards to connect with the too soft leather of her chair. Fuck, this was not good.

Rising to her feet, Kyra allowed herself to pace the room. It was hard to ignore how her feet took the same path Damian had cut earlier that day. Leah could be useful, could be a good source of information. Kyra's mind clung to the flimsy excuse, shoring it with hopes half believed in. Beyond what they could learn, the possibility of turning a Hunter to their side had further implications. Kyra couldn't name a single one, but it had to be worth trying. No wonder Damian thought she was an idiot.

Given time and the right information, she could convince Buddug of the uses of a pet Hunter, surely. It was hard to pretend she was a neutral party with a Hunter in her home. As though demons could be neutral.

A dark voice, deep at the back of her mind, almost quiet enough to pretend it didn't exist at all, whispered that there was another solution. It would be easy to allow Damian to take care of it, or Wendy, or to simply ensure the right words were breathed in Buddug's ear. There were so many options, so many ways in which she could clean her hands entirely of the situation and simply turn a blind eye. She didn't have to meet Leah's too innocent eyes, didn't have to think too hard on the angle of her head.

Kyra's stomach twisted sharply. Even as a half-considered thought, it raised her bile. She stopped before her book-lined wall, unseeing eyes traced spines well-worn and well loved. Unconscious fingers danced across paperbacks, hardcovers, and leather-bound tomes, pulling out titles without thinking. This on demon society, that on laws, Kyra eased books out slightly without actually pulling them down. When had she decided to entertain Leah's request?

Keeping a Hunter like she was a stray cat wandered in off the street. This had to be the dumbest thing she'd done. But that open curiosity, the way it burned from Leah's eyes...how would it react to the knowledge Kyra could offer?

Despite Damian's misgivings, there was an opportunity here. An opportunity Kyra couldn't waste.

It took three days for Damian to return. Three days in which Kyra had gnashed her teeth and chewed through the fragile skin inside her cheek. Three days in which everyone swore they hadn't heard from him, swore they knew nothing of his whereabouts. Three days in which Kyra had snapped and snarled and sulked in the safety of her office.

On the second day, following a particularly cutting remark to Wendy, the petite woman had bitten back. She had yelled across the vaulted foyer that there was no one to blame for his absence other than Kyra, the words delivered to the demon's retreating back, chasing her fleeing form into her office. Everyone had made themselves scarce as soon as Wendy had raised her voice, but the looks of sympathy Kyra received when she finally braved the kitchen told her the words had been well heard.

Even with the open sympathy, there was still a sense of judgment. It wasn't spoken, but no matter how sad the eyes that traced her stiff-backed stride, they agreed with Wendy. Kyra agreed with Wendy too in the darkest corners of her mind where she couldn't lie to herself.

So when Damian sauntered in, eyes dark and brows pulled down, acting for all the world as though he hadn't been gone, Kyra did what she did best. She ignored him, resolutely keeping her eyes on the paperwork before her while tracking his movements in her peripheral vision. He crossed the room, a wry twist to his mouth at her antics, before pulling up a chair. He collapsed in his usual artless sprawl, but there was a listlessness to it. As though it was more for show than anything, and his heart wasn't really in it.

"The Hunter still lives." It wasn't an accusation, a simple statement of fact. There was no bite to his words this time, no hint of judgment or condemnation, not even surprise. His voice was as flat as his posture.

"I've been questioning her."

"You've visited her once."

He had spoken to Wendy then. Kyra shifted, lifting her eyes properly from the paper before her, though she hadn't read a word since Damian entered. Or even before that, really. Damian had crossed his arms over his chest, eyebrow raised in question though his eyes were still carefully blank. His whole posture was careful, positioned exactly as it should be, as it would have been any other time during any other discussion. But everything felt wrong.

"It'll take some time to open her eyes."

"To your charms?" The pointed question had no right to cut the way it did.

"To some hard truths." Folding her hands carefully on the desk in front of her, Kyra projected calm confidence.

Damian sneered. "She'd have more use as a breeder."

"No." Kyra's voice was sharp, a touch louder than she expected, than either of them expected. "You will not..." She couldn't bring herself to finish, couldn't find the right words.

"At least Elizabeth wasn't human."

"We're not doing this again." Kyra placed her hands to the cool wood of the desk, fingers splayed as her palms pressed hard. The solidity of her desk was grounding, a reminder of her power. "You need to feed."

Damian's eyes hardened, his expression darkening. Kyra expected him to argue, to brush her off at the least. Instead, he nodded once, sharply, mouth thinning in anger.

Pushing herself away from her desk, Kyra crossed the space between them before he could change his mind. He stood at her approach, and for a moment, Kyra expected him to leave.

He fell into the easy synchronisation borne of years of repetition, facing Kyra as they both extended their arms. His glamour barely shimmered as he adjusted his height to match hers. Damian stood with his arms bent at the elbow, palms facing the ground. Kyra mirrored him, her own palms facing the sky, the closeness of him setting a tingle through her skin. The space between them was minuscule, fingers brushing wrists with every shift of their bodies.

Together they evened their breathing, quickly falling into a simple rhythm of in and out, perfectly timed so that every breath was taken in tandem. In time, they slowed their breathing to deep inhales and slow exhales, a sense of still calm enveloping them both. In, hold, out. In, hold, out. Kyra's mind quietened under the familiar ritual, thoughts drifting into nothing as she focused on the warmth growing between their hands.

Their hearts followed their breaths, falling into a synchronised beat. Kyra could feel the flutter of Damian's pulse against the tips of her fingers. Or was it just the echo of her own? Heat continued to grow between their palms, warming to the point of discomfort. It grew to burning, a small fire trapped between their hands. The air pressed tight between them was aflame, so hot and bright, Kyra was sure her skin would be red and blistered when they finally parted.

Still, she held herself carefully stiff, kept her breathing even, maintained the burning contact. If Damian felt the pain, it didn't show. He was as still as ever, eyes calm and mouth set. Kyra felt herself flinching, felt her face twisting with the pain. Her eyes were watering, but she held herself firm. The pain was temporary, she reminded herself.

Heat continued to blossom from where their hands touched, spiralling out to engulf her wrist, her forearms. Soon, her arms were on fire, her whole torso. Tears slid unbidden down her cheeks. Kyra imagined she could smell her flesh cooking, could feel her muscles stiffening as they broiled in her skin. Despite the fire between them, Damian's skin remained cool against her own.

Kyra wasn't sure if it was seconds or hours they stood there, hearts and breath in perfect time. Just as the pain reached its peak, far beyond where Kyra thought her limit was, exactly at the place she knew she could take no more, the fire began to die. The heat receded in waves, soothing coolness sweeping down from her shoulders. It wasn't a sharp cold like the kiss of ice but a gentle reduction of heat, a slow easing away from the fire.

It ebbed like a tide, drawing down until only her palms were warm. Damian's skin warmed, soaking the flames that had recently called Kyra's veins home. Like dry sand welcomes water, his skin drank in Kyra's heat until she felt cold. For a moment, as the fire drained from her skin, it felt like home, cold and safe. Damian stiffened momentarily, the burning pain racing through his body.

Kyra could think now, could count their breaths as Damian ate the power Kyra willingly offered. While it had felt like an eternity when it had been her aflame, it was only a second before it was over. Together they panted, slowly coming apart to fall into the chairs in front of Kyra's desk. They were weakened from the exchange yet satiated.

"I still think you're making a mistake." His voice rasped, rough with screams held tightly inside.

"I know." Her own voice was no better, throat scratchy and sore. The fight had left her, her energy drained and knees weak. Locking her legs stubbornly, Kyra rose and took careful steps back to her throne. The few steps felt like miles with Damian's eyes trained on her back. He probably had the energy to run marathons while Kyra was nearly defeated by the simple task of sitting, not falling, into her chair. It was hard to tell if he watched for weakness in order to judge her or to know when to catch her. She knew it was the latter but would always worry about the former.

"I could-"

She didn't let him finish the thought.

"No!" The word came out louder, harsher than was necessary. It was impossible to ignore the roiling fear that his words had unleashed in her. Kyra had expected the suggestion, had been waiting for it even, but that did nothing to prepare her for the stark terror it brought.

It had been impossible to avoid thoughts of Damian with Leah, his hands on her skin, his magic in her mind. Kyra's mind skittered away from the images conjured, her insides twisting painfully.

"It would be more effective..." she continued in a calmer voice, ignoring how it trembled slightly at the edges. "It would be a stronger statement if we didn't..." She couldn't even say it.

Damian's face was carefully blank as though his mind wasn't racing, as though he hadn't noticed and categorised every flash of weakness Kyra had shown. A part of her screamed that he would do it anyway, to prove a point, to save her from herself.

"Please." The word clawed from her throat, small and pained and laden with desperation it had no right to bear.

"Fine." It cut like a curse regardless of how flatly he said it.

Ozone flooded Kyra's senses with such sudden, shocking clarity, she barely had the time to snap her laptop shut before Buddug was stepping into the room. Appearing before Kyra's heavy desk, the other woman stepped into existence. Materialising on a lateral movement that would always be unsettling, no matter how used to it Kyra became, Buddug was simply just there in a space that had been empty a second before.

The exhausted pressure on her skull, forgotten in the hours following Damian's feeding, rallied to wrap itself tighter. Her eyes were aching, the muscles in her neck protested every movement, and her thoughts had slowed to a crawl. But none of this could be acknowledged, could be allowed.

"Buddug." Finding a smile or welcoming tone was beyond Kyra, the greeting carrying more of her feelings than she would have liked. Buddug, for her part, ignored Kyra's clipped tone and took the chair across from her. The long lines of her body, barely hidden by the clinging glamour of pale skin and form-fitting pants suit, were held at precise angles. Appearing just beyond middle-aged, the soft lines at the corners of her dark eyes highlighted the stark beauty of her face rather than detracted from it. Close-cut hair of a shocking silver only added to the air of matured grace. It had to be a coincidence that her features so closely matched Kyra's own, as though they were truly mother and daughter in more than just name.

"Kyranthine," she drawled once settled. Her eyes had danced from the chair as she sat, traced minute creases as she smoothed the legs of her pants, and carefully avoided Kyra entirely until she knew Kyra's fingers were flexing with frustrated anxiety. When Buddug did level Kyra with a stare, Kyra almost wished she had stayed looking around the room, engrossed in books, anything other than that heavy weight lodging itself behind her lungs. Buddug knew. "There have been Hunters in the area."

Speaking around rising bile, Kyra resolutely ignored the way her stomach turned lazy circles. "Yes." Her mind danced to excuses, to explanations and reasons and flimsy words that would be useless against Buddug's impending rage.

Buddug was her mentor, her mother. She was a member of the Council, and she oversaw The Rose and every other sanctuary in this corner of the world. She was historically vicious when it came to defending her kind, and even the smallest hint of a Hunter in one of her sanctuaries was sure to send her into a fury.

"Have they attacked?"

Kyra's head swam with how quickly the tension left it. Buddug didn't know.

"Yes, and I dealt with it."

Silence stretched between them, Buddug's gaze still heavy on Kyra's chest, but it was easier to return without the pressing panic. Leah would remain a secret. Damian hadn't told Buddug, not yet.

"And you still-"

"No." Kyra didn't let her finish. Her relief was fleeting. Of course it was.

"You can't deny," Buddug tried, frustration seeping into her voice.

"There's nothing to deny." Nothing to avoid, nothing to discuss. Kyra wrenched her eyes away. She wasn't avoiding that weighted stare, wasn't itching to slip out from beneath it and flee. Running her eyes over the comforting presence of her books, Kyra could almost pretend she didn't feel Buddug's gaze. "We're safe here."

"Safe?" Buddug was beautiful even when barking a mirthless laugh. Her sneer was lovely. "How many Hunters have attacked this past month? How long ago would that number have shocked you in the space of a year? How long since it was safe to live outside of these walls?" Kyra let her eyes pick out individual titles, wondering which Leah would find interesting. "You can't pretend they're not building up to something. You're the only sanctuary not engaging them, and I don't know how much longer I can allow you to shirk your responsibility." Maybe the study on humanity as a food source; no, too confronting. If only she had some taste for philosophy, though that would probably be overwrought. "They're building an army."

Kyra scoffed, pulled completely from her consideration of her library and turning her gaze back to a scowling Buddug. Still beautiful despite the twisted anger in her features. "They wouldn't attack us openly." Staying in the shadows benefited them all.

"They wouldn't have to." Buddug snarled. Emotion, white hot rage, coated her words. Kyra jerked back at the open display, hands drawing into fists subconsciously. As if she'd punch Buddug. As if Buddug would let her. "The Church has shown an alarming influence on politics," Buddug continued in a more even tone, but the rage still burned behind her eyes. "You think you'll still be safe if they control the police? You think they'll have to worry about the whispers of demons in the dark if they can just label us all criminals?"

"What, they'll just lock us all in prisons?" Biting back another scoff under Buddug's heated stare, Kyra couldn't stop the flow of words. "And when we don't age? When we don't eat or can't remember which face we're meant to be wearing? How will they explain that to our fellow inmates?"

"Did I really raise you to be so ignorant?" Buddug snapped, slicing through the bravado Kyra had been building. The twist of frustration on Buddug's face made her feel like a child again. For a moment, Kyra was barely twenty and crying as Buddug comforted her for feelings she couldn't control. She had been ignorant then too, stupid and foolish and a million other things Buddug had never raised her to be. "We wouldn't make it that far. How many would face accidents? How many times would guards look the other way? Or place weapons in our attacker's hands? How many more would just be starved with no access to each other? No access to food? How many would die for resisting before even seeing the inside of a cell?"

Every word, every accusation punched the air from Kyra's lungs until she was silently gasping for breath that wouldn't come. If Buddug saw her pain, it did nothing to stem the flow of her vitriol.

"You call yourself safe; you think this sanctuary,' Buddug spat the word like bile. "Is enough to protect you? You know nothing."

"I won't join your war," Kyra shot back, voice shaking with twisting guilt and shame and indignant anger. "It has no place here."

"It's been knocking at your door for years, and I've done everything I can to protect you." The words hissed low, a stark counterpoint to Kyra's own rising voice. "You won't get involved because you still think it doesn't affect you yet." Buddug's rage drained suddenly, replaced with something darker. Her face shifted into something akin to sadness, a look Kyra had never seen before, and it chilled her. "You won't fight for those of us who are already dead and dying."

"Your war—"

"It's not my war." Buddug's voice broke over Kyra's, still cold and empty but inexorable. "If you still can't see that..." she sighed, shaking her head to herself. "Sometimes, I wonder where I went wrong."

Before Kyra could find the words to respond, could arrange her thoughts into something that made sense, Buddug was out of her seat and stepping away. As suddenly as she had appeared, the flooding scent of ozone and emptiness of Kyra's office said she was gone.

It was an argument they had had a million times before and would no doubt have again; that it was a point of contention for years, did nothing to the rising shame Kyra felt.

Buddug knew she wasn't a fighter, knew that she wasn't made for that. Neither of them was, but Kyra lacked the fire that burned in Buddug's gut. Kyra lacked the sharp determination and steely rage that Buddug used to fuel her war. It shouldn't feel like failure to stay true to her nature, but in the cold space where Buddug had been, Kyra could only sense a lingering disappointment.

~ Six ~

Dragons chased Kyra in her sleep, with scales of fire and ice and air and earth. In every size and shape, they roared so loud her ears bled.

The monstrous beasts screamed their fury as they crossed skies and seas, closing in on all angles. Kyra stood stranded on a small island, a rock barely big enough to be granted such a generous name. Precariously balanced, Kyra fought the biting winds and crashing waves, turning in tight circles in a vain attempt to identify every threat and watch for each impending attack. They came from all sides, hurtling towards her with a singular fury.

Her hooves slipped on the water slick stone, sending her reeling into the freezing waves. The tide was strong, the waves high, forcing her head below swells whipped white. The sky, buried in roiling grey clouds, disappeared as water crushed Kyra under its overwhelming weight. She opened her mouth to scream, and her lungs immediately flooded. Her body burned, muscles screaming for air, eyes stinging from the salt water, heart straining to process the panic.

The dragons circled overhead, vultures awaiting their next meal. Some dove dramatically, wings folded close as serpentine necks stretched to breach the choppy waters. They cut through the waves around her, dark shapes moving below as they gracefully reflected the movements of their brethren above. They circled their prey, a small morsel, a sweet snack to be enjoyed but not enough to be savoured. Kyra could feel their claws slicing her skin, could feel their teeth breaking her bones. Through the fire consuming her, radiating from her lungs to the ends of her body, Kyra could already feel the tearing of flesh as they sectioned her out for their enjoyment.

Darkness rolled in around her, first slowly at the edges, eating away at the panic and pain before gaining traction. Her heart jumped over its beat, stuttering in her chest before pumping its last. Were her eyes still open? Black consumed her vision, consumed her mind.

And Leah called to her. A pale light, weak but insistent. Leah called to her, voice echoing across the distance. Leah called to her without fear.

Kyra tore herself from sleep, jerking roughly in the soft warmth of her nest, wings tightening protectively around her as she rolled to her feet, ready to face the foes of her mind. Heart racing, breath coming in painful gasps that weren't enough after the airless burn, it took too many moments for her mind to recognise her surroundings. Even safe in the knowledge she was in her room, blessedly alone, it took a concentrated effort to get her breathing under control.

Standing in her darkened room, everything washed in the dull grey light of the witching hour, Kyra took note of her pains. Her heart no longer pounded in her chest, but her ribs felt bruised around the edges. Her temples throbbed with panic and exhaustion, and her cheeks were damp with tears she didn't remember spilling.

She dragged herself to her bathroom but turning on the light felt a mistake when the harsh fluorescent attacked her eyes. Squinting in a vain attempt to stop the stabbing at the back of her eyes, Kyra glanced at her reflection to find a bleary demon staring back at her. Dark circles had taken up residence under her eyes, giving her a sunken, dead appearance. Still, she was beautiful. It made her sick.

Panic-numbed fingers fumbled for the tap, releasing a rush of water that splashed back with its force. Kyra adjusted the flow and lowered her head to drink directly from the stream. The bite of cold washed away the taste of sleep and the last of her panic. She couldn't decide what was more disturbing: the thought of dragons, long-extinct, chasing her or the relief she had felt at Leah's voice. Maybe Damian was right; maybe she should just kill the girl and get it over with.

Kyra stumbled back to bed, almost connecting painfully with the edge once she threw the room back into darkness. Maybe there would be safety in her new dreams.

~ Seven ~

When morning came good and proper, Kyra managed to greet it. She would never go so far as to greet it with a smile or ever be described as bright-eyed or bushy-tailed, given her kind had shed their tails countless generations ago. Some questioned if they had existed at all. But greet it she did, nestled in the corner of the kitchen with a steaming mug of coffee cradled in the safety of her fingers. A small collection of books sat at her elbow. No matter how hard she tried to ignore them, they shone like a beacon at the corner of her eye.

She watched from her quiet perch as various demons drifted in and out of the room. Some took a simple cup of coffee, much like her own, and climbed the stairs back to their rooms. Others gathered cereal and milk and bowls and made an attempt at a meal at the table. Most would still be sleeping, their work taking them into the early hours of the morning; for those, breakfast would be closer to midday. Damian was one of these, though he didn't work. He liked to see the end of the late shift off to bed, ensuring there were no complaints, no customers to ban or issues to resolve.

Still, he would be down in around an hour, ready to make a substantial breakfast for anyone who hadn't risen or eaten yet. True, demons didn't need nearly as much sleep or food as humans, but Kyra often worried he worked himself too hard. Not that she would say anything. And not that he would listen if she did.

Downing the last of her coffee, Kyra steeled herself for what she knew she could no longer avoid. Though that didn't stop her from carefully washing and drying her mug, then placing it back in the cupboard with its mates. With nothing left to delay her, no more excuses to hold her, Kyra collected her books and climbed the stairs slowly to the top.

Bypassing her own door, though sorely tempted to take sanctuary it offered, Kyra resolutely passed first Damian's room, and then Wendy's, both firmly closed against the world, before coming to a stop at Leah's. It was entirely unremarkable, the dark stained wood identical to all the others along the hall. It would be heavy to open, weighed down with so much uncertainty. In Kyra's mind, it became a thing made of stone, a barrier of insurmountable weight, too much to overcome.

It was difficult not to talk herself out of knocking, out of trying to pretend this was a good idea, out of everything. The books clutched to her chest were a comforting weight, their sharp edges digging in hard enough to cause discomfort. Kyra focused on the gentle bite of hardcovers gripped too tight in knuckles gone white, used the solidness of it to anchor her wispy thoughts. There was a Hunter beyond the door. A Hunter she had trapped but wouldn't kill. A Hunter she was determined to win over for reasons that still felt ridiculous.

She knocked sharply and let herself in before Leah could respond, or she could talk herself out of it. The Hunter was perched on her bed, but her hair was damp, and the room smelt faintly of floral shampoo. Wendy's clothes hung on her oddly, the finely tailored blouse too loose at the chest and the pants too tight around muscled thighs. Bent over a book, back arched in a way that would be uncomfortable after any length of time, it was hard to tell if Leah hadn't heard Kyra enter or simply had not cared to look up.

Caught in the doorway, one hand gripping the door handle while the other kept the grounding books pressed hard to her chest, it was hard to reconcile this easy creature with the Hunter she had first seen. Or even the snarling mess she had left in this room a few days ago. Words danced on her tongue, a strange sentiment about captivity suiting Leah, but Kyra knew better than to open with that.

"I've brought you more books," she announced instead, finally finding herself enough to enter the room completely. The door shut with the smallest snip, and it echoed in Kyra's head like the slam of a prison cell.

Leah's head jerked up in surprise, wide eyes sliding from Kyra's face to the gifts in her arm. Any shock was quickly forgotten in the wake of open hunger on her face. She shifted on the bed, pulling her legs under herself to rise, to get closer to the knowledge Kyra bore. Even in her rush to obtain more information, Leah's hands were gentle in collecting the book already in her grasp, a finger slipped between the pages to mark her place. Cradling the book in one hand, Leah shuffled to the edge of the bed, rising with a complete lack of grace or insecurity.

Kyra held out her offering silently, trying not to flinch back with how quickly Leah crossed the space between them. The Hunter was suddenly right there, the scent of her clean skin and perfumed hair clouding Kyra's head. This close, Kyra could see the darkened patches on her shoulders where her hair had dampened the fabric. Was it cold? Or did she simply not feel it with her mind so firmly turned to whatever it had been she had been reading? Warm skin brushed her fingers where Leah's hands spread too far, her grip too eager to get around the books to avoid Kyra's. It burned despite how fleeting the touch had been. It was an accident, but Kyra's skin sang with the warmth Leah had graced her with, no matter how briefly.

Leah seemed unaware of the touch or the way it caught Kyra's breath in her throat, the young Hunter already turned back to her bed. She collected a bookmark forgotten by her pillow, slipping it into what she had been reading to better turn her attention to Kyra's offering. Taking Leah's distraction as the opportunity it was to gather her thoughts, Kyra busied herself with dragging the only chair out from behind the desk. It was tempting to place it as she had done last time, halfway between the bed and freedom, but that didn't feel right. Instead, she turned it where it was, facing the bed and making herself comfortable with the desk and wall behind her. She still had a fairly straight line to the door, but Leah could easily block her path or throw her off course if she had half a mind.

Kyra settled herself with carefully crossed ankles and delicately folded hands in her lap, her smooth movements at odds with the increasingly dark thoughts clambering in her mind. It was far too easy to picture all the ways Leah could no doubt kill her.

Leah, for her part, was entirely unaware of Kyra or her internal struggle. Sat against her headboard once more, she was bent over the books now spread before her. The seams of Wendy's pants pulled alarmingly tight against crossed legs, but Leah paid the discomfort as much mind as she did Kyra. Her fingers, so long and still warm from the shower, danced over the covers as though they could absorb the information directly without having to crease a single spine.

"I suggest you start with that one," Kyra interjected when Leah's fingers hesitated on a leather-bound book that was as old as Kyra. The original outdated most surviving demons, but that particular translation had been commissioned the year of her birth. Leah nodded, still not looking up. She tucked the book in question closer to her pillow but didn't stop reviewing her options.

"Why?"

"You asked for books." Kyra shrugged, a nonchalant move wasted on the top of Leah's still bent head.

"You could have given me anything." Leah finally looked up, eyes shining with curiosity. "You could have given me some stupid romance novel or something." It was impossible to fully quell the scoff that brought, though the cheeky twist to Leah's answering smile said that had been the intended response. "Why these?"

"I wasn't lying when I said there's a lot we could learn from one another."

"I thought you meant that you would torture me for information when you said that, not give me books."

"You asked for them." This wasn't how this conversation was meant to go—not that Kyra had really planned anything beyond giving Leah the books. A sudden wave of fear washed over her, a half-pictured image of Leah tearing pages flashing through her mind. "I can take them back if you'd prefer."

Leah snatched the books up before Kyra could finish shifting forward, pressing them close. At least destruction didn't seem likely.

"No." Leah eyed Kyra with mistrust. Her grip didn't lessen until Kyra was safely relaxed back in her chair once more. "Thank you." The words were soft, a bare whisper.

Silence stretched between them. Kyra shifted in her chair, feeling there should be more to say. This felt like a momentous occasion, something to be marked with more than a few awkward moments of conversation. She was teaching a Hunter, giving knowledge that could almost definitely be used against those she was meant to protect. Leah, looking all the world like a guest and not the prisoner she was meant to be, was thumbing through the tome Kyra had suggested. Her eyes danced too quickly to be taking in the words with any depth, but she seemed unable to resist the call of knowledge.

"If..." Leah looked up sharply, meeting Kyra's eyes with that same burning curiosity that lodged a strange flutter in Kyra's middle. "If I have questions..." She trailed off again.

"I will answer them as best I can."

"When?" The question caught Kyra off guard, something she hadn't considered. "If I'm not to leave the room, will you visit me?"

"No." Kyra smoothed her hands over thighs, pressing hard enough to hide any hint of trembling. "No, umm..." The wall behind her pressed the desk closer, the comforting weight now insistent and heavy as it pushed her. Had those fingers been taught to snap necks like hers? "I mean, you don't have to stay in this room."

Damian was going to throw a fit. Wendy would have words. Pressing her hands to her stomach did nothing to stop the way it roiled.

She tried to hide the movement as attempts to smooth creases that didn't exist, quickly shifting her palms to run repeatedly over jean clad thighs. Memories of Michael flashed in her mind.

"It would be better, I think, if you met the creatures you've learnt to kill."

Leah flinched back, looking away. Kyra pressed on, mind scrambling to keep up with the way her mouth was running. It was easier without the weight of Leah's curiosity. "It would be good for you to see we're not so different, humans and demons."

Pushing herself to her feet, Kyra's hands spasmed into fists at her sides. "Just, if you have questions, come find me." Fleeing the room was the first sensible choice Kyra made since selecting the books that now littered Leah's bed.

~ Eight ~

Without pausing in the hallway and risking Leah chasing her deeper into The Rose, Kyra strode back toward the stairs that would hopefully take her to safety. Her glamour shifted, her control slipping in the solitude of the corridor, her features rearranging into one of her well-worn faces. By the time she was mounting the stairs to return to her office, she was once more the mature business-woman, the voluptuous figure encased in a pressed white shirt and tight pencil skirt. That it was the face that had killed Michael didn't escape her notice.

The simple act of stepping into her office was enough to ground Kyra, the familiar smell of books and sight of sun-kissed wood a reminder of her power here. This was her domain. Not even a too young, too curious Hunter could disturb her here.

"Bell." Putting a smile into her voice wasn't too hard when faced with the open anxiety on the face of the other woman in the room. "Are you okay?"

"Yeah." She started to rise from the chair before Kyra's desk but lowered herself slowly at Kyra's waved direction. "Wendy said it was okay to wait?"

"Of course." Kyra slipped into her own seat on the other side of her desk, schooling her expression into a warm smile tinged with concern. It felt wrong to be relieved that it was only Bell in her office, especially with the way she was twisting her fingers together in her lap. "What's wrong? Is this about what you wanted to discuss the other day? I'm sorry for not following up. I've been-"

"Busy, yes, of course," Bell cut in in a rush, words tumbling too quickly for her to silence herself. "It's fine. I mean, I'm fine." She forced a chuckle that only heightened Kyra's unease. "I just...I wanted some advice? Actually, no. This was dumb. Sorry." She rushed to her feet, movements as jerky as her words.

"Bell." The calm surety of Kyra's voice froze her in place. "Sit down." The younger woman did so silently. Even through her glamour, she was blushing, the colour of her cheeks rising. "Now tell me what's wrong."

"I think I'm in love." The words tore themselves from Bell's throat, cracking in the air where they fell in a tangled jumble between them.

Love. Shit.

"I know we're not supposed to. I know it's wrong. But he's just so sweet. I mean, at first, I just laughed him off. They all say they want to save us at first; it's kind of cute, but it never means anything." Now that she had started, it seemed Bell couldn't stop. "But he kept coming back with flowers and little gifts."

Kyra let Bell's voice wash over her, mind already compiling a list of things to do. Damian would need to know to ensure Bell's shifts were covered. Wendy would keep an eye out, make sure Bell had a clear escape route. She'd have to call one of the other sanctuaries; maybe Hannah had some room. There was time for that yet, at least a few months, but Kyra liked to be prepared.

"So will you meet with him?" The earnest hope in Bell's eyes twisted Kyra's heart, pulling it tight against her ribs as she forced a warm smile.

"Of course." Kyra reached across the desk, gathering Bell's hands in her own as she met her halfway. "I'm happy for you."

"Really?" Her hope was turning watery, eyes shining with tears that threatened to fall. "I mean, it's okay?"

Kyra squeezed Bell's hands comfortingly before pulling back to rest against her chair. "You're allowed love here." The lie tasted vile, but Bell beamed. "Now go pack; you have a whole new life waiting for you." Kyra waved Bell off, pretending not to see how the dam broke and tears spilt down her cheeks. That Bell would leave was a given—she wouldn't be able to continue to work with love so fresh in her heart. Even if he approved, she wouldn't have the confidence.

Turning to paperwork already completed felt like dodging a bullet and avoiding a responsibility she had no right to shirk. If Kyra had any sense, she would have tried to talk Bell out of it. Or at least warned her. If only history hadn't taught her better, hadn't taught her how likely failure was and how impossible it was to avoid.

Even bathed in sunlight, the harsh rays pooling across her desk to lick at her laptop and warming her fingers, Kyra felt a chill. Meeting Bell's John had done little to reassure her. Forcing a smile had been easy, even in the face of Bell's open glee, but ignoring the way her stomach twisted over the situation wasn't as simple.

Kyra couldn't picture his face, couldn't hear his voice, couldn't taste his scent, though it should still be lingering in the air. They had left less than an hour ago, heads bent together as they whispered plans Kyra hoped wouldn't fall through. She knew they would.

Her fingers tapped ineffectually at the keyboard, barely pressing enough to make a hollow sound. She didn't exercise enough pressure to type anything—not that there was anything open. The neat expanse of her desktop stared back. The sun wouldn't warm her, and the computer was mocking her.

It was a relief when Wendy slipped into the room, a more than welcome distraction to the tension building at her temples. It was barely midday, and she had a headache.

"What is it?" She failed to keep her voice even, but Wendy didn't even blink at the sharp edges to Kyra's tone.

"A new client." She extended a sheaf of paper once she reached Kyra's desk. There was something comforting in knowing that Wendy would sound bored in the middle of a battleground. Kyra took the paper, waiting for Wendy to continue before glancing down at the information carefully printed. "Lisa gave him a quick once over when he first came in. He didn't ask for what he really wanted, so she didn't offer." Kyra grunted to show she was listening, eyes darting immediately to the section labelled interests. "He left happy enough and made another appointment. I figured you'd want to handle it yourself."

"Thanks." Kyra tucked the paper behind a pile of bills. "Send me the details for his next appointment. And call Hannah."

Wendy nodded at each order but didn't leave. They watched each other for a long moment, Wendy's face carefully blank even as Kyra raised an expectant eyebrow.

"Yes?" she finally asked.

"Have you seen the news?"

"What?" Kyra didn't engage much in human affairs, the same way she avoided demon. Too much of a headache.

"They've passed this new law..." Wendy spoke slowly, selecting her words carefully. Or expecting Kyra to not completely understand. "Apparently, people aren't allowed in certain establishments after three in the morning."

"Certain establishments," Kyra repeated.

"Bars, clubs." Wendy shrugged.

"Brothels?"

"They didn't say it in so many words." Wendy rolled her shoulders, trying to resettle her glamour. It was a nervous habit that set Kyra's teeth on edge. Usually because it meant something bad was about to happen.

"Find out who we need to bribe."

"I don't know if it'll be that easy."

"Oh, come on. They call us the oldest profession for a reason." Kyra waved her hand, hoping it would dismiss Wendy's worries. "The humans have never been good at denying themselves anything. Even if they actually police it, it won't last long."

"If you say so." She sounded less than convinced.

"I do." It felt good to ease such a simple concern. The tendrils of relief seeped into the tension across her skull and prised it away. "Trust me; this is nothing." Wendy nodded, though it lacked her usual resolution. "Don't forget to call Hannah." She bowed her head minutely, turning on her heel sharply. The click of her shoes on the floorboards warmed Kyra in a way the sunlight had failed to.

~ Nine ~

"Mary's here." Wendy barely poked her head in the doorway, the words only half spoken before the other woman was bustling into Kyra's office like she owned the place. Like she belonged. Kyra couldn't fight her indulgent smile.

"Thank you, Wendy," Kyra called to her retreating back. This was an improvement; Mary burst in without warning more often than with.

Kyra watched the young reporter as she crossed the room, her thin frame and easy smile a distraction most fell for. No matter how sweet her demeanour, nothing could hide the sharp intelligence behind her eyes or the sharper focus that she wielded like a blade. Even now, sauntering the few steps between door and desk, her bright brown eyes danced across Kyra's desk in the hopes of picking up hints of a story.

With exaggerated calm, Kyra collected her papers and slid them into a drawer. Her laptop closed with a small click, and her smile was sharp when she turned it to Mary.

Mary, for her part, shrugged; surely Kyra couldn't blame a girl for trying. She was pretty in an unassuming kind of way, with brown hair and eyes that could have been found on any face. She was average in height and build, as though her creator had selected the base mold to make her, not bothering with any changes or real touches of difference.

Sliding into the chair across from Kyra, Mary's laser focus turned to Kyra herself, looking the demon up and down slowly as unknowable thoughts raced through her mind. In anyone else, her smug surety would have had Kyra's fingers curled into angry fists. On Mary, it just made her smile.

"What can I do for you today, Mary?" Kyra asked slowly. Settling her elbows on her desk, she rested her chin on steepled fingers. "I don't remember any new politicians visiting."

"Not that you'd tell me if they had." Mary grinned, the shark-like expression strange on her plain face. It wasn't just her intelligence that made Mary dangerous; it was her general ordinariness. She could hide in a crowd with ease and was often forgotten or over-looked. She used this to her advantage constantly, her forgettable face and strange non-uniqueness allowing her to blend into crowds and sneak into places she shouldn't be. If Kyra had met her earlier, had had a chance to utilise this to her own gain, Mary would have made a perfect spy. Instead, she used her ability to blend in to reveal truths to the public. "No, I'm not here on business. Not strictly."

"Oh?" It was hard to hide her surprise. Mary had never shown any interest in sampling the services of The Rose. "What's your poison?"

Even her laugh was forgettable. Not too loud or soft, like her voice, it was almost monotone but not enough so to be worth noting. "No, I'm not here for that."

"What, you just came for coffee?" Incredulity entered Kyra's voice. True, she considered Mary a friend but only in the same way she considered any human a friend. A work colleague at most. Someone who was pleasant enough to talk to but not a person to actively seek out.

"No, not that either." There was something else to the sharpness of her smile, an extra light to her bright gaze. All at once, Kyra was on edge, skin tightening as senses immediately tunnelled to focus on the woman across from her. Her throne-like chair suddenly felt more like a prison than a position of power.

Wendy slipped into the room before Mary could say any more, though her presence did little to ease the itch of danger between

Kyra's shoulders. Placing a mug of coffee before Mary and a glass of water at Kyra's elbow, she waited for Kyra's nod before leaving again. Mary didn't need watching, at least not by Wendy. Hopefully.

"No, I'm chasing something a little bigger." Mary sipped from her mug, eyes sliding closed in pleasure. While Wendy couldn't take a message to save her life, she was obsessed with good coffee and made the perfect cup for every visitor. Kyra waited it out, knowing Mary liked her drama and pushing the woman would only make her sulk. "You've heard of Richard Smith, I assume?"

"The conservative? What of him?"

"His new laws," she said.

"I've already had this conversation with Wendy, though I do appreciate your concern." Kyra sipped her own drink, fighting for an equilibrium that was never so far out of reach. "We've survived through stupider legislation."

"Oh no, these are new." Mary's grin took on a wicked edge. She loved knowing more than others, had made a career of it, but Kyra hated it when it was directed at herself. "He's taking the next step in his war on failing families. He wants to make adultery illegal."

Kyra didn't bother stifling her laughter at that. "I can see that going down well with his party. Half of them are regulars." Mary leaned forward with open hunger on her face before catching herself and drawing back. "No, I'm not giving you names." Mary shrugged her disappointment, unsurprised.

"His views are gaining traction," she said instead. "Those who disagree find themselves suddenly lacking in power and funding. Anyone he can't charm or bully quickly find themselves at the centre of a scandal."

"You sound almost impressed by that."

"He's good."

"He's going to put you out of business," Kyra pointed out. "Soon everyone will be following his rules, and then what? No scandals, no underhanded deals, no more cash under tables and late-night phone calls to tap.

"Richard Smith is trying to build a utopia, a world without sin."
She scoffed. Even if it risked her and her way of life just as much as
Mary's, Kyra knew humans better than that. "He's trying to force
you to go against your very nature."

"As though he isn't a risk to demons like you?"

"I wouldn't say that too loudly if I was you."

"Why, that's what you are." Mary was clearly put out by Kyra's
lack of reaction to the allegation. As though they hadn't been dancing around the subject for months. Or maybe Kyra had been dancing, sidestepping as Mary dropped hints and made digs. Reading
women was so much harder than men.

"Yes, but if Damian overheard you, he'd be very upset." Kyra
finished the last of her water with a delicate swallow. Knowing
that Mary knew was nothing compared to having the knowledge
spoken. It settled thickly in the air between them, tasting of Kyra's
own fear. "He doesn't take kindly to humans making such damaging
accusations."

"Are you threatening me?" There was a fission of terror beneath
the incredulity in Mary's voice. Kyra had misstepped.

"No, of course not. You're too useful to waste." Kyra smiled
warmly, though Mary's anger didn't lessen. "Besides, knowing puts
you at greater risk than me."

"What do you mean?"

"I mean, there are enemies and factions you know nothing
about that would prefer you silenced over watching a lynch mob
storming the place. Mutually assured destruction is a wonderful
thing. I'd tell you to quit while you can, but that would be pointless,
wouldn't it?"

Mary thought for a moment, disbelief and fear still at the forefront of her expressions, but Kyra could see the burning curiosity
too. "It really would." She spoke as though half distracted, mind
already whirling over possibilities and where to source more information. Kyra would have to call in a favour. Someone needed to
keep an eye on her.

~ Ten ~

"I have a question," Leah said in way of greeting, letting herself into Kyra's office without any hesitation. A part of Kyra's mind made a note to remind Wendy about announcing people before letting them barge in, but it was only a small corner drowned out by a flutter of anxiety and a suddenly racing pulse. Kyra closed her laptop with none of her usual calm surety, eyes locked on Leah as she hesitated in the doorway, a book clutched to her chest. "Is that okay?"

"Yes, yes." Kyra waved her in, gesturing to the chairs in front of her desk. She had told the Hunter to come find her if she had questions. Knowing that did nothing to stop the mammoth-sized butterflies who had decided to take up residence in her stomach.

"Tell me about demons." It was neither a question nor a demand. Almost like a suggestion, a hope Kyra would acquiesce with a touch of doubt that she would.

"What would you like to know?" Kyra waited for Leah to sit, hoping the brief seconds would give her brain time to catch up. It didn't.

"Everything."

The word carried more emotion than Kyra could analyse. It was laden with curiosity and a burning desire that was entirely foreign to her. Leah's eyes remained trained on her lap, on her twisting fingers over the leather-bound book Kyra had suggested she start with. Somehow Kyra doubted that was the only one she had read.

"You'll need to be a little more specific." Kyra made a show of leaning back in her chair, settling into her throne with more confidence than she felt.

"The Church teaches..." Leah hesitated, shooting Kyra a challenging look from under pale lashes. She was daring Kyra to scoff or laugh. The books had shown Leah her ignorance, and she was not going to abide by it any longer. It wasn't hard to smile gently at the Hunter, a soft expression of encouragement that shouldn't have had a place on Kyra's face. "The Church says there are three kinds of demons, but this"—she tapped the book sharply—"says four. But according to what I know..."

Leah shook her head, struggling with a lack of information. Kyra nodded slowly, waiting for a hint of question she could answer. "We were taught," the word twisted with disdain, "that there are succubi, incubi, and vampires. But this," her fingers twitched against the book, tightening alarmingly for a moment before a calming breath forced them loose. Kyra's pulse spiked at the show, very afraid that Leah would tear the tome. "This mentions fae and witches. Wouldn't that make five, not four?"

"It would if succubi and incubi weren't the same. I can almost see how humans would think we're not the same species; I guess a female peacock hardly seems the same as a male." Kyra spoke slowly, unpacking the misunderstandings in Leah's words. It was hard to not fall prey to her own curiosity, her own desire to understand just how wrong they had gotten it. "But that's not important," she waved away the point, conscious of the rising flush to Leah's cheeks. Information she had long taken for granted was new and wonderful to Leah, but she couldn't risk driving her away by appearing patronising, no matter how much she wanted to lecture on the idiocy of humans who thought they knew it all. "You want to know about fae and witches?"

Leah nodded eagerly, her initial shyness eclipsed by the burning need to know. Her face was alight with it, eyes too bright for Kyra to hold her gaze. Being the target of such intensity made her stomach swoop, not in familiar anxiety or concern, but something warmer and fuzzy at the edges.

"I'll start with witches." Kyra cleared her throat, ignoring the way the butterflies in her stomach had multiplied alarmingly. Though they hadn't lessened in size. "Witches are probably the closest to human. They live a bit longer and can use magic, but they look like you and eat like you and reproduce like you."

"Practically human then." Leah laughed, the sound breathless and lovely. "What kind of magic?"

"I don't actually know." Kyra shrugged, quick to continue at the falling disappointment on Leah's face. "I mean, I don't know how it works. But they can cast spells and enchantments."

"Like with wands?"

Shaking her head, Kyra searched for the right words. "It's less sparkles and explosions and more droning incantations and clouds of smoke. Mostly their magic is used to conceal and confuse. Our magic"—Kyra touched a hand to her own chest—"evolved to help us feed, a means to read human desire, mirror it, and heighten it as necessary. Their magic evolved to let them hide in plain sight, protect their homes from humans, that kind of thing."

"Evolved?"

"Look, I know the Church probably teaches creationism, but you're smarter than that at least." Kyra let a touch of teasing, a hint of flirtation, enter her voice. Leah's answering blush and small smile said the risk had paid off. "Though, truth be told, there are people much smarter than me who have devoted their lives to arguing how we came to be. I don't concern myself with it much. What's the point of knowing how everything came about?"

"And fae?" Leah prodded.

"The fae are gone." It should have hurt to say. There should have been pain or sadness or anger, anything other than a cold emptiness. "The last of their kind died before I was born."

"What happened to them?"

Words froze in Kyra's throat, stuck painfully where they couldn't break free. Would she choke on them? Would they be able to break themselves free? There was rage now, a burning anger that screamed in Buddug's voice. A frustrated knowledge that was beyond her ability to control, a situation she could do nothing to fix. An inconvenience she couldn't entirely ignore.

"They were effectively wiped out." Her voice was rough and raw with emotions she had no claim to, words heavy with meaning she had spent most of her life trying to avoid. "The Church hunted them down and eradicated them entirely."

"What?" Leah's open shock only stoked Kyra's rage into an inferno.

"They were slaughtered by you, by your people." When had she stood up? Her palms landed on the desk with a sharp slap, fingers clawing ineffectually against hard wood. She was looming, and Leah was shrinking back. It didn't bring her joy, didn't lessen the sudden boiling heat; it barely even registered. The truth was bitter on Kyra's tongue, and it was easier to blame Leah for sins long past than examine her own inactivity. "The Church culled them out of existence within a generation."

This had been a mistake.

Kyra let herself drop back into her chair. "Get out."

"But—"

"We're done here." Kyra was cold without the rage, the burning leaving her as quickly as it had ignited. Leah hesitated, wide eyes darting from Kyra to the book in her lap and back again, lips slightly parted in a question that would have no doubt rekindled Kyra's anger. She almost wished the Hunter would ask just to burn away the crushing void left by her fleeing emotions.

Leah, it seemed, possessed an ounce more of self-preservation than Kyra had given her credit for, silently leaving the room. Kyra kept her eyes trained on the far corner, pretending they didn't burn with tears. The sound of the door closing would have been a relief if it wasn't joined by Damian's scent. He had barely taken two steps past the door before Kyra was piercing him with eyes red from tears and a slipping glamour. "Not now."

He stopped dead, hands raising automatically in supplication. Concern twisted his lips into a frown as his eyes softened from shock to something too close to pity for Kyra's current mood. "I—"

Whatever he had intended to say, Kyra wasn't going to allow it. "Not now." The words cracked on a voice half-broken, too loud but still not enough to warm her cold insides. Walls of anger were always easier, cleaner.

"I'll come back later," he conceded, leaving as quietly as he had come.

The room felt even colder without either of them, though it had already been freezing without her rage. Rage that she had no claim to, mourning a loss she'd never understand, not entirely. Buddug was right: she was a coward.

Damian was good to his word, though later turned out to be a full day. At least Kyra's emotions were entirely under control by the time he cornered her in the hallway. He was simply there when she exited her room, despite it being a good three hours before he usually rose. It was more than an hour before she herself would usually be up, but sleep had been fleeting and tainted by the image of Leah's open fear. Fear of her.

"You good?" It was probably too much to hope for the pretence of small talk this early in the morning, this late in their relationship. Kyra nodded anyway, heading to the stairs and confident he would follow. His footfalls, silent under her own heeled boots, were in perfect time. "Erik brought a friend home yesterday."

A sharp question formed and died on Kyra's lips in the space of a few steps. Leah's face, painted in fear, flashed in her mind again. She forced it away with ruthless determination, pushing it down with her anger at Damian for not telling her earlier, anger at herself for not letting him. "How old?" she asked instead, leading Damian down the stairs.

"A few months at most."

The harsh press of nails into skin startled Kyra; she hadn't remembered curling her hands into fists. A few months, barely a child. A child in the body of an adult with too much strength and an unquenchable blood lust. And Erik had brought it here.

She was going to kill him, slowly, painfully. Were it possible, she would have drained him dry without giving him the pleasant dream.

"Where are they now?"

"I'm pretty sure Erik took him to bed."

"Go wake them." She stopped before her office door, turning fully to Damian. He kept his face impassive, but she could feel the judgement. This should have been resolved yesterday, the moment Erik dared to bring a fledgling into The Rose. But she had been too busy sulking after yelling at a Hunter. "I'll deal with it."

Not waiting for a response and unwilling to meet Damian's carefully blank expression, Kyra slipped into her office. Sitting behind her desk, she immediately regretted bypassing the kitchen. A coffee would have made the impending confrontation easier, more tolerable, but it was too late now.

Her fingers danced to her laptop, running along the seam of the lid without opening it. It was too early to start working, and there was not enough time before she'd be staring down two vampires of questionable intelligence and motives. Looking like she was waiting on them wasn't ideal, though. Kyra huffed a sigh of frustration, her only concession to a ruined morning, before opening her laptop and turning it on. Pretending to be busy would have to do.

It took less than ten minutes for the two men to slip into her office, more than long enough for Kyra to stew in her frustrations. Erik ducked his head on entry, whether to show respect or an excuse to fold in on himself, Kyra didn't care. Her attention was taken by his companion. Despite being only a few months old as a vampire, he hadn't been young when Erik got his teeth into him.

Shocks of silver sat over each ear, contrasted by his otherwise dark hair. Cropped close, it highlighted the sharp angles of his wide face. He could only be described as blocky, rough-hewn shapes piled together in a hulking form that easily dwarfed Erik. Kyra would have taken him as a bodyguard, not a lover.

He shifted slightly, the movement small on him but large in the room, placing himself between Kyra and Erik. She wasn't sure it was entirely conscious.

"Welcome." Keeping the teeth out of her smile was hard, harder than keeping the bite out of her voice. "Please, take a seat." She waved to the chairs more out of habit than any desire to be courteous, especially when that massive body set one groaning alarmingly. "Damian tells me we have a new guest." This was directed entirely at Erik, Kyra's smile sharpening slightly.

"Is this not a sanctuary?"

Kyra blinked in surprise. She had expected a voice like the body, deep and slow. While it was a rumble, the words were clear and almost clipped. Looking at him closely, there was a quiet intelligence behind his eyes. He was a greater threat than she had realised.

Leaning back in her chair, Kyra turned her attention to the newcomer entirely. Erik happily pulled further into himself, keen to be forgotten. "It is," she conceded at length. "But I must protect everyone here, not just every stray that appears on my doorstep."

The large vampire smiled slowly, the expression unsettling. It was predatory, which was to be expected, but also calculating. "Do you think I'm a threat?"

Kyra allowed herself the laugh that bubbled up. His smile didn't fade, didn't change.

"We all know you are, dear."

"Caleb," he grunted.

"Nice to meet you, Caleb." Kyra shifted forward, offering her hand. "I'm Kyra, your new boss." Caleb hesitated, glancing at Erik, who only nodded emphatically. He took her hand. "Everyone who lives here works. I'm sure I'll find a use for a man with your talents."

"And if you don't? Will I be expected to leave?" His grip was sure and strong, but he wasn't foolish enough to make it crushing.

"I will; don't you worry about that." Kyra's mind danced between possibilities, weighing risks and rewards and potential outcomes. She maintained her calm mask, meeting Caleb's eyes with her own steely gaze. "You will be welcome here as long as you can follow the rules."

"Rules?"

"Erik will be happy to explain, I'm sure. He is vouching for you after all." Kyra watched Erik swallow his fear with no small touch of satisfaction. "Now, if you'll both excuse me, I have work to do."

They rose in tandem, Caleb following Erik's lead out the door. That was a relationship Kyra would have to watch closely. There seemed so many ways it could go wrong, but at least Caleb didn't appear entirely lost to his new nature. His intelligence was a blessing, despite how much more dangerous it made him.

~ Eleven ~

Kyra had almost forgotten about the new client, though it had only been just over a week since Wendy slid his information into Kyra's hands. She had almost missed the small addition to her calendar, something Wendy had no doubt included when her emails had gone unanswered and loud looks ignored.

Wendy never openly told Kyra that she needed to feed, nor did she remind her in words that she had agreed to take on the client. If Kyra insisted, someone else would have seen to him. But if Kyra insisted, Wendy would have been at Damian's side in an instant, reminding him that Kyra hadn't taken her fill with the Hunter, hadn't eaten properly in almost two months. That would have led to an argument which would have ended with Kyra seeing the client anyway, so this felt more like the path of least resistance than actually giving in.

Waiting in a room on the second floor at the opposite end of her own quarters, Kyra tried not to pace or think of all the things she could be doing at the moment. The room was larger than her own, though it didn't look it with the additional furniture. An ornate wardrobe took one wall, the doors firmly shut on an array of toys she hoped she wouldn't need. A vanity of the same heavy wood was across from it, framing the large bed. All were made of dark wood and carved with vines.

At the sound of approaching feet, Kyra ducked into the adjoining bathroom. He entered, and Kyra reached out with her senses, with her magic. Sightlessly, she saw him, running formless fingers through his mind. His desire was low, closer to anticipation than need, but she could read the colours of it. It pulsed with a sickly light, tainted and nauseating. Forcing down bile, Kyra wrapped herself in a glamour he would find most pleasing before stepping into the room.

Keeping her eyes down and mind attuned to his lust, she more sensed than saw him flinch back as his desire spiked. The twisting guilt did little to settle her stomach, but that was easily ignored. She crossed the space between them, eyes trained on her feet. It was a strange line to dance, between innocence and seduction. Thinking overly long on it didn't help.

Kyra could feel him trembling even before she was close enough to reach out and touch. He fought his desire, fought to keep himself motionless. It didn't matter; she didn't need him to reach out. Stopping close enough to feel the heat of his body, Kyra paused, giving him the chance to make a move. When he didn't, something to be commended, she took his hand in hers while enveloping his mind in magic.

"My pet," he croaked out, the words spoken into the air and the space between their minds.

The moment their skin touched, she shed her glamour, her skin crawling in disgust as she discarded the vile disguise. In his mind, the scene played out according to his desires. Kyra pushed their shared fantasy into the darkest corner of her own mind, jerking his unresponsive body forward.

Manhandling a person was beyond her at the best of times, let alone with her mind half distracted in keeping them caught in a tenuous trap. Kyra shoved at his shoulders and somehow convinced his body to move without input from his mind. It was slow and shuffling, but he eventually fell onto the bed. For a horrible second that stretched to eternity, Kyra thought she would lose the physical connection. The fantasy would have remained, but the risk of him seeing her as she was grew too great without touch reinforcing the flow of her magic. Keeping one hand pressed to the side of his face, she used the other to dig through the bedside table next to her. The familiar curve of the talisman was a relief, her fingers closing around the cool comfort of hard stone wrapped in leather.

Kyra shoved at the drawer ineffectually. It caught at a strange angle and refused to close. Frustration threatened to seep into the fantasy, and she tried to ignore the uncooperative furniture in favour of clambering onto the bed above the sprawled form of her client.

There was an element of haste to her movements that had to be balanced with maintaining comfort and focus. She briefly considered attempting to lift his legs the rest of the way onto the mattress, his current position awkward at best, body twisted where it had fallen with his chest rolled to the side and head pulled to lay flat. His legs trailed down the side of the bed, knees wedged against the floor with little more than luck keeping him from sliding entirely onto the carpet.

Kyra folded her own legs close, shifting her grip so that his head was cradled in both her hands. His hair brushed her calves, and she resisted the urge to pull away.

He had begun moaning at some point, though it was impossible for her to tell if it was within the fantasy or into the warming air of the room. Kyra kept her mind as far as possible from the fantasy, the familiar disgust impossible to ignore or become accustomed to. Instead, she focused on the talisman in her hand, pressing it between her fingers and his forehead, ensuring it touched as much of his skin as possible.

Another flavour of magic leaked from the obsidian depths, wrapping itself around Kyra's questing fingers and dampening the fantasy. To him, it would still be sharp and real, but to Kyra, it was fuzzy at the edges, too far off to see clearly. Her mind squinted to keep it in focus. Hannah was getting better at making these charms; a few years ago, Kyra would have had to throw herself fully into the fantasy to keep the connection.

The body in front of her shifted, moans clearly heard. Her fingers itched to pull away, his desire a coating of slime she couldn't free herself from. Not yet.

Pushing her fingers deeper, pressing the stone harder into his skin, she flooded his mind with her magic. His answering lust rushed back into her, filling her middle, her stomach. Kyra expertly split her focus between the press of the warming stone, the rush of energy, and the carefully muted blade of her desire. She played the body before her and the mind under her fingertips, carving a song from his desires. A building crescendo of lust rang out against the pounding drums of his heart, the rising tempo racing to experience the final notes.

Too soon and not soon enough, it was over, the body before her letting out a pitiful whimper as the body in her mind roared. She knew without looking he had soiled his pants. A careless mistake. Maybe he wouldn't be too shocked to wake in the bath. It was too late to plant the image in his mind, their shared fantasy already dissipating into nothing, but a release that violent was possibly enough to cover the missing memories.

Kyra stood from the bed, tucking the talisman back into the bedside table as she clothed herself in a clean glamour. Her stomach churned, half-convinced she had just gorged herself on a meal on the edge of spoiling, full to the brim but unsure of the freshness of the food.

Manoeuvring him was no less difficult when passed out, and without the connection of magic, it was hard to convince herself he was worth touching. He was somehow heavier despite the glut of energy he had left in her, and she considered leaving him on the bed, maybe dropping him on the floor halfway to the bathroom or just fully clothed in the bathtub. Talking herself into peeling off his clothes was harder, every inch of skin reminding her of the rot in his desires.

Once naked, she filled the bath enough to cover his lap but not enough to risk drowning. Leaving him to die was more tempting than leaving him on the floor with stained pants. She made a tight bundle of his clothes and carried them with her to the door. They were passed off to the first person she came across, trusting them to see the offending items cleaned and returned before he woke. He'd be out for half an hour at least, almost exactly as long as the fantasy had felt for him. Kyra would be trapped with his taste for far longer.

Bell's tears seeped through the incorporeal fabric of Kyra's blouse to stain the skin beneath her glamour. They were warm and tickled as they slid slowly down her back, but she didn't pull away. If anything, she pulled the younger succubus closer, held her tighter. Even knowing it wouldn't be forever, wouldn't be close to the human lifetime Bell was dreaming of, saying goodbye was hard.

"You'll call," Kyra murmured into Bell's hair, auburn fire today. It wasn't an order or a request. It was a hope that would probably go unfulfilled. Kyra wouldn't hear from Bell, but others at The Rose would, and that would have to be enough.

Kyra focused on breathing Bell's scent and committing it to memory, trying desperately to ignore the small pile of luggage tucked in the doorway. Packed with clothes she didn't really need and a wave of gifts, it would feel light as air to Bell. To Kyra, it was a weight that wouldn't shift from her stomach.

"Kyra?" The soft voice was a fraction of a second behind the whisper of her opening office door. Neither gave enough time for Kyra to gently pull away from Bell. Not that she should feel ashamed for comforting a friend about to leave. If only logic worked on the sharp drop of her stomach at Leah's small gasp. "Sorry, I'll..." the Hunter faltered.

Schooling her features into something akin to calm, Kyra pulled herself away from Bell, her senses honing in on Leah. The Hunter was caught in the doorway, afraid to cross the entrance but seemingly frozen in place. Distantly, Kyra was aware of Bell dabbing at her eyes to fix Leah with a look of open curiosity.

"Leah, come in." Her skin buzzed, but the sensation felt distant. Everything felt distant. Stepping around her desk to her chair didn't ground her; it should have. "Sit." She waved at the seat across from her, more out of habit than thought.

Bell, sensing the dismissal that wasn't voiced, passed Leah on the way to the door. She smiled encouragingly at the Hunter, though it seemed lost on Leah, her own eyes darting between the two demons, expression blank but gaze flashing. She walked slowly into the room. A shutter had closed over her face, a tension held high on her shoulders.

"I have questions." Leah's tone was as guarded as her face, speaking only when she had settled in the chair.

"Of course." Kyra reclined against the soft leather of her chair. Did Leah expect her to linger on the anger of their last encounter? "I'm happy to enlighten you." Kyra winced, the words too patronising, but unsure of how to be reassuring. This was what she wanted, after all—to teach the Hunter.

"Vampires." For a long moment, Kyra worried that was Leah's question, a single word. Her hands were twisting in her lap, but she hadn't brought a book. There were no cues, no clues for Kyra to guess at. The silence between them stretched. "They eat people, like you do," Leah finally finished.

The flash of anger Kyra felt at the accusation was entirely her own. Leah didn't know any better, though that did little to reduce the indignant disgust Kyra felt. "No." The word was sharper than it should have been. "Vampires consume humans." Kyra's mouth twisted over the words, lip curling. "They feast on blood and life force and leave nothing but hollow husks behind when they leave anything behind at all."

"But they do kill?"

"Some don't." Kyra shrugged. "But most revel in the destruction of life."

"But you don't?" There was something to Leah's voice, the flat way she asked, that set Kyra on edge. The question felt deeper than wanting to know about demonic eating habits.

Shifting forward, Kyra fell into an easy position of elbows on desk and hands tucked under her chin. Open, easy, inviting. Maybe she could salvage this conversation yet. "As a species or personally?"

"As a species." Leah shot back, but Kyra felt she was more interested in a personal answer.

"Generally, we avoid it." It felt too much like a trap; there was a taste of bait to the questions. Kyra couldn't see the teeth, couldn't sense how to avoid them, but she could feel them biting into her skin. "Death isn't always avoidable, especially for the young and inexperienced, but it is hardly necessary."

"And you?" Darkness seeped into Leah's voice. "How many have you killed?" The question was a purr. If she hadn't watched it slip from Leah's lips, Kyra would have sworn someone else had spoken.

"How many demons have you killed?"

Leah stiffened in her chair, face briefly twisted with shame before falling back into the blank mask of anger. Kyra held her own emotions tight. She fought to remain passive as she watched Leah's thoughts whirl. She shouldn't have taken the bait, shouldn't have driven her own attack home. This wasn't going to help. She needed to stop letting Leah get under her skin.

"You can't pretend you haven't. Not even the Church would send people out without practical experience." The Hunter turned away, gaze falling to the ground. Did she wish it would swallow her? "Come on, how many? Or have you lost count?"

Fire licked at her words and her belly; the tattered edges of her control were slipping from her fingers as her mind conjured pictures of Leah soaked in demon blood. It was far too easy to imagine her hair a golden halo, slipped from her ponytail in the struggle, streaks of sticky blood caught on skin and strands where careless hands had pushed it away from her face. Her chest heaving with effort, shirt painted with splashes of viscera. Knife gripped in a fist drenched with someone else's life force.

"How many?" Kyra demanded in a low growl.

"Fourteen." Leah spat, voice tinged with pride even as her cheeks flushed in shame.

The word, the number, struck Kyra square in the chest, forcing air from her lungs as she fell back into the embrace of her chair. The soft leather and high back did nothing to comfort her. Her blood was ice, and it did nothing to fill the sudden hollow that was her chest. Such a high number for such a young Hunter.

Kyra's mind spun as it scrambled for numbers; how many died to train a Hunter? How many Hunters trained a year? They were so few to begin with. Knowing they were being systematically wiped out and facing the truth of it were very different.

"How many?" Leah threw her question back at her, but Kyra was too cold, too empty to flinch at the blow.

"Three," she answered without thinking, without pausing to consider lying. "A murderer when I was first learning to feed safely. A..." even in the chill of her shock, she couldn't find the right words. "A less than pleasant man that no one will miss, and the Hunter you arrived with." Kyra spoke tonelessly, not caring if Leah was listening, not caring if the words penetrated. They weren't piercing the panicked fog of her own mind. "I remember their faces, their scents. I can still taste them. Sometimes I dream about them." With a sudden sharp focus, Kyra brought herself under control and glared at Leah. "Can you say the same? Did you know the names of those you killed? Can you remember their faces?"

"We were trained," Leah spoke through gritted teeth, her own rage growing to match Kyra's. "They taught us not to care, not to think of it. We were killing demons. We were killing things. You killed—" She stopped short.

"People?" Kyra laughed bitterly. "You still don't think we're people do you?"

"You kidnapped me; you're holding me prisoner."

"And you came here to kill me. Don't pretend you're the hero here."

"And I suppose you are?" Leah's face shifted, anger falling away as she raised her eyes to Kyra's. She tilted her head, and it took Kyra's breath. "No, even you don't see yourself as the hero."

Her anger skittered away, fleeing under the scrutiny of Leah's curious stare. Rage had been warm, a barrier, a modicum of control.

"There are no heroes."

"No, there aren't," Leah agreed. They watched each other in the sudden quiet, Leah the picture of calm while Kyra struggled to find balance. Without the anger, without the fight, she was defenceless against Leah's too sharp eyes. "I can't remember their faces; I can't remember anything beyond the rage of blood. We were taught to focus only on that, only on the heat of battle, never the face across from us. We were taught to not see their faces.

"I can't remember their faces, but I can still hear their screams." Leah didn't drop Kyra's gaze, no matter how much she wished the Hunter would free her from it. "My trainers made me go again and again until I could do it without crying. Without flinching. I didn't get better at it, just better at pretending it didn't hurt."

"Shit." Kyra hadn't meant to speak, hadn't meant to shatter the fragile silence following Leah's words, but it had slipped out of numb lips. She was so young, barely more than a child, too young to be given such a darkness. Kyra's skin itched, buzzing with static that screamed at her to lash out, to hit and hurt those that had put the blankness in Leah's eyes.

"Maybe you're right. Maybe I am the monster here, not you." Leah's tone was aiming for light and missed entirely. The mirthless laugh that followed did nothing to reassure Kyra. "I'm sorry; I'll let you get back to work."

The casual emptiness to her voice left Kyra reeling, unable to understand what the hell had just happened, even long after Leah had left.

~ Twelve ~

Damian burst into her office, his scent roiling but not enough to cover the smell of human. Kyra looked up sharply as he bodily threw the man forward. The stranger stumbled, catching himself on the edge of falling. He whirled to face Damian, arms coming up as he fought his momentum to lunge at the demon. Wearing the mask of a bodybuilder today, Damian cut an intimidating figure, even if it did nothing to alter his own physical strength.

Fuelled by rage if the snarl on his face was any good indication, Damian was still able to catch the reckless man, pivoting easily. Allowing his attacker's momentum to drive them, Damian guided him around until he was being thrown towards Kyra's desk once more. Kyra watched as the boy caught himself on the edge of the hard wood, fingers curling into the solid weight before using it as a springboard to surge at Damian once more. Damian, for his part, was already squaring his shoulders in preparation.

"Stop." Kyra pressed the word directly into the young Hunter's mind, coating it in magic and a need to obey her, to please her. His head jerked back as her power blanketed his senses, a pained gasp falling from his lips. His whole body drained of energy, suddenly still except for a gentle swaying as he fought to keep his feet. "Come, sit down. Let's talk." Keeping her voice even, a low croon that would lick along his every nerve, Kyra drew on waves of power to ease his rage down to nothing.

He sat, movements jerky and not quite his own. Damian took the chair beside him, bemused smile tugging at the corners of his lips.

76

"Good." Kyra maintained her soft tone and softer brush of magic, pulling her senses back to allow his brain room to breathe without her cloying scent. "Have you come to kill me?"

"Yes." His voice cracked high. He looked even younger sat still and without the fire of violence twisting his smooth features. There were still traces of baby fat on his cheeks, his face not yet matured fully. Maybe it was the press of her magic, but despite his age, he still seemed to lack the innocence Kyra had found in Leah's eyes.

"Did you come alone?" Kyra could feel his mind balk at the question, layers of loyalty surging against the gentle suggestions her magic whispered in his ear. She pressed harder. He didn't have years of experience, no practical knowledge to defend himself with. A whimper escaped his lips as his mind fought and failed to stop Kyra's creeping influence.

"Yes."

"Put him with Leah." Kyra kept her focus on the boy, barely turning to Damian to give her order. She wove a fine net of magic, tangling it in the brightest parts of his mind. A spiderweb of power wrapped tight around his very core, gossamer-thin and impossible to be rid of.

"What?" Damian's smile was gone, replaced by a shock that was quickly being eaten by anger.

"Put him with Leah," she repeated slowly.

"So they can work together to kill you?"

"He's hardly in a position to conspire." They spoke over the boy's head, his eyes vacant and mouth lax.

"Then let me do the same to her."

"No."

"What's the point of keeping a brain-dead husk? It's almost as stupid as keeping a fucking Hunter."

"He's not brain dead." Kyra extended her senses and delved deeper into the mind before her. She didn't need to check, didn't need to confirm; she had perfect control of her magic. That didn't stop the spike of relief when she found no lasting damage. "He'll even go back to normal if I want him to."

"Kyra," Damian snapped, "we are not keeping another one."

Turning her attention to the Hunter, more to ignore Damian's glower than out of any great concern, Kyra's mind raced. Keeping him was a stupid decision, worse than kidnapping Leah. But could she kill him? There was no shortage of demons who would love to sink literal or magical teeth into a Hunter; she could have plausible deniability. He'd make a perfect snack for Erik's fledgling, if nothing else.

Leah's face flashed in her mind, and Kyra knew she couldn't do it. She had kept Leah and given her books to sway the Hunter to her side, not to weaken her own resolve.

"Just put him in with Leah."

For a moment, she was sure Damian would continue arguing or even just reach out and kill the boy himself. It shouldn't have been such a surprise, such a relief, when he did as asked. Standing slowly, he raised the Hunter with a punishing grip on the human's elbow. The whites of his knuckles did little to calm Kyra or her thoughts.

Kyra was better prepared for Damian's anger when he returned, the heat of it palpable as he strode back into her office.

"Give me one good reason why I shouldn't kill them both."

"I've told you-"

"You've given me excuses," he cut in sharply. "I've had nothing but excuses and a Hunter wandering the halls like she belongs here, but no explanation. And don't give me some bullshit about swaying her to our side—you two fight every time you talk." Kyra's teeth clicked together sharply. She wasn't pouting, wasn't sulking, and definitely wasn't cursing Wendy for telling Damian everything she heard.

"She's killed fourteen," Kyra said instead, voice barely above a whisper and more open than she wanted.

Damian threw his arms up dramatically. "And that's meant to convince me not to kill her?"

"It haunts her." Forcing herself to meet his fiery gaze, Kyra stressed her words. "She doesn't like killing, probably wouldn't want to hurt a fly. But she wants to know things."

"That's nice, your little girlfriend likes to read. That doesn't mean she isn't dangerous to us."

"She's not..." Kyra sighed. "It's not like that. Like you said, we can't talk without yelling. I just...I can't shake the feeling that she deserves a chance. I don't really want to prove her right—that we are monsters."

Striding forward, Damian fell into the same chair he had sat in less than half an hour ago. A tired hand pinched the bridge of his nose, his eyes screwed shut against what Kyra assumed was a headache. It wasn't the first she had given him and probably wouldn't be the last, though that didn't stop her from wincing in sympathy.

"So, we're keeping her because you want to prove we're not just the things that go bump in the night." Hearing it spoken aloud made it sound even stupider. "Okay, I can almost let that one slide if only because she hasn't actively tried to hurt anyone yet. But this other one? How much energy do you plan on using to keep him docile? And for how long? I can't believe he's as open to the truth as she is."

"I can't kill him."

"So don't. Let Erik do it, or that new one, Caleb." A small shudder trembled down Damian's shoulders at the mention of the new vampire. Kyra tucked the information away for a later discussion. "Keeping him here only increases the risk. Even if the Church doesn't send more, how can you be sure having another one around won't convince Leah they're in the right?"

"Killing him will only push her further away." But he was right—keeping the boy could be just as bad. "If you have another solution, I'm all ears. A solution that doesn't involve killing them both," she quickly clarified. Damian's scowl almost brought a smile to her own face. Almost.

"Okay, we can't kill the girl." He ran a hand through his hair, fingers seeming to tug it longer as his glamour shifted. "Killing the boy openly would be bad." Kyra nodded her assent as he paused to throw her a questioning look. "Okay, how about an accident? I mean, I'm sure it wouldn't take much to put him in a room with Caleb. It would take even less for Caleb to give in to eating him."

"Because that will go so far in convincing Leah we're not evil." Kyra dropped her head into her hands, elbows digging into the wood of her desk under the additional weight. The discomfort did nothing to calm her thoughts.

"Surely you can explain how..." he searched for the right word, "uncontrollable urges are for such a young vampire."

"Considering our last discussion?" Kyra huffed a bitter laugh.

Before Damian could venture another thought, they were interrupted by the creak of her office door opening. The well-oiled hinges were noiseless unless weight was applied in a specific spot. "Yes, Wendy?" Kyra asked without looking up, head still bowed over her desk.

"Was Leah meant to be escorting a young man out?"

Somehow Kyra managed to reach the door before Damian, half remembering vaulting her desk in her hurry. Wendy quickly stepped aside, though they probably would have simply gone through her had she not moved. Tearing around Wendy's desk, Kyra covered the foyer in steps that were far from graceful. Not that it mattered. Leah stood alone beside the door, arms crossed beneath her breasts and eyebrows drawn down in a frown as she stared out at the cool night beyond the glass of the automatic doors. The sensor picked up Kyra's movements and opened to let in a wave of fresh air, the cold curling around her bare legs. If Leah saw the movement or felt the chill, she didn't show it.

"What did you do?" Damian growled, looming on Leah's other side, hands in tight fists, rage barely restrained. He grew with every word, shifting from hulking bodybuilder to near giant. "Where is the other Hunter?"

Leah turned to him without fear, meeting his gaze unwaveringly before answering, "He's gone. I sent him home."

"What?!"

He lunged forward. Kyra matched his speed, throwing herself in his path, shoving at Leah's shoulder to get the Hunter out of his reach. Damian stared down at her, eyes flashing red, teeth turning to fangs, control slipping. Fighting down her own anger and a surge of panic that he may just strike her, Kyra held him with her gaze.

They shared a conversation in a moment, unspoken and loud in the air between them. He demanded blood and she asserted control, all without saying a word. After agonising seconds stretched into eternities, Damian tore his gaze away with a huff of frustrated defeat. Kyra eyed him for a few moments longer, ensuring he had really conceded.

Damian resettled his glamour, lips pulled into a scowl and arms folded tight across his chest the only signs of his anger now. Kyra nodded to herself, the situation under control for now. She turned to Leah, who had gone back to staring out into the night. The frown was less pronounced but still marred her face.

"Why?" Maintaining an even tone took effort, effort that was shaken when Leah didn't answer immediately. Acutely aware of Damian's simmering rage, Kyra kept her own anger in check. She reached out slowly, but Leah didn't seem to notice the movement or feel the hand on her shoulder. "Why?" Kyra repeated with exaggerated calm.

"He doesn't belong here," Leah finally replied.

"But you didn't go with him." The underlying question burned Kyra's tongue, aching to be spoken.

"No."

"Why not?"

"I don't belong there."

It was impossible to ignore the surge of hope, though the words weren't spoken. Leah's meaning was clear. Or close enough to what Kyra wanted that it didn't matter.

Leah didn't belong with the Church; Leah hadn't left. Therefore, she belonged here, at The Rose. With Kyra. The rush of that thought was followed by a sharp twist of guilt-laden panic. She wasn't meant to want a human, a Hunter.

"Wendy." Damian's growl broke the women out of their fragile reverie. Kyra hadn't even noticed Wendy follow them in their desperate charge from the office. "Take Leah back to her room, please."

Wendy stepped forward silently, softly taking Leah's arm to steer her away. Leah went limply, directed by Wendy's soft touch as her mind remained wrapped up elsewhere. Kyra wished she could read those thoughts, could see the images playing in the Hunter's mind, get an insight into what she would do next.

"I guess that solves our problem."

Damian's answering grunt told Kyra exactly how much he didn't appreciate her levity. Apparently too angry to discuss it further, he turned on his heel and disappeared towards the kitchen. Kyra, for her part, stood in the space Leah had vacated and stared out into the night. She knew she shouldn't linger; patrons would be arriving soon—the lull in busy periods was never long or guaranteed. Even her desire to avoid clients wasn't enough to pull her away, glued to the spot as she tried to imagine what Leah had been thinking, what had motivated her to free the boy. What had made her stay.

~ Thirteen ~

Magic compressed her skin tight against her flesh, a crushing hug that could easily slip from comforting to smothering if left unchecked. Kyra's glamour was heavy on her, pressing her into the shape of a small child. It would have looked ridiculous to anyone who entered the room to see a cherubic form with golden curls and large blue eyes perched behind an imposing desk and swallowed by the luxurious leather of Kyra's chair.

In truth, Kyra liked the feeling of being cocooned, of being small and cradled. It was a pleasure she indulged rarely, usually while reading and distancing her mind from the worries that plagued it.

The heavy paper was smooth between her fingers, and she breathed in the familiar scent indulgently. Thoughts of Leah threatened to break her calm, flickering at the edges of her mind in the moments it took to turn the page. Kyra ignored them as her eyes soaked in the words before her.

A new scent washed over her, cutting through the mellow aroma of books. Kyra adjusted her glamour with a sigh of regret, allowing her features to melt back into her favoured mask of hyper competent business woman. She was loath to let it go, but some things were better left unknown.

She waited, eyes still on the book but mind pulled from the words, but the door to her office remained closed. Seconds dragged, and a second scent joined the first. Wendy was speaking to Leah but neither entered.

Wendy's scent buzzed along the edges of Kyra's senses, a familiar sensation that spoke of protection and home. It was pale in comparison to Leah's. The Hunter overwhelmed Kyra, and no matter how she told herself it was due to the anger still simmering in her breast, that it was the bubbling disquiet in her stomach that made her so attuned to the human, the excuses rang hollow.

Even now, with Leah still loitering close enough to smell but not yet see or hear, Kyra's every sense was honed in on her, and it rankled. At some point, Wendy must have gone back to her own desk, her scent gone from under the haze that was Leah. Kyra shouldn't have missed the change.

Should she just open the door herself? Call out for Leah? Or use the phone at her elbow to tell Wendy to send the Hunter in?

Kyra's thoughts were on the precipice of spiralling into anxiety when Leah eased the door open. She watched the human from under dark eyelashes, keeping her head bowed over the book in her lap. It had looked so large in her other hands.

Leah closed the door as quietly as she had opened it, hesitating with her back against it as she appraised Kyra and likely tried to get a sense of her mood. Maintaining her still calm took greater effort than Kyra would like to have admitted, but she managed.

Painfully slow, Leah crossed the short space to the desk, hesitating again with her hand on the back of a chair. Her fingers were long and pale against the dark upholstery.

"Sit," Kyra ordered when it became clear Leah wouldn't otherwise. Her answering sigh was more of defeat than relief.

Kyra used the silence between them to her advantage, pretending to read words that had long gone fuzzy under unfocused eyes. In her peripheral vision, Leah shifted in her seat, hands playing restlessly with the hem of her t-shirt. It didn't surprise her that Wendy had gone shopping, only that it had taken her so long to notice. Leah filled her thoughts often enough that the change should have been obvious. Wearing pale blue today, a part of Kyra wondered how many near identical-tops Wendy had bought for her, selecting a range of colours with little care for style or fit. Not that Kyra could picture the Hunter in anything other than the comfortable clothes she wore. The idea of Leah in a dress or something form-fitting just didn't sit right.

Usually, Kyra wasn't patient enough for using silence to her advantage, much preferring the press of words or easy distraction of her body. Maintaining an icy visage was rarely useful in her everyday interactions. For Leah, for a woman, it would have to do.

"You wanted to see me?" Leah finally spoke after Kyra had read the same line for what felt like the hundredth time.

Kyra bit the inside of her cheek to avoid correcting Leah pointedly that Wendy had been sent to fetch her three hours ago. After the first hour, Kyra had decided that reading was a better use of her time than pursuing the Hunter. Letting Leah stew had felt the safer choice.

Leah crossed her arms over her chest, and Kyra struggled not to take some pleasure in her obvious frustration. She still didn't look up, instead taking her time to close her book and lean back in her chair. Folding her hands in her lap, she let herself meet Leah's gaze. There was a steeliness to Leah's eyes, a stubborn set to her face, though it was undermined by the protective position of her arms.

"You let the other Hunter go." Kyra's voice was calm even as her anger spiked. The distance of a night had dulled her curiosity and wonder to nothing, her mind no longer distracted by Leah staying. Her anger had festered as she had courted sleep and been denied, growing into a constant frustration that made her unbearable throughout the day. Wendy had almost snapped when Kyra demanded she get Leah, clearly relieved she was addressing the cause of her foul mood. "Tell me. Why shouldn't I kill you for it?"

"Because if you were going to, you would have done so last night." Leah's forced calm only caused Kyra's anger to grow. The fragile peace she had clawed into her mind earlier was gone, her fingers threatening to cramp in her effort to avoid forming fists. "He didn't belong here."

"And you do?"

The hard lines of Leah's face softened as her gaze melted, and she tilted her head to the side. Her arms fell to her sides, leaving her open and unguarded. She was back to reading Kyra. "I think I do."

A simple statement delivered with little emotion, and yet, it rang in Kyra's head. Her anger fought against a sudden buoyancy in her middle, a rush of butterflies smothering flames until her chest felt full of burning wings. It was nauseating and addicting, a buzz of sensations too big for her skin.

"Will you still feel that way when he brings others back?" Will you still feel that way when they set you free, Kyra desperately wanted to ask, the question dying on her lips with the light sensation that had come so close to enveloping.

"He won't."

"How can you be so sure?" Centring her anger was easy, safe. Kyra fed it and focused on it, pretending it was the only thing she felt. Pushing words out in a sharp hiss was better than thinking about the way her stomach was twisting. "You seem very certain for a naive Hunter. For a prisoner."

"He won't because the Church will kill him the moment he reports back. I had to convince him that you wanted him to go, and if he's still that obvious when he makes contact, they'll kill him before he has a chance to tell them I'm here." The hardness was back in Leah's eyes, flashing brightly as she spoke. "You really aren't as bad as you think you are."

"If I was as evil as you thought I am, I would have killed him." Kyra crossed her arms under her breasts and tried to pretend it wasn't a poor defence against Leah's too knowing stare.

"I don't think you're evil," Leah said with complete certainty, striking Kyra effectively speechless. Pressing her advantage, Leah leaned forward. "You're not evil. Demons aren't evil." She shook her head at this. "The Church lied; I can see that now. Maybe they're evil. I don't know. I don't even know what evil is anymore, but it's not you. So no, you won't kill me. I don't think you even liked killing Michael or letting other Hunters be killed."

Every word hit Kyra, knocking her anger further and further out of reach.

"I may be naive and a Hunter, but I know what I see, and that is a woman who will tear the world apart to protect those she feels are her responsibility. I stopped being your prisoner the moment you gave me those books. We both know I want to be here, and if I wanted to leave, you wouldn't stop me."

Leah's hands were pressed against Kyra's desk, but she couldn't remember seeing the Hunter move. Her eyes burned with a conviction that was almost frightening. Kyra didn't want to hear her truths but didn't have the words to silence the onslaught.

"If you want me to be a good little captive and stay in my room, fine. But don't think for a second it's not my choice too." Good to her word, Leah pushed herself up and away, her chair scraping loudly against the floor. Kyra watched mutely as the Hunter spun on her heel and strode from the room, taking the warmth of her fiery energy with her. Kyra remained glued to her chair, blinking owlishly, for longer than she cared to admit.

~ Fourteen ~

The slip of paper was innocuous, a sheaf of white printed with carefully formed letters, fold lines barely visible. The envelop had been equally nondescript, marked only with her name. Wendy shrugged off Kyra's questioning look when handing it to her, apparently nothing more than a strange addition to their daily mail. Kyra had twirled it between her fingers for a while before slicing it open with a letter opener that had been mostly decorative up to that point.

She had read the words quickly and then again slower. On the third read, they managed to seep into her mind, penetrating the panic that had gripped her throat at the inked seal in place of a signature. The shape was foreign to her, but the origin was obvious. The Church. Demanding Leah's return. So much for the boy being killed before he could say anything damaging.

Kyra wasn't sure if she was happy Leah was wrong in this case or not. Wishing death on someone so painfully innocent was beyond her, but she should have let Damian deal with it.

Her fingers tightened without thought, crushing the paper into a rough ball. When that didn't ease her panic, she tore it into increasingly small pieces. Once it showered her desk in shredded paper, she swept the mess into the small bin tucked beneath her desk. The pieces fell like snow, disappearing between other debris. It didn't leave her mind as easily.

The letter still weighed on Kyra's mind days later, though its remnants had been removed during the nightly cleaning. Perhaps it was lucky Leah was still avoiding her...or was she avoiding the Hunter. Just another worry to nag at the edges of her concentration. A part of her knew the business was suffering, should be suffering with how little she could focus. Admitting that it wasn't would have involved admitting how important Damian really was.

"He's requested another session." Kyra nearly jumped out of her skin at the sound of Wendy's voice. She hadn't heard the other woman enter her office, let alone cross to her desk and take a seat. "Are you sure he's not getting attached?"

"It's fine." Even clipped, her tone was a little too high, betraying the way her heart struggled to slow from a racing beat. Wendy hummed in disagreement but didn't push the matter, face blank and eyes down as she shuffled the pages in her hands. Reports that would be easier dealt with digitally but were printed in diffidence to her distaste for technology. "Someone else can see him; I don't need it yet."

"And his...desires?"

"Don't need to be completely fulfilled every time." Kyra ignored the sound of shuffling paper and the way it grated on her nerves. "Can you set up a meeting with Hannah? Tell her I need a new protection charm, sooner rather than later." Wendy nodded with each instruction, making notes in her tidy hand. "And can you check Buddug's schedule? I feel like she's due."

Kyra sighed, allowing herself to rub at her eyes. It was hard to concentrate with the threat of the letter still in her mind, but she could hardly pause for it. She pushed it to the back of her mind and re-centred her thoughts. There were always more worries than time. "Has anyone heard from Bell?"

"Amy says she's doing well." A strange tenor ran through Wendy's voice, setting Kyra immediately on edge.

"But?" she pressed.

"She refuses to meet in person, only talks on the phone."

For a second, all Kyra saw was red, blood rushing in her ears as her skin flushed with rage. Her glamour pulled tight as her more bestial side roared to the surface, her every nerve humming with energy that had nowhere to go. Taloned fingers dug into her desk, gouging long lines. The mask of humanity flickered and fell for a moment, her glamour falling away to show her true self as control slid out of her grasp.

Kyra breathed deeply, forcing her palms flat on the marred wood. She pulled her glamour back into place and knotted it with ropes of power and control.

"I was thinking of sending Caleb out to check on her." Wendy hadn't flinched at Kyra's demonic features, and her tone remained even. The only sign she was aware of Kyra's lapse in control was a brief glance at the scarred desk.

"No," Kyra matched Wendy's tone, pulling in calming air and pushing out the heat of her anger. "Send Erik. Caleb can't be trusted yet."

Her distractions were going to get someone killed at this rate.

Later, in the strangely quiet hours between waves of customers, Kyra took the opportunity to flee to her room. Finding Leah in the hall, back to her and heading in the same direction, she was struck by a sudden thought.

"I have a question."

Leah stiffened at the words, halting in the hallway but not turning around to face Kyra. Feeling her smile fall, the small spark of joy at turning the phrase back on the Hunter was lost in the tense line of her shoulders.

Rather than be cowed by it, Kyra pushed forward to close the gap between them as she spoke. "I was wondering how you always know it's me. At first, I thought it was because you keep coming to my office and maybe just assumed no one else would be sitting in my chair, but I've seen the way you look at the others. It's different when you look at me, even when we pass in the hall." It was awkward speaking to Leah's back, but Kyra couldn't trust the woman wouldn't flee if she made a motion to turn her. "Even when I'm wearing a different face, you always seem to know. How?"

Leah raised a hand, tucking her hair behind one ear. It was down today, as it had been most days lately. Blond locks trailed over a soft cotton t-shirt, the muted grey making her appear less washed out as though the gentle colour allowed her skin the room to glow. Kyra wished she would turn around, let her see her face, let her gauge her mood. Everything was starting to feel like a terrible mistake.

"I..." At least with her back turned, she didn't see Kyra jump at the break in the silence. "You hold yourself differently. With confidence but also apart. It's like even in a room full of people, you wouldn't let anyone touch you."

Kyra regretted asking. That she expected anything other than an answer with teeth was beyond foolish. The crushing weight of being seen was her punishment.

"Was that all?"

"Yes." Kyra allowed herself a full body shake, pretending it was to settle the tightness of her glamour and not the deadly calm to Leah's voice. "Yeah."

The Hunter walked away without another word, leaving Kyra wishing she hadn't approached her at all.

~ Fifteen ~

A small chime sounded from Kyra's laptop speaker, drawing her attention away from the books she had been staring at, or staring through, as her mind wandered aimlessly. Her meeting with Hannah was in five minutes–enough time for her to feel restless but not enough for her to actually do something. Looking sightlessly at the titles before her, part of her mind wondered which Leah would find the most interesting, which would pique her interest, which would have the Hunter returning to her door.

Kyra had never been good at waiting, feeling the seconds radiate tension through her body as they dripped by. Any attempt at distracting herself was futile. Huffing under her breath, Kyra gave into the restless energy lighting up her skin, pacing back to her desk to throw herself into her chair. The leather gave way under her weight, rising up to greet her, to encase her.

A quick glance at her laptop screen told her Hannah would be arriving any moment. Punctuality was hardly the witch's strong suit, but neither was consistency, meaning there was a near equal chance she would be early, or late, or on time. She often blamed focus intensive spells, but Kyra suspected it was merely a whim of a quicksilver mind.

Wendy's quick knock pulled Kyra from her musings, a soft sound to warn Kyra of Hannah's arrival. Standing as the door opened, Kyra moved around her desk to meet Hannah halfway. A darkly intimidating woman for those who knew better, it was always a shock to realise there were no lines at the corner of her eyes or grey in her hair. Hannah carried herself with a weight and confidence that Kyra long associated with beings well beyond her years.

This woman, barely tall enough to be called average, figure closer to chunky than curvy, could so easily be passed on the street without knowing the power she held. Between her youth, her dark skin, and her deceptively affable smile, many had met their end underestimating Hannah. It didn't help that she insisted on wearing faded jeans and overly large tops, drawing attention to her age at every turn. A beaten leather messenger bag hung from her shoulder.

"Hannah." Kyra smiled easily, honestly happy to see the other woman. She reached out arms wide to embrace, leaning down to press a kiss to each smooth cheek.

"Kyra, good to see you." Hannah returned the hug with a small laugh. "One day I'll visit, and it won't be on business."

Kyra waved her into a seat as she pulled away, moving around her desk to take her own. "That would involve one of us stopping working long enough to make a social call."

"True." Hannah settled herself comfortably, crossing one leg over the other before piercing Kyra with a stare that saw too much. "Wendy said you needed a new protection charm?"

"Yes." Kyra hesitated. Lying would result in a less than effective charm, but the entire truth would result in questions and a call to Buddug Kyra wasn't ready for. "For a human."

"You've taken in another stray? I always thought Wendy was the only human you could stand." Curiosity burned in Hannah's eyes, but she shrugged it off. "I'll need some hair, a week, and three full loads."

"One load," Kyra countered more out of habit than any desire to bargain. Agreeing instantly would have raised even further questions anyway.

"Two."

Kyra made a show of thinking, regardless of how willing she had been to pay much more. She would collect the energy herself. "Done." Opening the top drawer in her desk, Kyra pulled out a small Ziplock bag. A few strands of blond hair sat at the bottom, so pale and thin they were barely visible. Hannah took it without comment, slipping it into a pocket. "Payment on receipt."

"It's always a pleasure doing business with you." Hannah smiled as she stood, that same deceptive grin that had lulled many older and more powerful than Kyra. She didn't doubt that they were friends, just as she didn't doubt Hannah would slit her throat if it would protect her own kin. Hannah hadn't become the youngest leader of a sanctuary by accident, her raw power matched only by her shrewd mind. As long as their goals aligned, Kyra was fine.

"Oh, and the other thing?" Kyra asked as casually as she could manage. Hannah dug into her bag, pulling a small hardcover book from its depths.

"Not your usual fare," Hannah noted with a raised eyebrow. Kyra reached for the book and for a horrible moment thought Hannah would snatch it away. The witch relinquished it with a wry twist to her lips. Had she read Kyra's flash of panic?

"Sometimes, it's good to expand your horizons." She slipped the book onto the desk behind her, though it glowed brightly at the back of her mind. Hannah shrugged, the matter forgotten or at least not worth pursuing.

They embraced once more, both murmuring vaguely about seeing each other in a more social setting without the pressures of work. Once the pointless platitudes were over and she was blessedly alone, Kyra went straight to her laptop to pull up her calendar. A week, it was doable.

Rapid-fire typing filled the air of her office as she typed out a quick message to Wendy. A client would need to be found for her.

Once the message was sent, Kyra dug through her bottom drawer. Her fingers danced over cool glass, pulling out a small vial. Specially made, it looked like it belonged in some fantasy movie with witches and potions and dragons.

The fragile bottle was small enough to be easily engulfed by her petite palm. A nail prised the stopper loose as Kyra focused on slowing her breathing. Thinking only of the rush of air into her lungs, the slight burn of holding it there beyond comfort, and the inevitable loosening of her chest when she let it flow back out, it took no time for her thoughts to dwindle to nothing. Her heartbeat faded to a soundless, distant thing until even the wheeze of her breathing became nothing.

In that perfect stillness beyond reality, Kyra felt the energy settle in her gut. She wrapped her senses around it, gathered all it was into a bright pulsing ball, and shaped it into something near physical, something she could manipulate and move. With the energy in her grasp, she pushed it up and out, feeling the burning rush of bile as it rode the wrong way through her insides. As it crested, she quickly pushed the vial to her mouth, breathing the burning light into the depths of the glass. It flowed forever; she would be caught in this eternity, body spasming and throat burning, waiting for the energy to leave her.

Truly, it was over in a matter of seconds, the vial a hairbreadth from full, the clear glass dampening the luster of the energy within. It shone with a yellow light caught somewhere between brilliant and sickly. Replacing the matching crystal stopper with practised ease, Kyra observed the energy with a detached, clinical eye. Hannah would argue it wasn't a full load, but the potency and shade would make up for it.

Her laptop chirped again, this time with a reply from Wendy. She had a client in a few days. It would have to do.

Kyra hadn't expected the knock at her door, hadn't even realised Leah knew which room was hers. It shouldn't have been surprising, given how close it was to the room Leah had been given, but Kyra was still taken by surprise when she opened the door to Leah's gentle tapping.

The Hunter's face was guarded, her expression closing off more every time they spoke. Dropping her hand, poised to knock again, she wrapped her arms around herself, not quite crossing them but not hugging herself either. For a moment, Kyra thought she caught a flash of uncertainty, but Leah looked down and away before she could focus properly.

"I have a question."

Kyra's lips pulled up at the sentence without meaning to, the simple statement seeming to indicate things could return to normal. Normal, with a Hunter. Shaking her head to herself, Kyra stepped aside and waved Leah in, using the distraction of the woman entering her space to avoid bemused thoughts whispered in Damian's voice. Leah eyed her in askance but took the silent invitation for what it was.

She hesitated barely beyond the door as Kyra closed it after her. Leah surveyed the room openly, the movement of her eyes clear in the way her head tilted in familiar curiosity. Trapped between the Hunter and the door, Kyra tried not to think of how close the human was to her, tried to ignore the way Leah's body heat washed over her own form.

"Please sit." She gestured to the bed without thinking, not that Leah saw the movement. Still, she followed the slight push of air against her back and finally entered the room completely. Her steps were slow but sure as she approached Kyra's bed.

Leah arranged herself carefully on the edge, shifting awkwardly to avoid slipping backward into the dent of Kyra's nest. She glanced at the dip. "What's up with your bed?"

Kyra crossed her arms, feeling defensive. Why had armour ever gone out of fashion? "It's to accommodate my wings." When Leah only looked at her, waiting, Kyra continued with a sigh. "We drop our glamour to sleep. We allow our true forms to fully materialise around us, including our wings. Human beds aren't really built for that, so we build a nest where we can."

"Why don't all the rooms have beds like yours then?"

"Because humans ask too many questions."

Leah read the hint and chose to ignore it. "You don't..." she paused, looking for a polite way to word her question.

"No."

"But I thought...you know?" They watched each other for a moment, both equally confused. Kyra wasn't too sure what Leah was asking, what her assumption was. "Isn't it a constant need? An undeniable thirst? An insatiable hunger for sex?"

Kyra couldn't help but laugh. The words, absurd on their own, were made all the funnier by the confused earnestness in which they were delivered.

"I'm sorry, what?"

"You're a succubus," Leah spoke slowly, torn between the crumbling surety of her knowledge and embarrassment in her sudden naivety. "A creature whose sole focus is to..."

"To fuck?" Kyra supplied, the word harsh but her tone soft. "You think us mindless creatures driven by primal lust?" The flash of shame was all the answer Kyra needed. "And yet we're such a threat. Never mind that we are able to curb our desires enough to live full lives without getting caught."

"You're cunning-"

Kyra cut her off. "You do realise that many demons see humans as the lesser species? Unable to use magic, so bound to the technology you create to compensate, working so hard to extend the brief time you have. Just to waste it all scrambling for money and power that give you no real happiness." She shook her head, trying to dislodge the anger that had taken residence in her mind. Snapping at the girl wouldn't help anything. "A succubus feeds of a man's sexual energy, yes," Kyra continued in a calmer tone. "But we do this maybe once a month to survive. This is then passed to our incubus brothers who use it to impregnate women, allowing the continuation of our race."

"Wouldn't that just make more humans?" she asked. "Human semen or sexual energy in a human host?"

"I'm not a scientist or academic, but I believe the transfer from human to succubus, to incubus, to human changes the genetic material. It stops being human; your energy is just the carrier."

"Huh." Leah was tilting her head again, clearly processing the information Kyra had given. "Do you really see us as lesser?"

"Some do," Kyra admitted. "Personally, I don't see the point either way. We need you to survive, so why try and pretend we're something better?"

Leah rose suddenly, surprising Kyra enough for her to take a step back.

"Thank you." Leah smiled, bright and open and warm. "You've given me a lot to think about."

She left with as much fanfare and pomp as she arrived, leaving Kyra feeling confused and a little out of sorts. It felt like it should have been a momentous occasion or a terrible argument that came close to blows. Instead, she had told a Hunter—a Hunter of all things—something considered deeply personal. But they had had their first conversation regarding demons that hadn't ended in screaming or burning rage.

Kyra examined her words, trying to remember exactly what she had said. She didn't think she had said anything dangerous, anything that could be easily used against her kind. She tried to ignore the voice in her head that sounded too much like Damian, telling her that the safety of her people should have been her first concern, not an afterthought.

~ Sixteen ~

Words swam before Kyra's eyes, the sharp black blurry around the edges against the too-bright screen. Starbursts played across her vision as she rubbed the tired corners of her eyes, trying desperately to focus on what she was attempting to read.

Sleep had been impossible last night, her mind half convinced she could feel the warmth of Leah's body where she had been sitting, no matter how brief it had been. If Damian so much as suspected she was hunched over her desk, hiding yawns behind a clenched fist all because of a woman, he'd throw a fit. And he would be right to.

It was a stupid infatuation, nothing more. Something dangerous, true, but nothing to get so worked up over. And yet here Kyra was, slipping her head into her hands and pressing at her temples, trying to push treasonous thoughts and feelings out of her head.

It was a relief when the phone rang, the sound piercing the still air of her office and the beginnings of her headache. Reaching for the receiver without taking her eyes from the words that still wouldn't coalesce, Kyra spoke without focusing on either task successfully.

"Kyra speaking." Her usually clipped greeting was even more harsh today.

"Kyra," Mary's voice beamed down the phone line. "It's me, Mary." Why people always felt the need to lead with 'it's me,' Kyra could never understand.

"Mary." Finding a smile for her face was easier than for her voice, the upturn of her lips not translating completely. "To what do I owe the pleasure? A new story?"

"Is everything about work for you?" She laughed. "I can't just want to talk to a friend? Provide some friendly advice?"

"I like you, Mary, but I didn't know we were friends."

"I'm wounded." The cocky drawl belied her words. Kyra could picture the smile Mary was wearing, something that could almost be called bland if it weren't for the glint in her eyes. Kyra scoffed, taking the opportunity to close her laptop. Maybe the screen wouldn't burn so brightly once Mary had said her fill. "I actually wanted to ask a favour."

"Oh?" Settling back into her chair, phone tucked between shoulder and cheek, Kyra half wished she hadn't splurged on the wireless model. A cord would have given her another distraction, something to busy her fingers. Instead, she examined her nails, shifting her glamour to make them grow and change colours.

"I was thinking we could start an information exchange, you and I."

"And what would I get out of that?" Kyra was a little surprised it had taken Mary this long to come to her for information. Either she wasn't as brave as Kyra had thought, or she was more adept at research. "I hardly need to know the ins and outs of every back door deal that happens in the city."

"No, but you do need to keep abreast of Smith and his plans."

"Not him again." Kyra definitely didn't whine; her voice did not shift into something petulant. No matter how much she was beginning to hate his name. All she had to do was reach out and shift a few papers, and his smiling face would be gazing up at her from the daily paper. Wendy had insisted she read the article. "The Rose has stood for decades and will continue to stand for centuries." Kyra had said the same to Wendy this morning and had received a similar disbelieving scoff.

"You do realise his reach has extended beyond the city, right?" Mary dropped the smile from her voice and the laugh from her words, speaking slowly and deliberately. As though to a very stupid child. "His views are gaining traction, and there's more than one rumour suggesting he's got his eye on federal politics."

"Which will take him a few years at least. And during that time, someone else will take his place and carefully undo whatever damage he may have done to ensure their own interests continue to be met," Kyra replied with equal condescension. "I have seen this before and will no doubt see it again. Whether it be prohibition or prostitution, even if the men screaming for change really wanted it gone, the general populace wouldn't stand for it, not for long."

"How old are you exactly?"

Kyra stiffened, partially from instinctive indignation but mostly for giving away anything around Mary. She knew better. "Old enough to take offence at being asked," Kyra drawled with more calmness than she felt.

It was unlikely Mary could do anything with the information, it was no more harmful than her knowing Kyra wasn't human, but it still rankled. Mary laughed in response, allowing Kyra to get away with it this time. The reporter was probably already making plans to examine the ownership records of The Rose or something similarly annoying.

"I think you ignore Smith's power at your own risk."

"Thank you, Mary. I will keep that in mind." Kyra didn't bother hiding the chill in her voice. "If that's all, I have work to get back to."

Mary made a noise of disbelief but didn't argue further. Instead, she said her goodbyes and barely allowed Kyra to repeat her own before the line was dead in her ear.

Pointedly ignoring the still obscured newspaper, Kyra replaced the handset and turned back to her laptop. The screen was still insultingly bright, but at least it didn't ask her how old she was.

It took Kyra nearly an hour to give up on work in favour of caffeine, telling herself coffee would make everything better. The hour was late enough for the world to be dark beyond the walls of The Rose but not so late that clients were streaming through the front door. The Rose felt strangely still and lifeless, the calm before the storm, the held breath before it went sailing from lungs to lips to the air beyond.

The kitchen was silent when Kyra entered, the only sign of life a hunched back, the owner curled over what Kyra could only assume was a strong coffee. Too tired to focus on their scent, Kyra largely ignored her companion in favour of preparing her own fortifying brew.

Rustling fabric and a soft sigh were the only things that told Kyra the other person was not asleep where they sat. Not that she would have blamed them—a nap sounded wonderful right about now. A pity sleep couldn't be trusted.

Kyra kept close to the bench behind the person's back but made no secret of her presence. Drawers and cupboards were closed with her usual disregard for their structural integrity. She made no attempt to soften the sound of shifting mugs as she dug for the largest, her favourite, tucked away in the furthest corner to make sure no one else used it. The clattering of the spoon against the ceramic was sharp in the quiet of the room, but sugar was more important than maintaining silence.

Falling into a chair close enough to not be rude but not so close to invite conversation, Kyra inhaled the first half of her steaming coffee fast enough to burn a layer of skin from her mouth. Through heavily lidded eyes, averse to opening entirely until the caffeine hit her system, Kyra finally looked to her companion. Amused hazel eyes met her own, crinkled at the edges by a soft smile. Still short of full alertness, Kyra could only manage a small scowl.

"Hello," Leah murmured, voice low in diffidence to the silence around them. Would they argue this time? Kyra hoped not, not unless she was allowed to drink another coffee first.

"Hello," she parroted, hands wrapped around the heat of her mug, head bowed to keep the aromatic steam floating straight into her core. The first half of her coffee always went too quickly, too caught up in the need to get it in her body and humming through her system as soon as possible. The second half was slower, savoured as it suffused warmth through her.

She slowed to sip at a more moderate pace and tried to ignore the lingering heat in her cheeks that had nothing to do with the liquid in her cup and everything to do with Leah's smile.

"Want to see something cool?" The words hadn't formed in Kyra's mind, hadn't been a conscious decision. They just appeared on her lips and danced out into the world without her permission.

Leah raised an eyebrow in question, expression shifting into bemusement without losing the tilt of her smile. Ignoring the way it made her stomach warm, Kyra drained the last of her coffee, a part of her mourning the chance to truly enjoy it. Her chair dragged loudly against the floor as she pushed herself up and away from the table. Leah followed suit slowly, not rising until Kyra was waving impatiently from the door.

The Hunter trailed her silently as Kyra led her to the back stairs. She could feel Leah's curiosity like a physical weight across her shoulders, pinned in place by a burning stare that sent shivers down her spine. Resolutely pretending it didn't exist, much the way she pretended this had been a completely planned out idea, Kyra took Leah beyond the last floor and up another set of stairs, more out of the way than the first. Hidden behind a nondescript door, concrete walls and cold metal stairs took them up and beyond the top storey.

Kyra leaned heavily on the crossbar that acted as a handle to the heavy door, shouldering it open and nearly losing control as the weight carried it wide. Leah hid a smile behind her hand, letting Kyra usher her onto the empty roof of The Rose.

The night air was sharp and chill, blowing enough to nip at their ankles in a gentle breeze. Leah hesitated, looking over the hulking shapes of air conditioning units as though unsure of what she was meant to be doing. Maintaining the silence that now felt comforting rather than oppressive, Kyra nudged the Hunter with her shoulder, half pushing her. She took a stumbling step forward; Leah let Kyra lead her around softly whirring machinery and massive tubes to a quieter corner.

Kyra approached the edge fearlessly, lowering herself to sit with her feet dangling above what should have been a dizzying drop. Her eyes were focused upwards, though, taking in the few winking stars able to shine through the light pollution of the city around them. Even in the dead of night, during the witching hours where the world slept, there was still too much light to truly enjoy the stars.

Kyra didn't look over when Leah shifted beside her, taking the space next to her with less grace than Kyra had shown. Was she looking over the edge, eyes too easily drawn to the street below to enjoy the stars above? Kyra hoped not. There was a calming beauty to be found in the night sky, no matter how tinged it was with the sickly orange glow of human touch.

"You know..." Kyra very nearly jumped at the words, the first sound between them since the kitchen. Even with her eyes glued to the sky, her every sense was attuned to the Hunter beside her. "I spent many of my formative years wishing on stars I didn't really believe in."

"And now?" That wasn't what Kyra wanted to ask. She wanted to know what Leah had wished for, what her young heart had desired but knew was fruitless. "Do you still wish on them?"

"No," she sighed, the word quiet and broken on a voice barely above a whisper. "But sometimes, I think I might actually believe. I mean, in a world with demons and magic, what's a shooting star? Why couldn't it be real?" There was an ephemeral sadness to her words, a hint of melancholy so fleeting, Kyra wondered if she imagined it.

"So make a wish," Kyra challenged. There was a fragility to the mood, to the air around them. Kyra felt all the world like she was caught outside of reality, outside of the responsibilities and expectations of life. It made her eerily brave and uncomfortably vulnerable. There was nothing to hide behind up here, no work to turn to. Nothing but herself, Leah, and the sky.

"What if it doesn't come true?"

"What if it does?"

It was hard to keep her eyes on the stars, hard to not look over at the woman beside her. She could picture the innocent awe, the earnest contemplation. There would be a small frown between Leah's eyes, her brows drawn tight as her head tilted minutely to the side. Her lips would be pulled down slightly, barely a frown, serious and soft.

Kyra's fingers itched to reach out, to smooth the lines of Leah's face. She wanted to breathe the right words to convince her that wishing on stars wasn't a waste of time. She wanted Leah to whisper her wish, the words only loud enough for them, so that she may make it come true.

On that roof, her secret escape that she had never shared before, Kyra had a horrible realisation.

She loved the Hunter.

Fuck.

"If I make a wish"—Kyra felt Leah shift beside her, felt the sudden weight of her stare— "would you make it come true?" There was an offer to Leah's words, an invitation Kyra couldn't deny, but it fell on deaf ears. Kyra's mind had shut down, focused entirely on the warm feeling in her chest and what it meant.

Now that she had identified it, there was no escaping it. The way her heart would struggle to race and stop and skip a beat all at once at the sight of Leah's smile. The way her face warmed and stomach swooped and entire body felt too big, skin too tight. The gentle rush of adrenaline, the clutch of air refusing to exit her throat or enter her lungs.

"You're asking me?" The croak of Kyra's throat belied any attempt she could make at playing calm. "Do you really think a demon can make your dreams come true?"

Could you love a demon?

"No." She turned back to the sky. The word punched what little air Kyra had managed to get straight out of her chest. "I guess not." If Leah sounded defeated, it was only because Kyra was projecting, was hoping that their conversation meant something else.

"We should..." Kyra cleared her throat, trying to dislodge the sudden tightness. "We should get inside."

If Leah sensed the change in mood, she didn't mention it, just followed Kyra back into the belly of The Rose and the carefully constructed places Kyra had carved for them. Whether Leah knew it or not, within the walls of The Rose, she had a part to play and a role that Kyra wouldn't forget. Not again.

Much later, when the last of the workers had called it a night and the building was truly asleep and silent, Kyra laid awake. Curled in the warmth of her nest, wings pulled close and tight to block out the world, her mind still raced. The darkness was solid around her, a pressure she could feel along her skin, but it wasn't comforting like it usually was. There was no solace to be taken in the night because her heart still fluttered awkwardly, caught between racing and stopping. Sleep was beyond reach as long as her blood pumped thickly and her thoughts refused to quiet.

Love. It was hardly a sin she didn't know intimately, a mistake she hadn't made before. She thought briefly of Bell. It hadn't been a lie; love was allowed at The Rose. Just not for Kyra.

Stretching her legs beyond the safe cage of her wings, Kyra rolled to her other side, subconsciously shifting her body weight until there was no risk of damaging the fine membrane. She pulled her legs close again, ignoring how pathetic she must look, curled in a foetal position over a girl. Over a Hunter.

Damian knew. He knew the moment Kyra refused to kill her. A frustrated groan tore itself from her throat. It was hard not to agree with him in that moment. He should have just killed her, should have saved Kyra from herself. And he would know that she knew, and she wouldn't be able to avoid the gloating smugness he would no doubt wear at the realisation. Bastard.

Or worse, he wouldn't gloat at all. Would only look at her with barely concealed pity. He'd try to let her down easy, try to comfort her while explaining all the reasons why a human would never love her.

Clutching the pillow sandwiched between the curve of her arm and her head, she punched the softness with her free hand. This did nothing for her frustration and only managed to shake her hair loose, strands falling across her face to tickle the tip of her nose. Growling in the dark, she blew at them from the corner of her mouth, achieving the dubious result of making her hair dance briefly before landing across her face once more. Her hand was in front of her face, it would have been a simple matter to just brush the hair away, but the effort seemed insurmountable, her stubborn mind turning it into a matter of principle. Maybe distracting her mind with pettiness would allow her to sleep. Knowing her luck, probably not.

~ Seventeen ~

Kyra tried not to panic when her laptop dinged with appointments she didn't remember accepting. A client in ten minutes, followed by a meeting titled 'Buddug' with no further explanation. She had less than half an hour to consume the meal and return to her office for Buddug's arrival.

The harsh drag of chair legs on wood was drowned by the anxious pounding of blood in her ears. Her skin felt full of static, energy coursing in the microscopic space between her flesh and her glamour. Kyra moved quickly, striding from her office straight towards the back stairs. Wendy watched with open worry from behind her computer, a fact that only added to Kyra's disquiet.

The client Wendy had selected was a truly pedestrian offering, someone who would be filling but ultimately uninspiring. He was convenient in that he was the next scheduled appointment, so he would have to do.

The pulsating energy had barely settled in her middle before Kyra was redonning her glamour and exiting the room. The clock on the bedside table told her she had less than five minutes until Buddug was scheduled to arrive. Not even Damian received meals so hot.

In the safety of her office, Kyra shed her glamour with a sigh, the press of magic itching under waves of concern and undefinable trepidation. Even before Buddug's urgent request, her mask had niggled at her, her skin uncomfortable under the familiar press of her armour.

For once, the unfurling of wings, the stretching of cloven legs, was a welcome relief. It gave her a point of focus that wasn't roiling panic in a too-full belly. Running a hand over her hair without purposefully avoiding horns, Kyra let herself feel comfortable in her skin in a way she rarely did.

There was a slight smell of flowers in the air, leftover from the cleaners earlier in the day, made sweeter by the lingering summer heat. Her blinds were open to allow the afternoon sun in, painting her walls in a soft orange glow.

A low murmur of life filled the building, gentle and separate, far enough away that it didn't intrude on the quiet of Kyra's room but close enough to remind her she wasn't alone. She kept her mind on that, on the calm outside the walls of her office. It was safer, easier, than thinking of all the things that had to have gone wrong for Buddug to be arriving with such a pressing need.

She wanted to just enjoy it, live solely in it, while simultaneously trying to catalogue every part of it for future reflection. Her mind darted from the gentle light of the sun to the soft warmth against her skin, the beautiful contentment she found herself in. Her overactive brain committed it all to memory, something to be treasured and guarded closely. Something to be hoarded and held, kept deep and dark until it was needed.

The calm, like the moment, was fleeting. Buddug would be arriving soon, and Kyra would have her worries realised. Best case scenario, Buddug had over-extended herself again. Worst case...well, Kyra didn't want to consider the worst case.

Even without those concerns, there were other layers of danger she couldn't ignore. A note from Wendy, dropped on her desk when she had been feeding, claimed Leah was hiding in her room waiting for Kyra to visit. Damian had promised not to alert Buddug to the Hunter's presence, though it would have been the swiftest way to ensure Leah's demise. Kyra could never doubt him, could never mistrust him, but the worry was impossible to ignore. The rest of the citizens of The Rose knew to avoid Buddug at the best of times and had grown used to Leah's presence over the past few weeks. They wouldn't betray that secret.

Still, Kyra found herself up and pacing without even noticing the veneer of calm falling away. It was a recipe for disaster, so far removed from her carefully controlled world. It felt like there had never been a time when she had been in control, when her word was law, as though the power she had cultivated over the years had disappeared. How a human could have such sway was beyond her, yet Kyra was sure it was all Leah's fault. Somehow.

Five steps to the bookcase, tight about-face, and five steps back to the other book-lined wall. Sharp turn and five more steps. Kyra's heels clicked loudly on the hardwood floors, recently polished and glowing under the warm light of the sun. Her glamour had returned the moment her calm had left. She walked in time with her racing pulse, every step another pump of thick blood from her panicked heart. Her stomach turned itself over, bile rising to sit just below her throat, threatening to come further but unable to commit. Click, click, click, her steps and heartbeat were a rhythm, a long-forgotten song, almost remembered as it danced at the back of her mind.

The smell of ozone engulfed her senses, and she stopped pacing immediately, turning to face the space she knew Buddug would step into. She kept her eyes carefully averted as Buddug re-crafted her glamour, catching glimpses of dark bruises and dried blood. When she felt it safe to look, it was to see Buddug's familiar face. She had always refused to wear a human form when eating.

"Buddug."

"Kyranthine." They greeted in equally formal tones. Kyra could feel the tightness to Buddug's voice and could only guess at the pain her mentor must be in to show it so openly.

She itched to rush over to Buddug, take her in her arms, and hold her tight. She wanted to examine every wound and hurt, clean the marked skin and ease the pain that radiated from every injury. But her stoic mentor wouldn't appreciate the fussing, so Kyra bit her tongue and wordlessly ushered Buddug to the chairs arranged in front of her desk.

Facing each other, they allowed Buddug and Kyra to sit close, intimately so. Once they were both seated, their knees were almost touching as they leaned forward to hold hands in the small space between them. Buddug's skin was chilled and smooth, her flesh soft despite her years. Kyra shifted her grip, placing her hands below Buddug's, palm up. Buddug held her own hands above Kyra's, palms aligned so that fingers brushed wrists.

They fell into the easy movements of habit, bodies and breathing falling into perfect synchronisation in the space of a few seconds. The familiar burn, the way it warmed and grew to wrap around her senses, to wrap around her arms, was all something she knew so well. Even as the pain swelled to the point of unbearable, a little higher each time as her mind fought to adapt to it, there was a part of Kyra that was bored by it all. And then, like clockwork, the pain was receding, the cramping of her muscles loosening as Buddug's skin soaked in all Kyra had to offer. Under her carefully constructed glamour, torn skin would be knitting back together, forming scars that would only add to Buddug's beauty.

Coming back to herself, falling away from the strange, shared existence she held with Buddug while the older demon fed, Kyra felt solid and real. In the darkness of her office, the sun setting entirely as they sat, Kyra could almost pretend her life wasn't falling apart around her. Pretend her mentor hadn't come to her carrying the marks of a fight she couldn't join, pretend a Hunter wasn't a few floors above, pretend Damian wasn't waiting for her heart to break, pretend her sanctuary was still her own. There was nothing beyond the walls of her office, nothing but night sky and stars that couldn't mock her with ungranted wishes.

"Kyra." She stiffened at the sound of Leah's voice. "I have a question."

~ Eighteen ~

Kyra swore, scrambling to put herself between Leah and Buddug, mind racing to think of something to say, anything to postpone the inevitable. Buddug's head whipped around, eyes narrowing as she adopted a human glamour. Kyra fumbled her magic to follow suit and somehow managed to draw a glamour close before Leah opened the door entirely.

"Leah..." Kyra hesitated, searching for anything to say. "Now isn't a good time."

"Now is fine," Buddug cut in. "Come in, child."

Leah entered slowly, looking between the two women with open curiosity and a healthy dose of trepidation.

"Is this the journalist?" Buddug looked to Kyra, voice and gaze equally hard.

"No, she's, ah..." Kyra was a child all over again, dirty and about to receive a tongue lashing.

"I'm a Hunter."

The silence that followed Leah's words was deafening, a heavy thing that settled in Kyra's stomach with the taste of bile. Possibilities played out in her mind, potential reactions from Buddug and her likely plans of attack. Surprise was her preferred weapon; physicality had never been the succubus way. Yet the longer it took her to attack, the more Kyra feared she would simply launch herself at Leah.

"Kyranthine," she said slowly, voice frighteningly neutral. "Care to explain why there is a Hunter in your office and coming to question you no less?"

"She's my prisoner?" Kyra hedged.

"Yet she walks free." Buddug rose slowly. Kyra shifted, surreptitiously keeping herself between the other two. Buddug's unimpressed look told her she wasn't as subtle as she hoped. "What are you doing?"

"Saving my life," Leah said before Kyra could even begin thinking of a reason.

"Is that so?" Buddug turned her disapproval to Leah. "And why would she do that?"

"I don't know." Leah spoke with a calm surety Kyra envied. "But she knew I was sent here to die and decided to show me mercy."

Buddug was quiet for a long moment, considering Leah's words as her eyes bored into Kyra. Whether she believed Leah's words or trusted that Kyra wasn't making a terrible mistake was known only to her. "I think I'll visit with Damian."

She brushed past Kyra without any further ado, not even deigning to look at Leah as she left the room.

For a long moment, Kyra and Leah simply looked at each other, neither moving nor speaking, though Kyra could see the curiosity burning behind Leah's eyes. Kyra took a step, moving to enthrone herself safely behind her desk, yearning for the sense of power it usually gave her. Instead, she stumbled, legs weak from the session with Buddug and the sudden lack of adrenaline caused by Leah's arrival.

Before Kyra could fall or even drop more than a little, Leah was there. Her thin arms, surprisingly strong, slipped under Kyra's, pulling her up and close. Leah gently led Kyra around the heavy desk to lower her into her chair, moving with a focused purpose to ensure Kyra wasn't jostled despite the short distance.

It was an awkward and strangely intimate moment as Leah checked that Kyra was settled comfortably, concern painted on her young face in a way that made Kyra's heart clench. For a human, she was an adult, but for Kyra's years, she was still so painfully young. Her life, so brief and fleeting, so far removed from Kyra's own. She'd never be able to truly understand the things Kyra had known, had experienced.

"Are you okay?" Leah's words, spoken softly, broke Kyra from her trance. The Hunter was still too close, leaning over to look in Kyra's eyes, her gaze darting around Kyra's face to assess her state.

"I'm fine."

Leah pulled away, clearly unconvinced but unwilling or unable to press the matter further. Kyra ran a hand over her face, taking the cowards way out, using the movement to tear her eyes away from the worry in Leah's expression. The tangle of her emotions proved more draining than feeding Buddug.

"Who was that? What happened?"

"That was..." Kyra hesitated. "That was my mentor." Mother, life giver, future. Kyra's mind echoed, words dark and heavy. Buddug was angry; this was bad. She'd be hungering for blood and would expect it to be spilt for the good of The Rose, for the good of their people. And when she was done ridding their sanctuary of the Hunter presence, she would turn her attention to Kyra.

"Did she hurt you?" Leah's voice was distant, barely audible over the pounding in Kyra's ears, in her chest. Her heart was trying to break through her ribs.

"No," she said after a moment, realising the question needed a reply. How could she risk so much?

"Kyra." Hearing her name with such fear would have been comforting from any other Hunter. "I'm afraid."

So am I. The words caught in her throat.

"Don't worry. It's nothing," she said instead, unsure if the lie was for Leah or herself. She knew neither of them believed it either way.

"But-"

"I'm fine," Kyra repeated, a little too harshly according to the way Leah flinched back. "I just need to rest," she continued in a calmer tone.

Leah hesitated before nodding her assent, turning to leave without another word. For a moment, Kyra considered calling her back, considered telling her...what? That Buddug would do whatever she thought was best? That she was tired from transferring power, from ensuring her mentor continued to live? That she would make it all okay? As if that was even something she could do, something she could promise.

~ Nineteen ~

That Buddug left as quietly as she had arrived both frightened and comforted Kyra. She hadn't killed Leah, the Hunter still holed up in her room under Wendy's well instructed and watchful eye, but she also hadn't spoken to Kyra before returning home. Kyra only knew Buddug was gone when Damian strode into her office wearing a scowl darker than the night sky outside.

"You let her see the Hunter?" He demanded as the door slammed closed behind him. The walls shuddered under the sudden assault, but Kyra managed to avoid flinching.

"Yes, I went out of my way to antagonise our historically trigger-happy mother," Kyra drawled, hiding the panic still clawing at her breast under layers of sarcasm and forced calm. "Leah burst in as we were finishing up."

Damian fell into his usual chair, scowl still firmly in place though the fiery anger in his eyes had banked down to a quiet smolder. "She damn near ripped my head off."

"I'm sorry," Kyra breathed with naked sincerity. "I shouldn't have put you in the middle of all this."

"You shouldn't have kept the human in the first place." Damian snapped.

Sighing a defeat she wasn't ready to face, Kyra pulled open her top left drawer before she could talk herself out of it. She had bundled the carefully folded letters with a strip of white ribbon as though she could purify them, could remove the taint of their words and origin. She raised the pile but didn't immediately hand them over, instead turning them slowly between long fingers. It was hard to pretend her hesitation was anything other than fear.

Damian remained silent as Kyra spun the pages, gaze staring beyond lines of neatly printed words that melted and merged into a dark blur of panicked thoughts. The weight of her guilt made the paper burn in her hands, the tips of her fingers tingling with muted pain.

"These," Kyra breached the silence she had created, thankful Damian had allowed her the room to think and annoyed he hadn't pressed her sooner, "have been sent to me over the past few weeks. Sent by the Church."

He grunted, the sound torn from him with the power of a physical blow. Yet, he leaned forward and extended a hand to take them. He wouldn't abandon her, not now. It was hard to believe the truth of that statement, almost as hard as it was to find the fortitude to allow him to take the letters from her tense fingers.

She looked away as he pulled the ribbon off, forcing her eyes to trace the comforting lines of books, catching on well-known titles and caressing spines cracked with age and love and multiple re-readings. Every moment Damian spent reading deepened Kyra's panic, her stomach twisting in complicated knots. Her skin was tight and buzzed with energy, giving the roiling depths of her gut permission to swoop from her feet up to the bottom of her throat.

Kyra braved a quick glance up, finding Damian reading slowly. He turned each page over with a sharp calm so at odds at her own frantic panic fluttering low in her chest. Looking only had her stomach lurching to sit in her throat, so she turned back to the book-lined wall to avoid spewing bile across her desk. Air whistled dryly in her throat as Kyra fought down nausea, pressing her hands to her stomach in a vain attempt to hold herself together.

"Fucking hell, Kyra," Damian sighed, tone small and defeated. He tossed the letters back across the desk, letting them splay and splatter, their words lurching dark and large in Kyra's sight. Scrambling to collect them back into their careful pile, the band around her chest only loosened enough for her to breathe once they were safely back in her desk. Her chest was still tight, but she could get air into her lungs now. "The Hunter has to die."

"I can't." Not won't. No more excuses. "You know I can't."

"I know." He shook his head, though whether to deny it or just at her foolishness, Kyra wasn't sure. "But she can't stay here either. They're practically threatening a full-scale assault. Did you show Buddug these?"

"No, of course not."

"Good. She really would have killed the Hunter." He pushed himself up, falling into staccato pacing. The familiarity of the sight should have been comforting. Instead, Kyra felt her stomach churn with the added pressure of his worry. "Have you shown the girl?"

"No," she replied less quickly, shame leaking into the edges of her voice. Damian looked to her but didn't stop pacing, waiting for her to continue. "I was afraid she would leave."

He scoffed and tossed his head, pulling his gaze away sharply. She could read the frustration in his movements, keyed high alongside his distress. He stopped pacing abruptly beside one book-lined wall, gaze hardening as it bore into Kyra. "You need to tell her."

"I-"

"No, you will tell her. The only way we survive this mess is if she's entirely on our side. She won't be if she finds out you kept this from her."

"How could she find out?" Kyra narrowed her eyes, voice gone soft. He wouldn't dare.

"It's going to be hard to miss if a group of Hunters knock down our door to save her." His fire matched her own, the anger on his face open where she had tried to hide hers. "I warned you; I fucking told you—" He cut himself off with a growl.

"To be fair"—Kyra dropped her head into her hands, delivering the rest between clutching fingers—"you said she'd kill me."

The words drifted between them, the moment hanging on tenterhooks as Damian processed her words, processed his own roiling emotions. His laugh, while bitter, was a relief. The alternative would have probably involved thrown items and a splitting headache.

"I'll tell her," she conceded into the ensuing silence. He didn't answer, and Kyra was too much of a coward to meet his gaze.

She listened listlessly as he walked from the room and shut the door behind him. He didn't slam it, but there was more force used than strictly necessary. Kyra kept her head in her hands, wishing all the answers would just reveal themselves to her.

~ Twenty ~

Kyra could feel Damian's eyes on her keenly as she moved through the following days, though she could only guess if it was to ensure she kept her word or if he had noticed the signs of exhaustion she couldn't completely hide. A fog had settled over her thoughts, slowing her responses and leaving her mind untethered.

She could only hope he would think it a Hunter-based distraction. Something small and insignificant, nothing to concern himself with. Nothing to question Wendy over. Nothing worth storming her office. Of course, Kyra was never that lucky.

Her office door swung open with enough force to bounce against the wall, the impact echoing loudly in the otherwise quiet room.

Leah and Kyra both looked up in surprise, Leah's face heating with embarrassment as Kyra's warmed with anger. Damian may as well have been wearing a storm cloud for a glamour, his expression darker than his midnight suit. The top buttons of his crisp white shirt were left open, and his painfully beautiful face was made all the more striking by a shock of silver hair so at odds with his unlined skin.

"You haven't eaten," he accused, striding into the room to loom over the desk. Leah was forgotten at his elbow, her gaze darting between the two demons.

"I-"

"You are not fine," he cut her off savagely, anger flashing behind his eyes.

"I was going to say," Kyra spoke with exaggerated slowness, "I have eaten."

"Then why are you so tired? Have you kept anything for yourself?"

There was no way of answering that without giving away her transaction with Hannah.

"I should go." Leah began to rise. The air crackled with impending doom, sparks bursting through the fragile magic of their glamours.

"No, stay." Damian placed a hand on her shoulder, not pushing down but not letting her rise any further. His grip was steel, though he didn't dig his fingers in. Leah lowered herself quickly. Neither demon looked her way, their eyes locked in a silent battle.

"Let her go." Kyra's voice, while low, was pure menace.

"She should be aware of the damage she is doing."

"This has nothing to do with her."

"No?" He laughed in bitter disbelief, the sound twisted by fury. "You expect me to believe that your unwillingness to eat with any consistency has nothing to do with the Hunter?"

"I just haven't..." Kyra cast around for the right words, the right excuse.

"Had the time? Had the chance?" Damian supplied. "Noticed the bone-crushing fatigue you must be feeling. It's been over a month, Kyra. I checked the roster; you haven't had a full meal since she arrived.

"And don't try to tell me about the one before her." He gestured to Leah with a wave of his hand. "We both know you didn't feed from him, not like you should have. You do this every time, push yourself a little further every time, as though it won't drive you into an earlier grave, and I'm sick of it."

Both women sat stunned under his torrent. Leah's darting gaze slowed, eyes narrowing as she folded her arms over her chest and tilted her head, watching Kyra with an inscrutable expression.

Kyra fought to process the edges of sadness and defeat to Damian's anger. It made her heart ache.

"Feed from me," Leah offered into the silence, brow set stubbornly. Kyra opened her mouth to explain, gently, how sweet, while pointless, such an offer was. Instead, Damian just laughed cruelly.

"Doesn't work like that, Hunter. She needs a man."

"Damian, enough," Kyra finally found her voice, pinning her friend with a weighted look. "Thank you, Leah," she continued, turning to the blushing woman across from her. She shared her embarrassment but refused to let it show. "Your offer is appreciated but not necessary.

"I will feed tonight," she told them both, unsure of how to feel about the mirrored concern in their eyes. A part of her, still clinging to the vain hope that this would all end for the best, noted that the two of them would be a force to reckon with should they ever decide to team up against her.

Damian looked mollified, if only slightly. It was enough for him to leave without further complaint.

"Have you really not fed?" Leah asked in the ensuing quiet.

"No," Kyra confirmed softly, waiting for the next wave of rage.

"Why?"

"I don't know." It was the safest answer Kyra could think of. It was also the closest thing to the truth that wouldn't result in another argument. She was juggling so many balls, half of them studded with spikes itching to pierce her skin, and she didn't know which they were until they had already drawn blood.

"You should have fed off of the Hunter before me."

Leah's words shocked Kyra, more than the matter-of-fact tone she delivered them in.

"What?" As though she really needed it repeated.

"You should have fed from him," she said. "Michael. He would have still been strong even if he wasn't young anymore. Why didn't you feed from him?"

"He was-" Kyra cut herself off sharply. It wasn't a simple question to answer under any circumstances. To explain it to Leah would be impossible. "I had my reasons," Kyra said instead, voice gone hard to indicate the conversation was over.

Leah looked like she wanted to press the issue further. For a moment, Kyra worried she would, but instead, she lifted her book from the desk, settling back further into her chair to continue reading. Kyra watched her for a moment longer, already falling completely into demolishing the words presented before her. Michael had been good too, his desires still pure, even under Kyra's influence.

It wasn't that she couldn't feed from him so much as she wouldn't. He had seemed a good man if on the wrong side of a war he didn't really understand. Kyra didn't feed from good men. No matter how strong they were or how weak from hunger she was, she did not feed from good men.

Kyra had barely sent the message to Wendy before she was pushing her way into the office, papers clasped to her chest. Leah didn't look up from her book, the sound of turning pages a quietly comforting counterpoint to Kyra's sporadic typing. Wendy crossed the room with her usual focused walk, footsteps sharp but not obviously hurried. She came to a stop beside Leah, unknowingly filling the same space Damian had help not too long ago, the same tight, angry concern blazing in her eyes.

"These are booked in for tonight." She tossed the sheets down on Kyra's desk with open disdain. Though her head didn't move, Kyra saw Leah's eyes hone in on the pages with greedy curiosity.

"Thank you." Kyra sighed, trying to overlook the emotional humans before her. "I'll let you know who I pick."

"I suggest the first one." Wendy straightened, crossing her arms. The implicit dismissal was summarily ignored.

"Thank you. I will let you know who I pick," Kyra repeated forcefully. Wendy simply tightened her crossed arms under her breasts and shifted her weight, her pointed look telling Kyra she wouldn't leave the room until a name was given.

Knowing a losing battle when she saw one, Kyra admitted defeat gracefully, gathering the pages into a neat pile before flicking through them. The words were plain and clinical, the same notes held for every customer. Two were dismissed immediately, their preferences unsuitable. It was tempting to oppose Wendy's suggestion, but she was right as always.

Kyra handed back the papers. "The first one will be fine."

Wendy's smile was mirthless, a parody of victory edged in frustrated worry. Turning away from it brought little relief when it meant meeting Leah's gaze, her own concern just as naked and no less sharp for the way it cut into Kyra.

~ Twenty-One ~

Kyra took the stairs to the second floor of The Rose slowly, unable to shake the knot of anxiety that always came before feeding. She had been doing this for decades, but it never made it any easier. Knowing what she would face, knowing what she would have to do, churned her stomach in a mix of disgust and fear.

The lighting was soft and sensual in the room, everything prepared for her, for the client. Kyra shed the edges of her glamour like she was shedding clothes, doing away with the pieces that wouldn't suit the fantasy. Her body shifted, skin becoming near deathly pale while she gained additional flesh, adopting the visage of a voluptuous beauty. Her full figure screamed fertility and power, a natural upturn to her luscious lips giving the barest hint of a smile, just waiting to break free. Her hair, now dark and wild, bounced as she shook the last of her glamour into place. Eyes as dark as sin took advantage of the full-length mirror in the corner to ensure she fit the brief.

It was less in what he had requested than what Wendy had noticed that had Kyra attending this appointment. He liked his women sultry and powerful because he liked to hit and hurt, to feel strong, to exercise his will over someone who couldn't say no. Kyra pushed it out of her mind, stomach clenching with disgust as her vision clouded in anger.

Holding her calm became difficult as he strode into the room. He was a small man, a timid beast pulled tight, shackled in shame, and buried under self-loathing. Kyra had no sense of who he was or how he looked physically, his desires washing over her mind until that was all she could see. A yearning for power, for control, entwined so entirely with his lust, it darkened from a bright, burning red to coal black.

His lust was corrupted beyond recognition, a broken thing that coated Kyra with its foul taint. A thing to be used to stab and tear, to remove flesh from bone. And while it turned Kyra's stomach, it was so strong, laying thick in the air, that it called to her. Contradicting instincts fought in the back of her mind, her need to feed, to fuck, battling with her deep-rooted self-preservation and distaste for men. She pushed both aside, giving them as much mind as the tang of male lust in the air. All were irrelevant at this point.

Kyra adopted a sultry smile and stepped forward on feet lighter than her new size suggested. The curve of her lips hinted at sin even as she widened her eyes into coy innocence. The old tricks were a second nature, talents so deeply embedded in her psyche, she'd never be free of them. For now, they had a use, so she couldn't complain.

There were no words spoken as Kyra crossed the room, giving him the power, coming to him, allowing his lust to grow and growl between them. Words were useless, only things to get in the way. She raised a hand to cup his cheek but diverted at the last second, instead resting it on his arm to gaze up at him. For a moment, there were two of him, one large and imposing as he loomed over her, the other small and fighting to be big. It didn't matter which was the true version.

She didn't have to wait long for him to surge forward, crashing into her bodily and forcing her backwards onto the bed. That moment of contact, the burning of skin on skin as he manhandled her was all she needed.

In his mind, he was pushing and pulling, hitting and biting, and she was screaming just the way he liked. In his mind, she was sobbing for him to stop. In his mind, his fantasies played out in sharp relief. He could taste her blood, her cries, the salt of her tears on her cheeks. In his mind, he roared his pleasure as she whimpered.

In the cold of the room, he jerked on the bed, body thrashing momentarily. Kyra sat above him, glamour and mask of humanity gone, clawed fingers cradling his head gingerly. Despite the low light, Kyra could see the damp darkness on the crotch of his pants. It had been careless of her, maybe cruel, but what was done was done.

It was a quick but filling meal, the rush of energy torn from him with a bored disregard. His essence sat thick and heavy in her stomach, leaving Kyra feeling vaguely bloated and considering a short nap.

Instead, she pulled her hands and mind away from the now sleeping man. Kyra wiped her fingers on the sheets, though it did nothing to rid the feeling of dirt on her skin. When she looked up, it was to find Leah in the doorway, mouth agape and eyes wide. Her gaze darted from the man on the bed to Kyra and back again.

"Is he..." She pulled her eyes away when they landed on the damning spot on his pants. "Is he dead?"

"No," Kyra replied slowly, stepping away from the bed in an attempt to distance herself from the loathsome reality of her eating habits.

"So, that's what you look like." Leah's gaze had settled entirely on Kyra now, running up and down her form unashamedly.

Kyra froze at the words, realising how naked she truly was. Her glamour fell over her skin, a door slamming closed in Leah's face. But it refused to hold, shimmering and failing. The man's energy, still raw and hot in the pit of Kyra's stomach, fought to break her concentration. Leah's searching gaze found the flashes of inhuman skin in the cracks of Kyra's carefully crafted human mask.

"Don't hide it." Leah darted further into the room, hand raised as though she could physically break through the glamour.

Before Kyra could reply or run, the man snorted in his sleep, rolling over into a more comfortable position. They both turned to him, eyeing him with a mix of trepidation and disgust. Kyra hesitated, wanting more than anything to avoid the conversation that was about to take place but knowing that the stubborn set of Leah's face was spelling her doom.

"Come on," Kyra sighed, leading Leah from the room.

The walk to Kyra's room was uncomfortable, though blessedly quick as they climbed the back stairs in silence. Every step felt like a step closer to her demise, a death row inmate walking to the electric chair. Her mind conjured images of Leah looking at her in disgust, much the way she had looked at the sleeping man on the bed. It didn't matter that she was a Hunter, that she was here against her will, that she had come here for the sole purpose of killing Kyra. The thought of being on the receiving end of Leah's disdain was frightening. The open curiosity and wonder in Leah's eyes were quickly forgotten under the spiral of Kyra's darkening thoughts.

"What were you doing there?" Kyra asked, a vain attempt to avoid Leah's vitriol.

"Damian said you were in there." It was decided; Kyra was going to kill him. "Can you show me again?" Though she didn't want to believe it, there was clear excitement in Leah's voice.

"Why?" Kyra's tone was defensive. She couldn't help it.

"You looked beautiful." Leah said it with such open honesty, it was hard for Kyra to discredit it.

Kyra hesitated. This was a mistake. Every fibre of her being screamed at her not to do it, not to let her guard down. Not to trust the human.

Taking a deep breath, Kyra forced her racing thoughts and heart to slow. Leah waited patiently, standing barely two steps into the room, giving Kyra all the space she needed. Hazel eyes held only wonder, and Leah's entire body was loose and at ease. Kyra appreciated her obvious care in making it Kyra's choice, but a part of her wished Leah would just force the issue and demand Kyra bend to her will. The fact that she wanted Leah to make those demands and knew the Hunter never would told Kyra that her panicked instincts would go ignored once more.

Letting her glamour fall, the magic slid off her skin like water, revealing her true nature to Leah's curious gaze. They stood there in silence, Leah drinking in Kyra's form as curiosity warred with another emotion Kyra couldn't place. There was a heat to Leah's eyes that caused Kyra to flush, self-conscious and painfully bare without her glamour. Her nakedness went beyond the lack of clothes on her body, as though her very soul, the core of her being, was flayed open to the Hunter.

Knowing Leah was drinking in the purple flush to her skin, the lilac tinge muted in the glow of artificial light, warmed Kyra's cheeks further. Leah's eyes trailed over Kyra's humanoid and decidedly demonic features with equal heat, an open fascination flashing across her face as she took in the long curve of Kyra's wings. The darker violet of her wings' membrane made her pale skin glow in comparison, even as they curled around her body protectively, attempting to hide at least some of her figure. This didn't stop her cloven hooves from being visible, of course, the dark fur giving way to flawless skin at the top of her thighs.

When Leah stepped forward, it took every ounce of Kyra's self-control not to step back. She allowed the Hunter to approach slowly, Leah moving as though dealing with a cornered animal. Kyra wasn't sure if that wasn't an accurate assessment.

No matter how slow her approach, how much time Kyra had to prepare, it was still a shock when Leah placed a gentle hand on the upper arm not blocked by her impressive wingspan. The touch was soft, a caress that felt too warm, too familiar, though Kyra didn't pull away. Leah took the invitation it was to trail her hand up and back, fingers pulling away from skin to dance along the thin membrane of Kyra's wings. They twitched under Leah's hand, instinctively pulling in.

"Sorry," Kyra murmured, so low it was almost inaudible, unwilling to break the trance they found themselves under. "They're fragile."

Leah adjusted the trajectory of her hand, instead lifting it to Kyra's face. Her skin, warm and unbearably soft, rested against Kyra's cheek. She hesitated a moment, caught between searching Kyra's eyes and tracing the curve of her short horns. Questing fingers gave in to temptation, trailing to the tip of the closer horn before slipping back down to run through the hair that surrounded it. It was an inky black, like the fur on her legs, though far softer than the coarse pelt covering Kyra's calves. Leah's hand shifted, curling to cup the back of Kyra's skull.

"I'd very much like to kiss you," Leah breathed, the words dancing across Kyra's lips. When had she gotten so close? Kyra couldn't do anything but nod, following the coaxing of the hand in her hair. As if in a trance, she tilted and leaned forward.

Leah met her halfway, pressing her lips against Kyra's. It was warm and chaste and heartbreakingly perfect. The touch was fleeting, over before Kyra could fully appreciate it had begun. Yet it left her lips tingling, her face flushed and heart racing with the silent promise of more.

When they both pulled away, Kyra was met with a radiant smile, one she had no choice but to return. Leah's cheeks, usually so pale, were pink, the colour high and warm. Her eyes were bright, shining in a way Kyra associated with the discovery of new information, not a barely-there kiss shared with a demon.

"I, um...I better go." Leah laughed awkwardly. She turned to leave, and though Kyra searched for something to say to make her stay, nothing came to mind before Leah slipped from the room.

~ Twenty-Two ~

It wasn't until much later, in the early hours of the next morning, that Kyra realised the gravity of her mistake. Not only had she kissed a human, a Hunter, but the look on Leah's face said it hadn't been a simple, sweet kiss. Laying in the warmth of her nest, wings pulled tight and close, Kyra replayed the moment again and again. The look in Leah's eyes, the bright glint of something Kyra couldn't name...it wouldn't leave her alone.

In the dark, safely hidden and alone, Kyra remembered the bundle of letters kept locked tight in the drawer of her desk. She remembered the newest letter, hand-delivered by a wide-eyed boy too young to be stepping foot in The Rose. It wouldn't be long until the innocence was banished from his face, but for now, he had looked at Kyra with open fear. The letter, addressed to Leah directly, had spoken of a sickly mentor pleading for her to return if she could. Kyra's fingers had itched to tear and destroy, remove any hint of guilt. She hadn't, though keeping it filled her with a quiet sense of dread.

She had to tell Leah. That had been true even before they kissed, but now it was unavoidable. More than that, she had to let her go. Kyra couldn't keep her locked away anymore. She should have let Leah go the moment she stopped viewing the Hunter as a prisoner. She should never have kept her in the first place, though she could never regret letting her live.

Kyra groaned under her breath, rubbing at her face as though it would help organise her thoughts, as though it would magically

131

dislodge the perfect solution from the dark recesses of her mind. Instead, all it did was create dancing lights behind her eyelids. Not for the first time, Kyra missed the ease of life before Leah, when things made sense, and the natural order of the world hadn't been turned so thoroughly on its head.

Dawn was barely a whisper of a promise on the horizon, but Kyra had given up on sleep hours ago, the night spent tossing and turning while her brain and stomach tried to decide if kissing Leah had been a stupid decision or not. While the fact that she was questioning it at all seemed a good indication of the answer, Kyra couldn't bring herself to actually regret the action. That Leah had initiated it, had been the driver of the embrace, had little bearing on the way Kyra placed any and all blame squarely on herself.

And while from the outside, it had been a chaste, innocent thing, Kyra knew better. She knew her own heart, the beat falling out of rhythm momentarily at the thought of Leah. Knew her own desires. She was a demon, fast approaching the end of her first century, and yet she was like a child experiencing puppy love for the first time. If it had been happening to anyone else, she would have said it sickening.

None of this helped the way her stomach twisted at the memory of the letters tucked in her desk. Her mind was running a tight loop, thoughts on repeat as she replayed the kiss and then reminded herself of the consequences of her lies.

Dragging herself out of bed felt like a momentous victory. The small effort, though repeated so many times previously, had felt beyond her in the washed-out grey of pre-dawn. The next step was pulling a glamour over her features, the shimmer of magic on her skin humming a dissonant note. For the first time in her life, her glamour felt like an oppressive mask, ill-fitting and painfully restrictive, rather than the shroud of armour it had always been.

Walking to her bathroom felt insurmountable, feet momentarily glued to the floor as her legs filled with concrete. Kyra knew she needed to move, needed to put one foot in front of the other to cross the short space between bed and bathroom, but the orders of her brain were ignored by her muscles.

The weight of guilt sat heavy in her gut, laden with trepidation and a sense of giddy anticipation. It was an odd, unsettling mix of emotions in her stomach, making her regret ever eating, or waking, or even existing.

She wasn't hiding in her office, no matter what Damian may think, smirking at her from across her desk. He knew. The knowledge shone with the mirth in his eyes, and it irked Kyra. She had no idea how he knew, just that he did.

The mischievous glint in his eye, the knowing way he had laughed at her look of panic at the door opening, he had to know. Kyra was sure he had planned it too, though she couldn't figure out why or what he had hoped to achieve. The whole situation was a headache she wished would just go away. As though her life had ever been that simple.

"Is there a reason you're here?" Kyra finally asked when pretending to be busy did nothing but make his smile grow. Damian hadn't spoken since sauntering into the room and falling into the chair, splaying his limbs in a way that didn't look comfortable. He had been content watching Kyra pretend to read files and check emails. He hadn't even cracked when she had written up a mock email, the draft dissolving quickly from an expletive-laden rant directed at him into garbled gibberish formed by hitting random keys in a way that threatened the structural integrity of the keyboard.

"It's okay. I can wait." His smile grew, the bastard. "I can see how busy you are."

Kyra closed her laptop with a sigh, finally meeting his eye head-on. "What do you want?" He was a pale beauty today, with short blonde hair and eyes that shone with a green light. His features were pointed and otherworldly, and Kyra would have forgiven a human for thinking him some kind of fairy.

"Did she kiss you?"

"What - How did you-" The heat suffusing her cheeks told Kyra her attempt at indignant protest was suitably undermined. Though the speed and vehemence at which she protested was just as telling.

"I passed her as she was coming out of your room." Damian shrugged. "I could taste it in the air, though I still don't understand why you didn't go further. She would have been more than happy to fall into bed with you."

"That's not...we're not..." Kyra drew a deep breath, fighting down her blush and rising panic with ferocity. "It's not like that." Damian's raised eyebrow begged to differ. "And you shouldn't have been lurking."

"I thought you'd be happy at least. You got your Hunter, she wasn't scared off by everything, and she isn't mad about the letters." Her stomach twisted with the all too familiar shame, and it must have been clear on her face. Damian's expression shifted immediately from gloating to confusion before slipping straight to frustration. "You didn't tell her?" The question was almost a curse, his voice caught between indignation and pure anger.

"I-"

"What have you been doing the past few weeks? She's in here every other day." He was out of the chair and pacing in a blink, the movement so well known, the measured tempo of his steps could probably lull her to sleep. If they weren't the soundtrack to her every mistake.

"We've been talking." It sounded pathetic, even to her own ears.

"Talking? You've been canoodling." Kyra spluttered at the accusation, at the word. Canoodling. As though she wasn't nearly a century, as though Leah wasn't a grown woman. "I can't believe you let it get this far without being honest."

He spun to face her, too angry to pace. "Actually, no, I can believe it. Rather than open up to her, rather than risk being vulnerable," he hissed the word, making the edges sharp enough for it to lodge deeply in her chest, "you just decided you'd keep her here and not tell her the truth. You let her fall in love with you while she's your prisoner."

"She's not," Kyra tried weakly, not entirely sure what she was denying.

"Leah will always be your prisoner as long as you keep her here. Yeah, she's allowed to walk around and probably leave the building, but you're keeping her here by force as long as you don't tell her the truth."

Her stomach had relocated, but she couldn't figure out if it was in her throat or at her feet. The sting of tears at her eyes was hardly a surprise. The way bile clawed at the back of her throat was new, her mouth flooding with saliva as her body prepared to void everything she'd ever eaten. Was it even possible to vomit up pure, sexual energy? She didn't want to find out but felt she would have no choice shortly.

"What do you care?" she bit back, clawing at any shreds of anger to keep her stomach in place. "She's hardly your favourite person."

"You've made her a member of our family." He loomed despite his slight stature. His hands were curled into fists where they pressed into the hard wood of her desk. Kyra couldn't tear her eyes away from the contrast of alabaster skin and warmed polished wood. "You let her wander around and make friends. You let yourself fall in love with her" He scoffed at this, but Kyra was given no respite from his tirade. "She's shown that she's not going to kill us all. She's even proven she loves you horns and all. One thing, Kyra, you only had to do one thing. You couldn't kill her; you wanted to keep her, and all you had to do was be honest."

Damian fell back into the chair he'd vacated with a heavy sigh. "When the Church does attack—" Kyra opened her mouth to protest but thought better of it under his withering glare. "When they do attack and they tell her you kept this from her, who do you think she's going to side with? It's only a matter of time before she's standing between us and them, and you can't afford to give her any reason to choose them. Because you've made it quite clear you can't kill her if she does."

"I've really fucked up, haven't I?" She didn't need his answering scoff. "Fuck." Dropping her head into her hands, she pressed her palms into her sockets. Starbursts fired behind her lids, but they did nothing to erase the world around her.

#

Calling Leah into her office was relatively easy, though the smirk Wendy shot her at the instructions did nothing to help settle her stomach or guilt. The wait for Wendy to return was a whole new level of torture.

Kyra couldn't help but picture all the ways the conversation could go wrong in painfully etched detail. Every situation was worse than the one before, culminating in a parade of conversations that ended in her own death with Leah's fingers wrapped around her throat. Though they were used to holding books, they would be strong and sure, tightening to crush her windpipe under inexorable pressure. Would she hear the cartilage give way? Would she feel it crack and splinter?

"Kyra?" The soft question of Leah's voice pulled her from morbid thoughts, but her gut refused to settle. "Wendy said you wanted to see me?" Leah stepped into the room with a quiet confidence, a gentle mischief shining behind her gaze. Her face was open and honest and heartbreakingly innocent.

"Yes. We need to talk." Kyra cleared her throat roughly, trying to push past the lump that was her stomach. "Sit." The Hunter took the indicated chair as ordered. Her smile faded, but it didn't slip away entirely.

"I was hoping we could do a little more than talk." She leaned across the desk, placing her elbows on the wood to prop her chin on folded hands. The flirtatious smile twisted at Kyra's insides. She wanted so badly to give in to the offer there.

Kyra tore her eyes away from the tempting tilt of Leah's mouth. Her gaze fell to the neat pile of letters on her desk and her resolve hardened. "While that is a very enticing offer," she breathed, telling herself she wasn't stalling, "I don't think that would be wise."

"Why? Do you regret-"

"No." It would have been a simple lie, a convenient excuse, but Kyra couldn't do that. "But you might." The words burnt her tongue, but she forced them out anyway. "I need to tell you something." The words fell in a rush from her lips as though pausing would allow them to catch in her throat or dry on her tongue. "The Church has been sending letters—demands, really–that I let you go. At first, I burnt them out of habit, I guess. Denying the Church what they want is kind of second nature at this point. But I didn't tell you. I think I was scared you would try to leave. As if you weren't my prisoner already.

"Shit, this is so messed up. I am so messed up." Kyra dropped her head, cradling it in her hands. Her thoughts raced, and her mouth struggled to keep up, words becoming muffled by the barrier of her tightening fingers. "And then they kept coming, every other week, and I couldn't keep burning them, so I hid them. And we kept talking, and it felt like we were becoming...friends? I don't know; maybe it's all just in my head. But it felt like maybe you were questioning the Church and their teachings, and you were starting to see that it's not as black and white as they'd like you to believe.

"And every new letter, I'd think to myself, 'This is it, I'll tell her about this one.' But I didn't, obviously. I just kept pretending they didn't exist because it felt easier. Even when they started addressing them to you, promising all would be forgiven. As though they wouldn't kill you the first chance they got. Or what if it had all been a lie, and you were just going to spill all our secrets to them? I don't know. Maybe I should have killed you like Damian said.

"But I couldn't. Not at first and definitely not now. Because you stopped being my prisoner the first time you said, 'I have a question' and I actually, stupidly, answered you. What was I thinking?" Kyra laughed bitterly, finally looking up but still unable to force herself to look at Leah. Instead, she looked over the Hunter's shoulder at nothing. "Damian would say I was thinking with my dick if I had one. But it wasn't that either. There's just something about you. I wish I knew what so I could dig it out and finally breathe.

"Sorry, I'm getting off track." Kyra's eyes swept past Leah to her desk, to the still carefully folded letters. "After last night, I knew I couldn't keep them any longer."

Leah eyed the letters like a primed explosive, waiting for it to go off between them. None of her natural curiosity was in her eyes, which did nothing to ease Kyra's low, simmering panic. It felt like an eternity passed in the moment, both women staring at the innocuous pieces of paper as though they were the source of all evil, the home of a dark force yet unknown but definitely to be feared.

With slow movements, Leah lifted the letters, turning the carefully folded paper between her fingers, unstaring eyes watching the edges twirl lazily. Kyra watched her closely, gaze darting from the letters to Leah's face. She couldn't decide if she wanted Leah to never read them or just get it over with.

The slide of paper against paper, a dry rasp that Kyra had come to associate with the Hunter, was loud in the office and cut across the sound of their breathing. Kyra's heartbeat hammered in her ears as she watched Leah read the words quickly, bright hazel eyes darting across the pages. Then she re-read them slowly, much like Damian had. Unlike Damian, her face remained neutral, carefully calm.

After reading the letters more times than Kyra thought strictly necessary, Leah's gaze slightly unfocused. Kyra ached to know what she was thinking, what she was feeling, for any hint of how this was all going to end.

Seconds stretched into a panicked eternity for Kyra's frayed nerves before Leah finally looked up. Unshed tears shone in her eyes, and there was a hardness to the set of her jaw. Anger was written clear and large across her face, but Kyra refused to look away, refused to flinch back. This was justified, she reminded herself. She deserved whatever Leah decided to give. She was prepared to be lashed by words or by blows. This was justified.

"How long ago did this come?" She held up the most recent missive. Despite the fury on her face, her voice was calm and even.

"A few days." Kyra wasn't as composed, her voice carrying the slightest tremble. None of this was meant to happen. This wasn't the way things were meant to be.

"And you kept it from me?"

"Yes."

"And if we hadn't kissed last night, you still would have kept it from me?"

"Yes." Kyra drew a shuddering breath, needing to explain, to try and fix the gaping hole she could feel growing between them. "I'm sorry. I should have told you from the beginning."

"But you didn't trust me?" The question wasn't malicious, but it made Kyra flinch just the same.

"No." Her assent was small, defeated.

"And now? Do you trust me now?"

"Of course." Leah raised an eyebrow at Kyra's response, delivered too quick, too loud. It was all too little, too late—that was becoming increasingly obvious. "I mean, I'm telling you, aren't I? You're a Hunter, you came here to kill me, but I'm letting you go now. You could tell the Church about everything you've learnt, and they could use it to wipe us all out if you wanted."

"But you don't trust me not to? You think I'd actually do that?"

"I don't know what to think." Kyra hadn't meant to yell, hadn't meant to let her voice rise and break with more emotion than she knew how to handle.

For a moment, they looked at each other, Kyra panting slightly following her outburst, Leah still carefully blank. Leah's pale eyes no longer glistened with tears; her gaze stony, a shutter had closed behind her eyes. Kyra could feel the telltale pinpricks behind her own eyes, the burn of waiting tears still familiar no matter how she had convinced herself to stop crying as a rule.

Kyra forced the tears aside, forced her breathing to calm, forced her racing heart to slow. This wasn't her. She wasn't a flighty girl barely in her third decade. This wasn't her first love. This wasn't love at all. This was barely even a crush, nothing to get upset over.

Leah was a Hunter, a prisoner, someone held here against her will. There was nothing between them but a messed-up case of Stockholm syndrome. Thinking otherwise was stupid, and keeping Leah in The Rose any longer would only prolong the suffering Kyra had already put them both through.

"I think I understand now," Leah broke the silence. Emotion appeared at the cracks of her carefully cultivated armour, a mixture of pain and sadness tightening the corners of her eyes, pulling her lips down into the slightest of frowns. "We'll discuss this further when you've calmed down."

"There's nothing to discuss." Liar. "You need to go." Coward. "You don't belong here. You never did. You were my prisoner, and now I'm setting you free." Her mind screamed obscenities at her, flaying her thoughts to match the raw, naked pain of her heart.

Leah studied Kyra, visibly digesting her words and suddenly calm tone. Kyra knew she saw right through it. She may be able to half convince herself, but Leah was too smart, too perceptive to accept Kyra's lies as anything other than a pathetic attempt at saving herself. Leah saw it all and still nodded her assent.

They sat across from each other, holding the other's gaze with unwavering eyes, both knowing exactly what was happening. Knowing this was a road to heartache, that this had been doomed from the start. They both knew the other wanted to fight on some level. They both wanted to try to save this, just like they both knew it was pointless.

Kyra's mouth and mind set stubbornly, and she only just fell short of folding her arms tightly across her chest. Even if Leah wanted to fight it, wanted to convince Kyra that she could be trusted despite being a human, despite being a Hunter, it would have been a losing battle.

"Then I will leave," Leah finally managed to say, rising slowly, letters still held limply between her fingers.

"Pack your things and go." As though Leah owned anything in her room. The clothes were bought by Wendy, by Kyra. The books borrowed from the various inhabitants of The Rose. But Kyra knew that. She was giving Leah an excuse to take things with her, to take mementos and keepsakes in case the Hunter didn't want to forget them. As though it was a kindness, not an excuse to ensure Leah suffered as she would, never able to truly shake free the time they had spent, the memories they had created.

~ Twenty-Three ~

The upside to spending the majority of her time in her office was that it was harder to accuse Kyra of hiding. It didn't matter that Leah was currently a few floors above, packing her bags. She could almost pretend it wasn't happening, that the woman had never come into her life in the first place.

It was hard to ignore the gaping hole in her chest, the empty space where she knew her heart should have been, though. The edges were bloody and raw, tender and leaking pain in radiating waves throughout her entire body. Forcing her mind to focus on the paperwork before her, on the numbers and requests and million little details that made up running The Rose, Kyra pushed everything else to the back of her thoughts.

Her door swung open with sharp force, bouncing off the wall to be carried into Mary with the momentum. She batted it away without slowing her step, ignoring the way it remained ajar as she strode into the room. Her steps were hurried, just shy of falling into a jog. Rather than coming to a stop at Kyra's desk or falling into a chair without invitation, the nervous energy in her body kept her moving. Barely pausing to meet Kyra's eyes, Mary immediately began pacing in front of her desk. Maybe she should paint a track on the floor or simply trust her friends to wear away a path in the hard wood.

"What's wrong?" Kyra demanded, mind jerking away from her own hurt to assess the woman before her.

"I think I'm being followed," Mary snapped, anger fighting with fear in her voice.

"Are you sure?"

"Yes...maybe." She let out a shaky laugh. "How do you know if you're being followed? This is my first time." Her hands raised to her head, threading in her hair to grip at her skull. The sharp clicking of heels against floor didn't slow even as her grip turned white-knuckled.

Kyra was out from behind her desk and pulling Mary into a hug in a flash. At first, Mary struggled, restless energy demanding to be expelled, but Kyra just tightened her grip until the woman slumped in her arms.

"Tell me exactly what happened," Kyra ordered into Mary's hair.

"I don't know. I keep seeing these people," she mumbled, weak voice muffled by Kyra's shoulder, but the demon refused to loosen her grip. "Not always the same ones, but they're still the same. They dress too alike, hold themselves with the same danger. At first, they appeared near the office, but I've started seeing them outside my apartment building and when I'm out. I saw one when I was meeting with a source the other day."

"Were you followed here?" Kyra couldn't help but picture faceless watchers outside The Rose, and her arms ached to tighten around Mary. She pushed the urge away, knowing it would only feed into the human's own fear. Her mind continued to conjure images of watchers and stalking shadows that would see Leah leaving in a matter of hours if they didn't go when Mary did. It had to be the Church; Kyra was sure of it.

"Probably? I don't know." Mary's arms twitched against her sides, caught between pushing Kyra away and holding her closer. "I'm sorry. I didn't know where else to go."

"No, it's fine." She'd need to tell Wendy, have any lurkers dealt with. Damian would probably need to be informed as well. Maybe Erik and his boy toy could be trusted to clean up any stragglers. "It's good you came to me. I won't let anything happen to you."

"I'm sorry," Mary muttered again, but her arms came up to return Kyra's embrace rather than push her away. "I guess this is what I get for digging."

"I did warn you." Kyra's chest loosened minutely at Mary's laugh, the sound nearly genuine this time. She began to pull away slowly, giving Mary time to adjust to the shift. The reporter jerked away as though surprised she had placed so much weight on Kyra.

Another short laugh, this one muffled by hands wiping at damp eyes, Mary visibly fortified herself with several deep breaths. By the time they stood a few steps apart, Mary had pulled herself together, though she was still well short of calm.

"So, what do I do?"

"You do nothing." Kyra indicated she take a seat, opting to sit beside her rather than circle back around the desk. "I will organise for someone a little more friendly to keep an eye on you and hopefully scare off your unwanted guests."

"Will you have them killed?" There was no fear to the question, a strange determination shining in her eyes. This disturbed Kyra more than learning that Mary was being followed in the first place.

"Not if I can avoid it," she answered honestly. Mary didn't need to know it would be almost entirely unavoidable. Demons killed Hunters; it was a matter of self-preservation. "But it won't be your concern, I promise. You won't even know they're there."

"Thank you, Kyra." Mary breathed easily for the first time since she entered the room. She slumped in the chair, the restless energy that had filled her moments before gone in a rush of gratitude. The implicit trust that Kyra would fix it, would keep Mary safe, should have warmed the demon. It did nothing against the frozen hole in Kyra's chest.

"Why don't you stay the night? I'll have a room made up, and I can send someone to pick up some essentials from your place." Kyra placed a hand on Mary's knee, squeezing reassuringly. "I'll have you escorted home in the morning. You'll feel better after a solid night's sleep." For a moment, Kyra thought she'd refuse,

Mary's jaw set stubbornly now that the threat had seemed to pass. Maintaining a calm yet determined gaze, Kyra effectively stared Mary into submission until the reporter was nodding slowly. "Good. Wait here a moment. I'll get it sorted for you." Kyra gave her knee one last squeeze before standing.

Wendy was sat at her desk, a game of minesweeper large on the screen of her computer. Kyra hadn't even known that still came loaded on computers.

"I need you to have a room prepared for Mary, preferably close to mine. She'll be staying the night. I also need to speak with Erik and Caleb, as well as anyone else currently on cleaning duty who can be trusted to leave the building. Mary's had some unwanted visitors." Kyra turned sharply on her heel, fully intending to stride back into her office without waiting for Wendy to respond.

"What about Leah?" The question struck Kyra between the shoulders, carrying all the weight of Wendy's disapproval.

What about Leah? In a moment of madness, Kyra almost allowed herself to voice her immediate reaction. She almost ordered Wendy to make Leah stay, to lock Leah in her room and keep her under constant surveillance so that Kyra could rest easy knowing the Hunter was safe and well at all times. But Wendy wouldn't follow that order. If anything, the too blunt woman would tell Kyra to ask the Hunter to stay herself rather than keep being a coward.

"Tell Leah she should wait until morning to leave. Don't tell her why, just say, I don't know, a good nights' sleep will do her good or something." Kyra closed her office door before Wendy could reply, before she was done speaking herself. She told herself it was because she needed to make sure Mary was okay, not because she was afraid of discussing Leah. Or worse, seeing the pale woman and being at the receiving end of a too knowing look and an infuriating head tilt.

Mary appeared less frantic in the morning, a solid night's sleep seeming to have done her a world of good if the smile she greeted

Kyra with was anything to go by. The kitchen was quiet around them, the whole building seemingly asleep in the still early morning. The reporter was curled over a mug, wisps of steam curling softly around her face, nose dangerously close to brushing the surface of her coffee. She had looked up long enough to identify Kyra and smile her greeting before leaning back in to attempt inhaling her coffee.

Moving further into the kitchen, Kyra set about making her own cup, needing the warm embrace of caffeine. She had barely been up an hour, and a headache was already forming behind her eyes.

Leah had finished packing last night. She hadn't found the courage to actually talk to the Hunter, but Wendy had told her in a flat tone that Leah would be leaving first thing in the morning as instructed. A part of her had wanted to sleep through the day, just avoid the entire thing, but that would have involved finding sleep in the first place.

Kyra clutched her mug tightly, using the warm ceramic to hide the tremble of her fingers. Rather than flee to her office, she sat across from Mary, hoping her returning smile wasn't too tired at the edges. There was no way she'd tell the human what had her so despondent. At least her glamour hid the dark circles and bloodshot eyes. Heat seeped into the skin of her palms, the ceramic burning her flesh uncomfortably, but she only pressed harder against it.

"Thank you for letting me stay," Mary broke the careful emptiness of Kyra's mind. Dark thoughts had been pressing at the edges, but they were easier to ignore when Kyra focused on the woman before her.

"It's fine." Kyra waved away her gratitude dismissively. "Erik should be ready to leave with you whenever you're ready to go."

"Is he..." She gestured at Kyra but refused to speak any further.

"Like me?" Barely waiting for Mary's confirming nod, Kyra laughed her off. "Of course not." Telling the reporter she was about to be followed home by a vampire would have been stupider than letting a Hunter live. "He'll keep you safe."

Mary opened her mouth, no doubt to thank Kyra again. Heading off another tangle of emotions she was too tired to deal with, Kyra made a show of draining her still-hot coffee. The liquid burnt bitterly on the way down, peeling a layer of skin as it went.

"Just don't forget to say bye before you go."

Dropping her mug in the sink, Kyra smiled once more in farewell before striding out towards the foyer and her office. If she kept moving, steps long and sharp, maybe she wouldn't have to feel the emotions clawing at the corners of her mind. This hope was depressingly short-lived as Kyra was forced to stop short in the shadows of the hallway.

Leah stood by Wendy's desk, a backpack at her feet, the thick canvas bulging. The corners of more than one book pressed from the inside, seeking to break free. They didn't want to leave either.

At Kyra's order, there would be a small phone somewhere in that bag. It was programmed with Wendy's number and probably her own, though she hadn't wanted it to be included. She wanted Leah to have a link to The Rose that wasn't laden with too many things left unsaid. There was also a book, written in demonic runes, that Kyra had agonised over.

She doubted anyone in the Church besides Leah could read it, but it was still knowledge they didn't need to have. It was a philosophical text, something Kyra had hunted down specifically for Leah. The Hunter had proven herself to be a quick study of demonic writing, and Kyra hoped contextual clues would help her decode the more complex passages. She had begun drawing up a rough translation guide a few weeks ago, something she would never finish now.

Leah wasn't alone; a small gathering of demons huddled around her to say goodbye, though Kyra's gaze had no trouble locking on the human. It was hard to hear the words shared, but it wasn't hard to guess from the looks of sadness. Andy would be telling her that this was her home now and that she didn't have to go, the words mumbled into Leah's hair as they embraced. Lacey, tearing up, pressed a delicately carved box into Leah's hands, no doubt holding one of her favourite jewellery pieces. Leah protested briefly but was firmly rebuked.

Watching from the safety of the shadows, Kyra tried to pretend her heart wasn't clenching at the sight, her stomach lurching as Leah broke free of the demons to walk towards the door. She hesitated beyond the range of the sensor, head bowed as she paused for a moment. But she didn't look back, didn't see Kyra in the hall fighting every urge to make her stay. A step forward, a rush of cold air Kyra couldn't feel at this distance, and Leah was gone.

A small, secret part of her heart hoped Leah would return, would get a few steps down the street and realise this was wrong, but acknowledging that hope would be as stupid as making the Hunter stay. Would be as stupid as not killing her in the first place was.

Kyra couldn't bring herself to regret it, not even as her stomach swooped to new lows when the doors whooshed closed. Not even as her heart squeezed so hard, she feared it had actually stopped.

Taking advantage of the gathered crowd, mingling and sharing their shocked grief in muted whispers, Kyra darted to her office before they began to disperse, before they could notice her. She clutched at her chest as she stumbled through the door, shoving it closed behind her as tears sprung in her eyes and her heart thudded roughly against her ribcage.

Leah was gone. The thought hit like a tidal wave, pushing inexorably against Kyra's skin, a constant pressure that only grew with each passing moment. Pain and anger and hurt and sorrow mounted at the edges of her mind, pilling up against her walls until they flooded over the top. They rushed down her barriers, the pressure creating cracks. Spiderwebs of weakness spread under the weight, her carefully constructed barriers losing chunks as the waves of emotions swelled. Holes exploded as tears began to fall, little leaks quickly succumbing to the pressure.

Heavy sobs wracked her body, her whole frame rattling with them as her mind gave way, crumbling like dust to be carried on the torrent of her emotions. Kept so tight and close, they burst with a fury Kyra hadn't thought possible. Tears ran thick and un-bidden down her cheeks, her sobs rising into muted wails, her pain wordless but not voiceless.

Lashing out blindly, she swept the contents of her desk onto the floor. She roared with a broken rage as papers fluttered, pens bounced, and her laptop landed with a sickening crunch. Kyra spun to find something else to break. Her book-lined walls seemed to laugh at her, silently mocking. Her fingers twitched, ached to rip them from their shelves, rip the pages from their binding, rip the very words from the paper.

But she couldn't. She could picture the horror Leah would wear if she knew Kyra had harmed a book, and that single thought crushed her.

Guilt rose with the acid in her stomach, shame settling like a weight over her shoulders as the image of Leah's contempt warred with that of Leah's back, leaving The Rose as though it had never meant anything. As though Kyra had never meant anything.

Kyra fell to her knees, the edges of scattered pens digging painfully into her flesh. But that was a minor annoyance, a hurt barely there compared to the ache in her heart. With her head in her hands, tears still falling, she pressed her palms against her temples as though she could squeeze the pain out. Squeeze out the insidious thoughts, force out the darkly whispering voices that this was all her fault, that this was the logical end to the situation. How could she expect anything different? She knew there was no happy ending for a demon, no happy ending for her. This whole thing had been doomed from the moment she decided not to kill Leah.

Huddled on the floor of her office, body curved as she tried desperately to pull into herself, Kyra continued to weep. A sobbing ball of pain, her wings closed tight around her, though she couldn't remember when she had lost her glamour. The air was warm around her, but it did nothing to ease the ball of ice lodged firmly in her chest.

~ Twenty-Four ~

Damian strode into her office much the way he always did. He fell into the chair opposite her desk, as he always did. The stare he fixed on her was new, though, a strange combination of exasperation and concern.

"It's been a week," he said.

"I know."

"And you're still sulking."

"I am not sulking." They both knew it for a lie, but Damian was good enough not to scoff audibly. Or comment on the new laptop Kyra was pretending so hard to be focused on.

"You're taking this worse than Elizabeth." The exasperation was winning out, though he did have a point.

She had cried over Elizabeth, this was true, but she had also switched to mounting fury in just two days. It had taken more than a week to work the anger out of her system, but that particular heartache hadn't affected her work or the running of The Rose. She knew this was, something that only compounded the mix of pain and guilt that coloured her every waking moment. Her dreams were of gentle kisses and fuzzy images of more that would never come to pass. It was pathetic.

"You shouldn't have let her leave."

"What?" The accusation, clear in his voice, brought Kyra's head up sharply. "You wanted me to kill her."

"Because I thought it would save you from exactly this." It would have been a poor justification from anyone else. Kyra had known

Damian more than long enough to understand and partly agree with his reasoning. "This was never going to be anything other than a mistake, you and I both know this, but that doesn't mean you should just keep making things worse."

"And what do you propose I do now?" Kyra ran a hand through her hair, ash blond and short today. Her washed-out features were close to Leah's own, but Damian was nice enough not to point that out either. "Find her? Go to her? Profess my undying love and ask her to run away with me?"

He shrugged. "Why not?"

"Because you were right. She's a Hunter; I'm a demon. I should have killed her the moment she crossed the threshold. I'm the biggest idiot in existence. Happy?"

"Do I look happy?" he growled, leaning forward, anger flashing. Kyra hesitated, actually looking at her friend, her brother, for the first time in a long time. Under the aching perfection of his glamour, he looked tired. His eyes were shadowed and tight with stress, his mouth slightly downturned. She could never remember him wearing such sombre features.

No matter the face, regardless of the mask or glamour, Damian always carried himself with an inner strength. He had faced so many challenges at her side, had guarded her back against countless dangers. Whether it was stray Hunters or the looming threat of war, Damian had protected Kyra and The Rose with unwavering fierceness. He pulled no punches in the privacy of Kyra's office and gave her enough pieces of his mind to create a clone, but he never backed down.

Now he just looked defeated and worn out. His face reflected her mood, and Kyra didn't know how to give him the same sense of strength he'd provided her so many times before. Another weight added itself to her heart, another knife of guilt slid into her gut. This was her fault too.

"I'm sorry," she whispered. "I'm sorry," she repeated, louder if no stronger. "What do I do? How do I fix it?"

"Not by playing the victim," he groaned, rubbing at his eyes in frustration. "Or by blaming yourself any more than you have. And definitely not by wallowing in your own self-pity."

Kyra bristled at the words, no matter how true or warranted they may have been.

"Then how?" She tried to bite back the hiss of her tone but failed.

"Go get your girl back."

"It's not that simple, and you know it."

"Why?"

"Because I held her here against her will. She was my prisoner, Damian, not my girlfriend. She was here to kill me, to kill us, to kill everyone who lives and works here. She's a human. She's barely more than a child, even by her own standards. She's going to live and die within a fraction of my lifetime. She will grow old and grey, she will become frail before my eyes, and I won't change. Even if what she thinks she feels between us is honest and not a result of being held here. Even if she doesn't resent me and all I've done. Even if she comes back of her own free will. Even if I'm wrong on those counts, she will still be human, and I will still be a demon, and there is nothing that will change that."

"Are you done?" The hint of a smile was back. And while it filled Kyra with relief, it also frustrated her. It was hard not to feel he was laughing at her, mocking her pain.

"What, that isn't enough for you?"

"Oh, come on, Kyra. You're being dramatic."

"And you're being flippant."

"Have you stopped to think, to realise, that I know what she was feeling?"

"Lust, desire, not love. Not what matters." Kyra sneered, fighting down rising hope ruthlessly. "I don't know what you want of me. What do you want me to say? What do you want me to do?"

"I want you to not give up to start with." Damian matched her heat with his own frustration. "It wasn't just what I could smell from her; it was the way she looked at you. The way she almost bit my head off when she thought I was a threat. She thought we were—" Damian cut himself short, face twisting into disgust. Kyra's own expression mirrored his with rising horror.

"Well, even if that were true..." She coughed uncomfortably. He was as good as her brother, not someone to... She couldn't even bear the thought. "You were the one telling me not to get attached in the first place."

She shook off her growing disgust. It was easier, and preferable, to sink back into the safety of indignation and frustration and the million other burning emotions that churned with the acids of her stomach. It all made her want to be sick. Made her want to yell and break things and just rage against the injustice of the world.

"I was wrong." The words, and the even gentleness they were delivered in, were enough to bring Kyra up short if not stop the simmering anger. "You idiots fell in love. Now I've got to pick up the pieces again. So go get your girl."

"It's still not that simple."

"So simplify it." Damian pulled himself to his feet, face set in stubborn determination. Kyra hated it when he got mulish. "Give it time if you think it needs time, but you need to toughen up and actually do something. You can't hide in this office, in The Rose, for the rest of your life. And you'll never forgive yourself if you don't at least try."

Kyra hated it when he was right even more.

Hours later, after successfully doing some work in between simply pretending, Kyra passed through the kitchen on the way to her room. So much of the past week had been a blur of barely restrained tears and the aching wound in her chest. She'd read her reports, signed her paperwork, completed her tasks by rote. Even coordinating ongoing protection for Mary, working with Wendy to create an effective roster that would balance the safety of The Rose and the reporter, was all done in a trance. These were all important things, but they couldn't hold her attention.

Now, her mind refused to stop prodding at the memory of Damian's words. She replayed them again and again, as though the repetition would shake loose an appropriate course of action. As though she wasn't just using them as another excuse to torture herself.

She knew he had a point, to some extent. Yes, she felt something for Leah, something strong and true. But she couldn't be sure Leah felt the same, and even if she did, that didn't make her own points any less valid. There were still issues regarding age and the simple fact that the human would be dead within a fraction of Kyra's own life. Wasn't it better to suffer now before she got in too deep than build a life with Leah and be crushed when she passed on?

Even without the fact that she was a human, she was a Hunter. They'd be the target of every faction, demonic or otherwise. Every sanctuary on earth would see them as a threat to their carefully cultivated protections. The Church would see them as the ultimate abomination, the epitome of evil. Demons would see them much the same—an obscenity, a violation of the natural order. Never mind that a succubus wasn't meant to fall in love. Never mind that romantic feelings were anathema to their kind, and loving someone of the same gender was even worse.

Kyra took the stairs slowly while her mind raced. Her thoughts sounded weak even to herself, all a pathetic attempt to convince herself. She knew it was a lost cause, but that didn't stop her dwelling. Damian had been right; she was sulking. She was wallowing in self-pity because that was easier. So much easier than admitting Leah was gone, was never coming back. It was safer than hoping Leah would come back. It was better to stay in this place of pain, where she was the only one to suffer, than just cut out her heart completely like she should.

Lying to herself used to be easy. Now it just made her sick.

The moment the door snipped shut, Kyra let her glamour fall. Her steps were sluggish as she slipped into the bathroom to confront her reflection. For a second, it felt like she was seeing Damian's face again. The same tight shadows hung around her eyes, and the same downward curve had settled on her lips.

"How long are you going to do this?" she asked her reflection. "Another week, a month, a year?" A lifetime?

She scoffed, turning the water on. It was icy, bouncing off the sink to splash against her fingers. Kyra didn't let it warm before scooping some up to throw on her lowered face. Now dripping, she faced her reflection once more. She could almost pretend the redness to her eyes, the dampness on her cheeks, was all due to the water on her face. She turned the faucet back off with a twist of her wrist. "You make me sick."

Face still damp, she moved into the bedroom, falling into her nest in the vain hope that sleep would come quickly. While she begged for dreamless rest, a part of her couldn't help but hope for the pleasant images of Leah's face turned to her own and the ghostly sensation of lips on hers. It would only lead to heartache in the morning when she would wake and realise it had all been a cruel trick of her imagination, but for now, she allowed herself to find a weak solace in the dreams.

Kyra indulged in a sleep-in, something she hadn't done in the years since Elizabeth left. It was a quiet morning in the way that there was no paperwork to check, no need to be the shoulder to cry on, no calls to take or supplies to order. It was blessedly silent, and for a while, Kyra could pretend her world wasn't falling apart around her. She could pretend there wasn't pain waiting just outside the door. She hated herself for relying on such pathetic lies, but she knew getting out of bed would be impossible without them.

It was well into midmorning by the time Kyra pulled herself from her room, The Rose already coming to life around her. Damian would have made breakfast long ago, and any scraps would have long been eaten. Wendy would have been at her desk at least an hour and would probably be onto her tenth game of Solitaire. Some would be starting their shifts as others made their way to bed after winding down at the end of a long day.

Kyra forced herself to focus on these little things, on the mundane. Keeping her mind on the minutia of the day-to-day meant there was less room to dwell on Leah. So Kyra thought of the demons curled soft and safe in sleep behind closed doors and calmed minds. She thought of those preparing for work, whether it be with a quick snack or a soothing book or even meditation, their minds carefully clear to allow sole focus on their clients.

More demons again walked the halls, not every denizen of The Rose dedicated to the pleasure of others. Many pushed cleaning trolleys and hauled laundry from strictly physical encounters, most yawning around boredom.

They'd exchange words when passing or when huddled around strategically placed cleaning closets to restock. They created pockets of gossip and impromptu classrooms as knowledge was passed from old to new.

Despite the lack of human workers, the day-to-day operations of The Rose were positively mundane. Even with vampires and witches working alongside succubi and incubi, magic was rarely relied on beyond hiding particularly stubborn stains and reading the desires of clients.

Kyra felt a strange mix of relief and disappointment when she found the kitchen empty. Even the peripheral appearance of company would have been nice. Just another person to share the space with so she didn't feel so painfully alone. Though, it was nice to avoid the looks of sympathy from those who were meant to respect her, not pity her. At least Buddug didn't know about Leah's departure, about Kyra's heartache, about the furtive glances full of shared sadness that were quickly becoming the norm. Because despite Damian's best efforts, despite his warnings and admonishment, despite his loud exasperation, Leah had well and truly wormed her way into the hearts and minds of everyone at The Rose.

Pouring herself a mug of coffee, Kyra fell into a chair at the large table. The empty expanse of polished, well-loved wood made her feel small and alone. Kyra tried to pull her mind from dangerous thoughts of Leah, sipping absently at her coffee. The liquid coated her tongue in burning pain, but even that didn't penetrate the fog circling her head.

Someone had left a newspaper on the table, and Kyra pulled it to herself, thankful for any kind of distraction. A vaguely familiar face was emblazoned across the front page, but the memory was too far buried to be worth pursuing.

Damian was right, of course. Her behaviour affected more than herself, and her staff, her family, were more important than self-indulgent sulking. Her eyes ran mindlessly over the headlines and articles, phrases jumping out and away, nothing quite piercing the fog that surrounded her thoughts. Another mouthful of coffee—it seemed to have increased in temperature as the burning spread to the roof of her mouth. The Family First Program sounded vaguely ominous, especially when headed by a deeply religious politician; Kyra wondered when they would be seeing him at The Rose.

This was a waste of time, sulking in her kitchen, moping about like a lovesick child. It was pathetic. It was beneath a succubus, beneath someone as powerful as her. Kyra downed the rest of her coffee and pushed herself up from the table, the wooden legs of her chair dragging loudly. She set her shoulders with determination.

A small, broken woman had walked into the kitchen, but it was Kyra's preferred visage of confident businesswoman who strode out again.

~ Twenty-Five ~

The careful visage of powerful businesswoman carried Kyra to the foyer, where it flickered and threatened to fall at the sight of a bent figure over Wendy's desk. Wendy had an arm wrapped around Bell's shoulders, cradling the succubus close as she tried to encourage her to move. Rushing forward, Kyra slipped her arm around Bell's waist, taking a share of her weight from Wendy, allowing them both to manoeuvre her towards Kyra's office.

They were a slow, silent procession, only able to move in halting steps broken by muffled whimpers of pain. It took all of Kyra's self-control to keep her grip loose and gentle, her fingers itching to claw and fist and draw the blood of whoever had caused Bell pain. As if she didn't know. As if there was any question. But the anger was for later; now was for healing.

As soon as they had Bell deposited safely in a chair, Kyra glanced to Wendy, orders clear in her eyes. She knew Hannah would be there within the hour.

Kyra sank into the seat beside Bell, unsure of where to place her hands, how best to offer comfort. It struck her that she'd been in this position far too often recently, sitting across from someone she cared about as they fell apart. Tears streaked down Bell's face, her glamour flickering over her skin as she fought to maintain control. In the flashes between magic, Kyra could see darkened bruising.

"He said he loved me." Bell got out between sobs, voice high and hiccupping.

"Shh." Kyra brushed at her damp cheeks, keeping her touch as light as possible and trying to avoid mottled skin she couldn't see. Words bubbled and caught in her throat, platitudes and empty comforts spoken too many times to help. Knowing nothing could be said to help only made her impotent rage burn brighter. "You're safe now," she said instead. "We'll get you cleaned up, and I'll organise a place for you with Hannah."

"What?" Bell looked up sharply, glamour finally falling completely as her control slipped beyond saving. Her skin, usually a pale sky blue, had darkened to cobalt in places. Patches of discolouration decorated her torso in large swaths, some marks faded and green with age. "Please don't send me away. I'll be good."

Kyra's heart clenched at the words. She was pulling Bell into a hug before she could think to avoid pressing against her fragile form.

"Of course not," she breathed into Bell's hair. The other woman's arms were quick to return the embrace, squeezing Kyra hard, clearly afraid to let go. "I would never. I just thought..." It was hard to find the words to finish. "I thought you'd want to forget about him, about this place."

"Never," Bell breathed with venom, her tone harsh despite being muffled by the flesh of Kyra's shoulder, despite the tears trying to drown them both. "This is my home." A hint of uncertainty entered her voice.

"This will always be your home," Kyra agreed, lifting her head to rest her chin in Bell's hair. She ran a soothing hand down Bell's back, letting the younger demon sob gently against her shoulder.

Once Bell was safely tucked away and sleeping, Kyra called Caleb into her office. Erik would have been her preference, but Wendy had pointed out it was his turn on Mary watch.

"Yes, boss?" He stood before Kyra's desk, back straight and face stony despite his flippant tone.

"I need you to deliver a warning." Tapping her fingers against the wood of her desk, Kyra wondered if she should have waited for Erik to return. "Only a warning, mind you," she stressed.

"Okay." His answering shrug did little to comfort her. Still, she slid a piece of a paper across the desk to him, a face and address printed near the top.

"You will find this man and tell him, gently, that he is no longer welcome here. Understand?" Caleb picked up the paper and studied it closely, committing the face to memory. "Understand?" Kyra pressed.

"Not a problem, boss." A dark smile spread across his face, and Kyra sorely hoped this wasn't a bad decision.

That Caleb returned in a matter of hours wasn't disturbing. What was disturbing was the smile that split his lips, his grin predatory and full of teeth. If Kyra hadn't been in the foyer, leaning over Wendy's desk to coordinate payment for Hannah's healing, she wouldn't have seen it. If Erik hadn't been returning from his shift, she wouldn't have known the cause.

"Why do you smell of blood?" Erik barked, alarm making his voice stronger than his habitual snivel. The tone alone would have been enough to catch Kyra's attention, though she was already watching Caleb with a growing sense of trepidation.

The hulking vampire shrugged carelessly, smile growing as he preened under the sudden attention. "I was just following orders." He waved nonchalantly. "Right, boss?"

"What did you do?" Kyra breathed pure malice into the question. Wendy stiffened beside her, sensing the growing pressure in the air. Erik's survival instincts must have been screaming at him, the smaller man stepping away to ensure he couldn't be caught in the crossfire.

"I warned him like you said." Caleb shrugged again, this time a little more self-consciously. "But he didn't like that. He said something about Bell being his, that we couldn't keep her from him, so I removed the threat."

Kyra pinched the bridge of her nose. Shit. Turning from Caleb, pushing him entirely from her mind, she pierced Erik with her gaze. He froze, already halfway across the room and inching towards the hall to the kitchen. "Go clean it up," she ordered. He nodded once, turning immediately to head back out. The droop of his shoulders said he was happy to be free in one piece.

Kyra turned to Wendy and continued barking orders. "Clear the roster on Mary. Caleb will be taking the majority of shifts. Give him enough time to sleep and eat but nothing more.

"And you," she spun back on him, taking no small joy in the lack of grin. "You will focus on keeping Mary safe and nothing else. Unless her life is immediately in danger, you are not to hurt a single soul. I don't care if a Hunter has a knife to your throat; you are not to fight back unless she's about to get hurt. Do you understand me?"

"But-"

"Do you understand?" She punctuated each word slowly, voice rising sharply to echo back at them against the vaulted walls. She should have insisted on having this conversation in her office, the walls thick enough to deaden even the loudest screaming.

"Yes, boss." He looked away as though that could hide the burning anger in his eyes. She'd have to watch him closely in the future.

~ Twenty-Six ~

Exhaustion settled heavily on Kyra's shoulders, weighing down her every step as she made her way to her office. Another restless night was topped off by sitting with Bell as Hannah worked her magic. Most of the bruising had been eased to nearly nothing, but the tension in her eyes would take more to fade. More time, more space. Things Kyra couldn't guarantee, not indefinitely.

A nervous energy shot through her every time her mind turned to Bell, skittish thoughts of how long it would take the younger demon to recover, whether she would recover at all. Such thoughts were laced with guilt but unavoidable.

Moving with a purpose she didn't quite believe in, Kyra strode past Wendy's desk and threw open the door to her office as though preparing for a fight and expecting to go down swinging. Coming up short, Kyra turned back in the doorway, looking over her shoulder to Wendy. Wendy, for her part, seemed completely unaware of her boss.

"Wendy," Kyra called with a dripping sweetness that would have sent a lesser mortal running. "Who is this in my office?"

"Don't know." She shrugged.

"Who let her in?" Kyra asked, smiling with teeth while her fingers twitched against the urge to pull into white-knuckled fists.

"I did."

"Why?" Kyra elongated the word, drawing it out to give Wendy plenty of time to consider her mistake.

"Because she asked to see you." Wendy suddenly looked up from her game, thoughtful. "I think that was half an hour or so ago."

Kyra sighed to herself, steeling herself against what would no doubt be an awkward meeting. Inside, she seethed, mind already preparing what would be a tongue lashing for the ages. Externally, she turned a wooden smile on the woman sat at her desk and almost faltered when she was faced with an all too familiar head tilt. The angle was wrong, but it was a rude shock nonetheless.

"Welcome to The Rose," Kyra spoke as she walked, offering a hand to the woman when she drew parallel to the chair. The woman eyed it for a moment, face blank, before taking it with her own in a surprisingly strong grip.

Beyond her middle years, the woman had creases in the corners of her eyes and sprinkles of grey at her temples that stood out sharply against the dark brown of her hair. There was a cruelness to the woman Kyra couldn't place. Maybe it was the disapproving turn to her mouth or the way her gaze raked over the demon, noting every flaw and clearly passing judgement. It may have even been the way she seemed to be looking down her nose at Kyra despite not even displaying basic courtesy in rising to greet her. Instead, she remained seated as they politely shook hands, though Kyra was willing to concede that may be because she had been left waiting for an indeterminate amount of time.

"How may I assist you?" Kyra maintained her calm dignity as she settled into the seat and authority of her chair. Ensconced in the familiar comfortable leather, Kyra almost felt back on sure footing.

"You can start by answering a few questions," came the brisk response delivered in a clipped tone. The woman's voice was as severe as her face, the whisper of a sneer at the end, as though any answer Kyra could give would never be good enough anyway.

"I'd be happy to." Kyra allowed her smile to widen, showing teeth that ached to sharpen into fangs, preferably against bones. "Though it'd be nice to know who I'm speaking to."

The woman didn't even bat an eye at the rebuke. "Claire. I'm a colleague of Mary's."

Kyra wanted to snarl, smile held by the skin of her teeth. Every scrap of her self-control kept her from lashing out at the reporter across from her.

"Ah." Kyra bit back further words. "And what would you like to discuss?"

"Is it true you pedal minors to your sick clientele?" While it was far from expected, the accusation barely had Kyra batting an eye.

"Huh, that feels rather like a loaded question, doesn't it?" Kyra refused to allow her smile to slip, though throwing Claire bodily out of her office just became rather tempting. "While I'm not going to ask why you'd think such a thing of my completely legal and professional establishment, I will assume you have nothing approaching solid proof because you're not here with the police. And before you think that isn't a denial, plausible or not, I want you to listen very carefully to my next words." Leaning forward slowly, smile still in place, if not a little steely, Kyra waited for Claire to inch forward to better hear. "If you ever make such an accusation about me or my employees again, you will live a very long, very regretful, and very, very painful, life."

Claire recoiled, mask of distaste falling under shocked fear. "Is that a threat?" she spluttered.

"I believe so, yes." Kyra settled back against her chair, finally letting her smile go. Her cheeks hurt from the stiff grin, but the terror in Claire's eyes made it entirely worth it. "Just so we understand each other, Claire, let me get a few things straight.

"I like Mary, but her presence is tolerated at best." Kyra held up a finger as she spoke, raising a second as she moved on to her next point. "I don't like you, which I'm starting to suspect is mutual." Third finger. "Every employee within The Rose is an adult, is here legally"—as much as a demon could be legal—"and would be extremely upset to hear such accusations.

"Now, while this is a free country with freedom of the press and so on and so forth, I'm going to have to ask you to leave. This is private property, and you are no longer welcome."

"You're hiding something. I know it," Claire snapped, hands gripping the desk before her as though afraid Kyra would physically remove her. The nails of Kyra's glamour sharpened under the cover of her desk, fingers twitching in the desire to form talons to tear and rend flesh.

"That's nice, dear. The door is that way." Kyra turned pointedly to her work, flicking her laptop open in obvious dismissal. Anger swirled in her gut and her mind, but this human wasn't going to best her.

Claire let out a series of strangled noises, each angrier than the last though none approached actual words. Eventually, she flung herself from the chair, striding from the room in a whirlwind that almost made the bitter churn of Kyra's rage worth it.

Kyra waited for a slow count to a hundred before rising from her desk and following. Popping her head outside the door, she wasn't surprised to find Wendy reading a small book, held low in her lap.

"Wendy?" The other woman made a small noise of assent but didn't look up. "The woman that was in here? She is not to return. Ever."

"And if she does?" Wendy asked as she turned her page, only mildly interested.

"Kill her."

Wendy knew better than to question the order and knew from the cold steel of Kyra's voice that it was not one to be ignored. If her boss decided someone was a threat, then they were to be treated as such.

Kyra retreated back to her office, forcing the encounter out of her mind. There was no doubt Claire would continue to cause trouble or at least attempt to, but Kyra could at least keep her away from The Rose. Away from her family.

The day was ending when Damian strode in, the setting sun sending streaks of red and orange against Kyra's office wall. Her eyes were beginning to strain in the falling gloom, but the colours painting her office were too pretty to disrupt with a light. Damian took one sweeping glance of the room before flicking the light switch, shaking his head to himself at Kyra's half-hearted glare in response.

"You don't have the face for glasses," he chided. Kyra raised an eyebrow, focusing briefly to shift her features and add thin-rimmed spectacles to her outfit. Damian only laughed in answer, sliding into the chair across from her.

"You're in a good mood," she noted dryly.

"Buddug called for you."

"And you're here to gloat before she tears me a new one?" Kyra guessed blithely.

"No, I'm here to suggest you lie."

"A course you've historically advised against," she said.

"Because it usually backfires for you." Damian shook his head. "I know she's going to ask about Leah, and I know she'll drag us both over the coals if she knows we let her go."

"Which is why I was going to tell her that Leah is dead." Kyra was almost insulted by the surprised look she received. "I've been dealing with Buddug longer than you've been alive, remember? Despite what you may think, I'm not a complete idiot."

"I never said you were." Out loud. "I just wanted to make sure you were ready to face her. Face this."

Kyra appreciated the sentiment, even if it wasn't really necessary. There were more important things to worry about now. Not that Damian could have known that.

Sighing to herself, Kyra pinched the bridge of her nose against a forming headache. She should have called him in as soon as Claire left.

"What's wrong?"

"A reporter." Kyra glanced up in time to catch the strange twist of emotions crossing Damian's face. He had never approved of Mary learning their secrets and was clearly afraid Kyra would repeat the mistake. "She made some serious accusations."

"The usual?"

"Worse." Kyra hesitated. Even here, with Damian—someone who had faced the worst the world had had to offer at her side—Kyra struggled to force the words out. Luckily for her, Damian knew her well enough and understood the minds of those who despised them. It was sickening to watch the play of realisation, disgust, and fury roll across his face.

"Is she..."

"Dead?" Kyra laughed bitterly. "Not yet. Wendy understands that if she returns, she's to be dealt with."

"You don't want me to have a word with Erik?"

"No, not yet," she said. "I may contact Hannah, though, see why her charm isn't doing its job."

Damian's mouth twisted as though fighting the sudden urge to be sick. He fought it down and nodded his understanding. Kyra had it in hand; she always did.

"Do we know who?"

"There's only one client." Driven on by Damian's raised eyebrow, Kyra explained haltingly, "Wendy thinks he's becoming attached to me, but I won't ask anyone else to deal with it. If he's resisting Hannah's magic, I'll have to come up with another solution."

"Do you need any help?"

"You can report to Buddug for me if you'd like?" Kyra spoke lightly, trying to break the bleak mood that had fallen over them. Damian barked a laugh, not expecting the request.

"You're on your own on that one, sorry." He lifted himself from the chair, his smile shifting to something softer as he paused before turning away. "You'll be fine."

"I know." Kyra waved him off, fighting down sudden waves of emotion. A surge of love and respect for him hit so hard and fast, it had tears prickling at the corners of her eyes.

Damian gave her a final small smile, no doubt reading the overwhelming rush of emotions and knowing she wouldn't appreciate him drawing attention to it. He left her alone to pull herself back together, and not for the first time, Kyra wished she had the right words to thank him for all he did for her.

It was a completely level-headed Kyra that left her office, any residual anger over Claire, grief over Leah, or solace from Damian pushed aside. There would be time for them later. It was a lie Kyra often repeated to herself, though she never really intended it to be. There was just always too much to do, too many things to manage. But Kyra would die before giving up the sanctuary she had built and fought to establish for herself and her own.

~ Twenty-Seven ~

The door closed with a whispered snip of wood against wood. It was loud in her dark, empty room, making the space feel cavernous and oppressive. Kyra let her glamour fall and walked towards the small table nestled in the corner. The heavy mantle of responsibility didn't fall away as easily, clinging thickly to her shoulders.

A crowded, makeshift altar of light wood awaited her, a hand-carved bowl taking up most of the tabletop. It was barely larger than her two cupped palms and circled by a scattering of thick candles, a smaller metal bowl filled with soft sand, and a stick of unlit incense tilted at a sharp angle in its holder. None of it would have been necessary if Buddug had simply deigned to use human technology, but she was too afraid to lose the old ways.

Kyra spent a long moment examining the water in her scrying bowl, the surface unbroken as her eyes saw beyond it into the twisted lines of her life, the knotted emotions of her heart, and tangled responsibilities of her existence. A dark melancholy gripped her, a sudden and stifling feeling of helplessness.

The world was too big; there was too much happening around her. She was spinning out of control with no anchor to hold her, no moorings to keep her steady. Kyra's breath came short and sharp, her hands jerking forward to grip her altar as her heart kicked into a higher gear. Water or wind rushed in her ears, the sound formless but roaring, drowning out the blood pounding across her skull.

Leah was gone, probably never to return. Her heart squeezed, trying to tighten against the empty ache, trying to fill the hole in Kyra's centre. Instead, the searing darkness ate at her edges, spreading to consume her. How long would it take? How long before she was nothing but an empty shell, a husk walking and talking but feeling nothing.

Leah was gone, and Mary was in danger, and it was only a matter of time before Bell would have to leave, have to flee the dark memories and darker thoughts. There was a growing list of people Kyra couldn't protect, couldn't save. How long until the rest left? How long before they moved to other sanctuaries, to join the war or seek greater safety? How long until it was only Wendy and Damian left, until they were gone too?

She was wheezing now, her breath struggling to force itself past the constricted passage of her throat. Her heart was racing, battering against her chest, but the sensation was fading into nothingness. Everything was fading into nothingness as bright spots danced across her vision and the edges darkened.

Her fingers, sharply taloned, slipped against the wood beneath them, her grip failing. Kyra stumbled, legs weak, arms unable to help support her. Still, her mind continued to race, thoughts running in tight circles to chase darker and darker visions of the future.

The Rose was under attack, the threats imminent and unavoidable, and they would be all the more deadly because of her selfish desire to avoid the conflict entirely. There was something lurking on the horizon, the presence dark and looming. Something large, something that hungered, something that would not rest until it destroyed her and everything she had ever cared for.

Buddug would see through her lie. This would be the final failure, the excuse her mentor needed to turn from her entirely. Then she would lose The Rose; she'd lose her home and her people. She wouldn't be able to protect them, and they'd all flee. It would be slow at first, in ones and twos, until it would become a wave of people. Within a fortnight, a month, after a mass exodus, she would be alone.

The tips of her fingers were numb, the sensation spreading in a relentless pressure of near painful pins and needles. Her eyes were pressed tightly shut, but she couldn't remember closing them. The darkness of her eyelids was shot with red as though she could see the blood flowing beneath her skin, carried by the racing beats of her heart. Her breathing had slowed from panicked, shallow gasps into halting heaves, though her brain still swam with the lack of oxygen. It was all going wrong, and there was nothing she could do to slow the encroaching decay.

"Kyranthine?" Buddug's voice was sharp but distant, fighting to break the screen of terror surrounding Kyra's mind, forcing its way across an unanchored connection. "Kyranthine!" she demanded as though sensing the smothering cloud hanging thick in the air.

Kyra jerked at the sound of her name, the word like slaps. But they were distant, delivered without feeling, without strength. Buddug's voice, straining across all the space that separated them, was a whisper barely there. A part of her imagination, her mind playing another cruel trick, her brain finding another spike to press into her flesh and pierce her core. Her mentor's voice, tinged with growing panic with every utterance of her name, was just another weapon, another means to cut and cause pain. Buddug's concern was as false as her voice, something to be questioned and mistrusted. Something Kyra wanted so desperately, it hurt.

"Kyra." Buddug's voice was full of emotion, shock and sadness, concern and gentle admonishment, the word a whisper on the edge of Kyra's mind. A hand, real and solid, still cool from the frozen burn of breaking space, grasped her shoulder. Clawed fingers, sharp and biting, rested gently even as they urged Kyra to find her feet. Instead, Kyra fell the rest of the way to the floor, collapsing with a broken sob as tears broke free.

Strong arms engulfed her, pulling her tightly against Buddug's chest, the familiar warmth and spiced scent only encouraged Kyra's tears. Buddug said nothing as she stroked Kyra's hair, silently letting the younger succubus relieve emotions held too tight for too long. Whether it was hours or minutes, Buddug maintained her silence as Kyra wept, not even breaking it to offer words of comfort. Kyra didn't need anything more than the warmth of Buddug's embrace and the fingers drawing carefully through her hair.

Finally, slowly, her tears tampered off, her sobs breaking into shuddering breaths before Kyra calmed completely. Buddug didn't slow her hand or ease the grip she held Kyra with. Even as Kyra's breathing slowed to something approaching normal and her fingers eased their grip on Buddug's shoulders, arms loosening but not moving, Buddug kept her measured strokes. Still, nothing was said between them, the moment stretching into oblivion as Buddug's gentle hands lulled Kyra into sleep.

Kyra woke some hours later, curled in the centre of her nest of a bed. Her head ached, her eyes felt grimy, and the idea of more sleep was tempting beyond measure, but Kyra forced herself up when she remembered Buddug's warm embrace, the ghost of hands briefly running down her hair. A quick glance around revealed her desk put to rights, the candle blown out and water emptied.

The clock on her wall said midnight had passed, but Buddug wouldn't have left yet. Kyra ducked out of her room and crossed the short space to Damian's, slipping through the door without knocking. Damian and Buddug let their conversation trail off, creating a space on the bed between them without looking up. Kyra took it wordlessly. They sat in silence, taking strength from one another. In that moment, Kyra could pretend her heart didn't feel broken, that Buddug wasn't disappointed in her, that things weren't so desperately out of control.

Maintaining his silence, Damian lifted a hand to squeeze Kyra's shoulder briefly before standing and leaving. Alone with her mentor, a woman she respected and feared in equal measure, Kyra was painfully aware of her heartbeat all over again. Her palms turned clammy, and her breath shortened, wheezing at the edges as Kyra fought to suck it deep.

Sensing her distress, Buddug resumed the careful stroking of Kyra's hair, controlling and calming the rising panic immediately. Kyra revelled in the feeling for a moment, taking guilty comfort from it before pulling away resolutely. Buddug allowed her arm to fall, and if the distance hurt her, she didn't show it.

"Damian informed me of your Hunter's demise." Buddug's tone was calm, the words delivered as carefully as such a statement could be. Kyra was thankful for Damian's lie, thankful he had delivered it for her. "No matter how unwise, I know you felt some attachment for her. I am sorry."

Kyra couldn't help the bitter laugh that escaped her lips, the absurdity of the situation too much to bear.

"Thank you," she said, controlling the wild spike of emotions through sheer force of will. Kyra had almost forgotten she could, the frayed edges of her feelings so torn and sensitive, it felt like she would never be normal again. Clawing back some semblance of control, some measure of power over herself, over her life, Kyra took a deep breath that grounded her. "It had to be done."

"Know that I am proud of you." The words warmed Kyra, a sentiment rarely spoken aloud though often displayed in small smiles and the fierce way in which Buddug would defend her. It didn't take long for the low swoop of guilt, a bitter twist to her stomach, to freeze her blood.

Kyra nodded resolutely in answer, afraid to speak, afraid her expression or tone of voice would give her away. Afraid she'd betray herself. Afraid the truth would pour forth in an attempt to receive further comfort, advice, and some slice of knowledge. An indication of what to do, an idea of a solution.

"Thank you," Kyra forced out again, squashing the tangle of emotions roughly. Pressure was beginning to build behind her eyes, settling at the edges of her temples. The threat of a headache was preferable over the crush of emotions.

~ Twenty-Eight ~

There was a pervasive temptation to avoid work, avoid feeding, and just curl back up in a ball. But that would have been sulking, and she had promised Damian, and herself, that she would stop. Relapse aside, she needed to keep her strength up.

That didn't make the situation any easier, sat in her usual place above the head of her client, fingers pressed to his forehead around the cupped talisman in her palm. Pulling his energy into herself while keeping distant from the fantasy between them, Kyra allowed her mind to wander as much as was wise. Her thoughts drifted to Leah, to the lack of communication, but were quickly pulled back. She had spent too long trying to convince herself that maybe the Church had confiscated the small phone, or maybe Leah just hadn't found it slipped between carefully folded clothes yet. They were more comforting than the growing dread, the fear that she was dead or uninterested in reaching out.

The body between her legs stirred, breathing turning laboured. Kyra responded immediately to his growing unease, focusing entirely on their connection, on her magic, and the way it pulsed through the dampening weight of the talisman. Something wasn't right.

Before she could identify the problem, before she could even react, his eyes sprang open, and he twisted bodily away from her. He clambered awkwardly over her legs, twisted and bent in ways human legs shouldn't be, before stumbling to his feet. Wild eyes darted around the room, and Kyra used the moment of panic to wrap herself in a glamour. The acrid taste of fear in the air said she had moved too late.

Kyra didn't rise, afraid of provoking him further. Instead, she pulled herself in physically while preparing to lash out with a blade of magic, honed and eager to bite into his lingering lust.

"Where?" His voice was hoarse, rough with the sounds she had been pulling from him. "What?"

"Come back to bed," Kyra purred, lacing her words with tendrils of desire and a compulsion he couldn't ignore. "Come on, baby. We were having fun." The expanse of her pale skin was on show, wearing only a scrap of ruby lace that could barely be called a negligee.

"No, you were-" The words caught in his throat, too terrible to bear.

Applying more pressure, more magic, Kyra felt her smile turn sickly—not that he'd notice under the blanket of lust. "Come on." She cooed again, layering the magic so deep, a part of her worried for his continued sanity. And yet, he hesitated.

Her fingers tightened around the talisman, the edges of the stone cutting into her flesh. Kyra swore silently that she would have a very pointed, very loud conversation with Hannah.

The rustle of sheets broke the silence as Kyra slipped from the bed. He drew back but didn't step away, didn't attempt to leave the room. Slowly, maintaining eye contact and the press of magic, Kyra reached out to him. He closed his eyes at the touch of her hand on his cheek, body leaning into the contact even if his mind still rebelled against her. The physical contact lit her senses on fire, sharpening the taste of his lust once more. Wielding her magic less like a knife and more like a sledgehammer, Kyra set about turning him into a puddle of incomprehensible need.

When she was done, his vile taste still at the back of her throat and quiet snores ringing in her ears, she left him where he lay on the bed. She donned her favoured glamour and strode from the room, trying to ignore bitter coating on her tongue.

The first thing Kyra did when entering her office was grab her phone off the desk. Dialling from memory, she let her anger bubble as the line rang in her ear.

"Kyra," Hannah answered sharply, the drone of voices low but persistent in the background. "Now isn't a good time."

"No, it's really not," she snapped. Taking a deep breath, Kyra fought to moderate her tone before continuing. "I have a client who is proving less than receptive to your talisman."

"I'll be right there." The line clicked in her ear, and then Hannah was stepping into the centre of the room. Kyra tossed her phone carelessly back on the desk. "Take me to him."

Kyra made no effort to hide her frustration or slow her steps for the shorter woman as she led Hannah up the back stairs. It didn't take long for Kyra to leave the witch behind, which stopped being satisfying when she was forced to wait impatiently outside the door separating her latest problem from the rest of The Rose. Her foot tapped rapidly against the polished wood, and she folded her arms over her chest as she watched Hannah hurry to catch up. Once Hannah was only a few steps away, Kyra opened the door and gestured for Hannah to enter first, following close on her heels.

The room was still dark, the air warm and damp with the smell of sex, broken by deep breathing that tipped into snores randomly. Hannah moved with the same confidence and purpose she always did despite being faced with a situation Kyra was sure she'd otherwise have avoided. Without flinching, Hannah pressed a hand to his forehead, her eyes becoming distant and unfocused as she used her other senses. Kyra remained beside the door, arms still pulled tight across her body.

His energy continued to churn in her stomach with something deeper than her usual distaste. It was something beyond the taint of his desires, beyond her disinterest in his form. It could have simply been the abrupt change in fantasy, the disruption to her meal, but it was hard to be sure. The burning light felt heavy and wrong in a way Kyra couldn't quantify, couldn't explain.

"Well?" she barked into the quiet, more to distract herself from the urge to be sick than any real expectation that Hannah would have an answer by now.

"He feels..." She paused, eyebrows furrowing in confused concentration. "Different. Like there's something else in there, something that snarls and shies away from my magic." Hannah drew away slowly, uncertain curiosity in her now focused gaze. "I can take him if you want."

The offer was flippant, carefully casual. Kyra knew agreeing would be a mistake. "No. Just make sure he doesn't remember anything that happened here."

"Are you sure? If he could break through the talisman, I'm not sure how effective it would be."

"Yeah." Kyra waved her off with forced indifference. "I'm sure it'll be fine." Hannah narrowed her eyes, gaze darting between the sleeping figure on the bed and Kyra's defensive form. It wasn't until Hannah nodded that Kyra felt her chest loosen enough to breathe comfortably. Not that the curiosity had faded from Hannah's eyes. The stubborn set to the witch's jaw should have been a warning signal. "You make sure he's good to go, and I'll get your payment."

Part of Kyra didn't want to leave her alone with him, but she wouldn't be gone long enough for Hannah to do too much damage, and the witch wasn't foolish enough to actually steal a human. Still, she kept her steps long and fast, pausing only long enough in her office to syphon the still roiling energy in her centre into a vial. Hannah was still standing over him when Kyra returned, but she wasn't touching him, only watching.

"It's done?" Kyra held out the vial, waiting for Hannah's confirming nod before releasing it to her warm fingers. The vial quickly disappeared into a pocket of her tailored blazer. "A pleasure as always."

"Good doing business with you," Hannah agreed. Turning towards the door, she stepped into her own sanctuary without breaking stride.

Alone in the room, save for the still sleeping man, Kyra couldn't shake the feeling that there was more to this. She was missing something, but it was hard to think beyond the gentle waves of her stomach. Even with a portion of it given away, it still refused to settle in her gut.

Rather than risk being seen when he woke, she left the room once more. Kyra found herself in her room, in her bed, without really meaning to go there. Wrapped in the safety of her nest, finding sleep was easier than finding answers.

~ Twenty-Nine ~

"Mary's dead."

Despite being a demon, despite living on earth with fleeting mortals and Hunters dedicated to eradicating her kind, Kyra had never been able to get used to death. Whether through encroaching old age or a wasting sickness, even brutal murders or those who fell victim to the insidious voices telling them to end their own life, Kyra could never get used to it. But for someone like Mary, arguably in her prime, someone Kyra assumed removed enough from her world to be safe, someone she was actively protecting, it felt doubly unfair.

"How?" Kyra finally forced the question past the lump in her throat, her heart lurching out of rhythm. Her fingers felt numb, as did her mind. Everything felt far away and washed out and removed. Nothing felt right.

"She was torn apart. The police have no idea, but it looks like..." Wendy trailed off. She didn't need to finish the sentence; she could read Kyra's horrified realisation in the way her eyes widened.

"Do we know who?" She felt like throwing up, like emptying her stomach of everything she had ever eaten, everything she had ever considered eating. Images played out in her mind, a compilation of memories and what she assumed Mary's body must have looked like. Vampires were messy eaters by nature, but they weren't stupid. Mary was left to be found.

"Erik is making the rounds, but he swears it wasn't one of his." Wendy shrugged uncomfortably, clearly having more to say but unsure of how to voice it. "He says there's something off about it. That it doesn't look right."

"What do you mean?"

"He thinks it's staged. Not enough was missing."

Wendy's tone was calm, bordering on flat, and it made Kyra's stomach clench painfully. Bile burned at the back of her throat, bitter waves of acid rising rapidly to coat her tongue. Usually, Wendy's calm was a source of comfort and strength, but it felt fragile today. She liked Mary too, in her own way.

Kyra sucked in a deep breath, ignoring how it shook at the edges, and forced her mind and heart to slow. Memories of Mary— her smile when she talked someone into a corner, her honest laugh when caught off guard—tried to intrude on Kyra's mind. It was hard to bury them, but they weren't useful right now. Later, Kyra would examine them, hold them close, and let them feed her rage before taking revenge.

"Find out everything you can," she ordered, striding past Wendy's desk to slip into her office. "And get me Caleb."

In the cool safety of her office, alone in the darkened room, the setting sun painting the walls in reds and oranges as the light faded into night, Kyra still refused to let her emotions win. Her anguish, a bright pain resting above her heart, was something to be held close, to be cultivated and tended. It was a fire she would keep burning, a blaze she would feed her sorrow until the culprit was found, and then she would release it to engulf those responsible.

Snatching her phone up, Damian's name flashed on the screen briefly before she held it to her ear, listening with impatience to the ringing.

"Yeah?" He sounded tired.

"Mary's dead."

"What?"

"Mary's dead. Wendy says it's probably a vampire, Erik swears it's none of his, but I'm bringing Caleb in."

"Kyra, breathe," he tried to soothe over her rapid-fire speech, his words trampled by her momentum. Stopping wasn't an option.

"I'm going to find who did this and make them pay." A darkness had entered her voice, something unrecognisable in shades of black and red, the colour of pain and blood. Her words were a tide, spilling from her in uncontrollable waves of rage and grief. "I will tear them apart, Damian. They will weep for what they have done."

She barely heard the sound of the door opening over her own voice, over the pounding blood in her ears tinging everything crimson. It was a shock to be pulled suddenly into somebody's arms, her body freezing in the split second it took her mind to process and recognise Damian's scent.

She fell easily into his embrace, her clawed fingers bunching the material of his shirt as she buried her face in his chest. When had she lost her glamour? Hot tears streaked down her face. When had she started crying?

Her rage fought to maintain control, fought to overcome the crushing weight of her grief, but it didn't stand a chance. Sadness rolled over her, but the burning need for justice refused to be extinguished. Even as she wept, her mind spun with the ways she would get revenge.

Every day that passed without finding Mary's killer grated on Kyra's nerves. Another nail pressing into her flesh, another point of pain lodged beneath the surface of her skin. Her fingers itched to dig it out, to claw out the infectious rage before it festered along the already aching edges of her chest.

"Talk to me," Damian demanded, sat in his usual spot with his usual sprawl. The familiarity did little to ease the crush of emotions constantly threatening to engulf her.

Her instinct was to brush him off, tell him there was nothing to discuss, that she was fine. But when had that ever done her any good? Sighing in defeat, Kyra closed her laptop and forced herself to meet his gaze. "When did everything go to hell?"

"Around about the time you decided to take over this place," he responded immediately. "Not that it was much better beforehand."

Kyra couldn't help the dry chuckle that broke from her throat, the sound shocking. She had given up on ever laughing again.

"You can't give up." Damian's eyes softened, the concern there warming her where it would have made her uncomfortable before.

"I won't. Mary will be avenged."

"I wasn't talking about that."

Maintaining Damian's gaze suddenly became a lot harder, the worry in his eyes shifting from warming to burning as her cheeks flushed with blood. "I..." Kyra swallowed thickly around the lump in her throat, unsure when it had formed. "I mean, she hasn't reached out. I left my number for her, but I haven't heard anything, and it's not like I can just find her on social media or whatever." As though she hadn't already tried with nothing more than a first name and a face that haunted her to go off. "If she doesn't want to be found, I can't change that."

"And if she does?"

"It'd be nice of her to give me a sign if that's the case."

"And if she can't? If she's in danger?"

Kyra's stomach did a spectacular impression of a trapeze artist, swinging wildly from her throat to her feet and back again at the thought. Even with the buffer of distance and time, Leah still managed to play havoc on Kyra's insides. He was only voicing her own concerns, but hearing the words spoken aloud only drove the spikes of fear deeper, only made them more real.

"And if she's not and she hates me?" It took every ounce of Kyra's strength to break the encroaching silence, though her voice was small and weak between them. Voicing this fear, the deepest and darkest from the furthest corner of her heart, felt like flaying her chest. She could feel her ribs cracking, bending open to reveal the gaping maw where her heart should have been, the space red and dripping and icy in its desolation.

"Is it really safer not knowing? She could be-"

"Don't," Kyra cut him off, knowing exactly what he was going to say. If the words were spoken, they would be true, and then there really would be no hope. "She's fine. She knows too much for them to..." Shaking her head to herself, Kyra pushed on. "She's too valuable now."

As though she didn't know full well what the Church would do to get the information they wanted. If Leah wasn't giving it willingly, if she hadn't simply told them everything the moment she arrived... Kyra wished she could talk to her, if only for a few minutes, just to know she was okay, unharmed. Even if it was only to hear that Leah hated her, as long as she was okay.

Damian reached across the desk, placing his hand over Kyra's trembling fingers and squeezing briefly. Through the pinprick pain of threatening tears, she smiled weakly at the gesture. It was a small comfort but better than facing the crush of panic alone.

Her thoughts danced between too many horrible possibilities for her mind to properly process, each nothing more than a smudge of pain that screamed at her. Leah bloody and beaten, Leah sneering her disdain, Leah broken and lifeless.

"Kyra." She pulled her hands away reflexively, hiding any sign of weakness. Wendy didn't even acknowledge Damian's presence from where she stood in the doorway, let alone the way he had been holding her hands, holding her together. "There are some people here to see you."

"Who?" Her voice was rough with emotion. Clearing her throat almost brought a fresh wave of tears, her body determined to stay with the pain.

"Detectives."

"What about?" Law enforcement were easily dealt with for the most part. Something was wrong; that much was clear in the tension of Wendy's shoulders and stiff back.

"Mary." The name brought a fresh rush of anger, pain, and guilt. She should have been driving the investigation, not getting caught in more pointless wallowing in heartbreak.

"Send them in," she ordered.

"It's..."

"What?" Kyra asked, the word tinged with impatience and frustration that had no right to be directed at Wendy.

"They're both women." It was a small, innocuous thing. Or at least it should have been. But for Wendy to be noting it with a weighted look, it had to have meant something.

"I can stay," Damian offered.

"No, that would only look suspicious." Kyra turned back to Wendy. "Send them in." She carefully adopted the glamour best known as the owner of The Rose as she spoke. The mark of the businesswoman matured by the passage of time, she was a striking beauty made all the more lovely by those years. Lines at the corners of her eyes and silver at her temples highlighted her authority and gave weight to her power.

The detectives entered under the direction of Wendy, passing Damian on his way out. Wendy hesitated briefly in the door as though debating whether Kyra would be better served by her remaining in the room, but Kyra waved her away. Wendy made sure to give a pointed frown before slipping out of the office.

Kyra's visitors stood stiffly before her desk, both adopting a seemingly unconscious pose of legs shoulder-width apart and hands clasped behind them.

Kyra rose smoothly, extending her hand to the older of the pair. "Welcome to The Rose." She smiled blandly. "How can I help you, Officers?"

The first woman took the offered hand, shaking it firmly. Dark in hair and eyes, she was of an age even with Kyra's glamour, at the peak of her maturity and on the precipice of beginning that dreaded descent into old. Despite the stiffness of her back and the weight of her career, there was a softness to her gaze and a readiness to smile at the edges of her lips. While her features were plain, neither pretty nor ugly, Kyra knew immediately she was a beautiful creature, radiating warmth in equal measure to her quiet confidence and strength.

"Detective Hyland. This is Detective Boyd." Hyland gestured to her partner. Kyra slipped her hand and smile to the younger woman.

As in all things, the universe found balance in putting Hyland and Boyd together. Young enough to be considered inexperienced, Boyd was pale in the way Hyland was dark, the colour almost reminding Kyra of Leah, though the countenance couldn't be any different. Stern seriousness shaped every line of her face, from the harsh nose through to the strong jaw, the chiselled lines of her features made all the more stark by the downward turn of her mouth. While Hyland's handshake had managed to remain friendly despite its strength, Boyd's felt like an open threat, a challenge that Kyra burned to accept.

Indicating the chairs across from her own, Kyra enthroned herself with careful carelessness. They wouldn't unnerve her. Under the pressure of discovery, it was easy to forget how close to crumbling she had been.

"We're here about the murder of one Mary Magda," Boyd announced in clipped tones. There was nothing conversational about her voice; her words delivered with a surety that Kyra would answer their questions, would give them what they wanted, whether she liked it or not. The impotent rage Kyra had first felt at Mary's death was quickly returning and finding a target in one Detective Boyd.

"How can I help?" Kyra said instead, maintaining careful neutrality.

Before either could answer, could question, Wendy pushed open the office door with just enough force to be obvious. Balancing a tray stacked with glasses and a jug of water, she kept her eyes downcast as though she could blend into the background. Kyra noted the tall glasses without seeming to even glance at Wendy. She hadn't expected Wendy to serve Boyd first, but too many years of these games ensured she didn't let her surprise show. Kyra waited patiently until Wendy had placed the glasses, poured water into each, and was about to slip from the room once more before calling for her.

"Wendy, sorry, could you please let Damian know we'll need to move our meeting forward?" Wendy nodded her assent, the ghost of a smile pulling at her lips as she left.

"Did you know Ms. Magda well?" Boyd ignored the water placed before her in favour of pulling a small notebook and pen from the pocket of her dark suit jacket. Both women were similarly dressed, as though still in the habit of wearing a strict uniform of navy blues.

"Well enough," she replied. "We were friendly but hardly friends."

"You don't think it odd, a reporter and a whore being friendly?"

"Brothel owner," Kyra corrected with a smile of sugary sweetness. "And we found it easier to be polite."

"You don't seem all that upset by her death." Boyd's every word seemed a challenge. Kyra felt her smile crack and falter. Hyland at least seemed to sense the imminent danger, inserting herself smoothly into the conversation.

"What my colleague means is, was Mary acting strangely the last time you saw her? Did she give you any reason to be concerned?"

"Did I think she was in danger, you mean?" Kyra let her smile drop entirely, taking a drink of the cool water before her. This wasn't a game worth playing anymore. "No, I didn't know someone was going to kill her. If I had known, if I had had even the slightest inkling of what was going to happen to her, I would have..." Kyra brought herself up short. A deep breath, a second, a third. She hadn't buried the hurt as well as she had thought she had; the pain was too close to the surface. "I don't know what I would have done, but I wouldn't have let it happen."

"Did she have any enemies that you knew of?" Boyd didn't even have the decency to look shamed by Kyra's display of emotion.

"She reported on politics. Maybe she learnt something dangerous there." Kyra sighed. It wasn't some politician that had done away with Mary; her body had been mutilated too deliberately to be anyone beyond the demon community. But that wasn't something to be shared. "I'm sorry, I wish I could be of more help. If I knew something, you would be the first to know, if only to ensure justice was served." Appearing to be honest, disarmingly so, was easy.

As easy as reading the mistrust in Boyd's eyes.

"If you think of anything..." Hyland rose, pulling a business card from her pocket while motioning for Boyd to follow her example. "Please give us a call."

"I will." Kyra rose with them, remaining standing until they had left.

Damian slipped back into Kyra's office almost immediately after the detectives left. Wendy's assessment had been accurate, as it always was, and women of Boyd's potential were too rare to pass by.

Kyra was already moving around her desk to take the chair Hyland had vacated when Damian stepped into the room, settling herself as comfortably as possible before holding her hands out while she waited for him to take the other seat. He positioned himself around her, knees brushing and palms touching as they fell into the familiar rhythm of shared breathing. It came easily with Damian, easier than any other incubus she had ever fed. Within moments, they were synchronised in heartbeat and breath, falling into an easy rhythm subconsciously.

Heat built quickly along Kyra's arms, growing near burning but never quite reaching the level it did with Buddug. She could trace the path of the energy as it built and flowed from her core through to the connection created by their hands. Kyra could feel Damian drinking it in, soaking in the warmth to fill his belly, to fill the aching hole that gnawed from his centre. It was over in moments for all that it lasted a lifetime.

"Give it a few days, then pay our new friend a visit." Kyra pulled herself up, stretching her body gracelessly just to hear her joints pop.

"Wendy seems confident it will take." Damian followed her lead, his own full-body stretch an artful splay of limbs. He shifted in the chair, turning to face Kyra as she moved around her desk.

"And she has an eye for it."

"We sure paid enough for them." Damian hummed. "Are you okay?"

Kyra fell back into her chair before answering. "Not really, but I will be." He smiled encouragingly, knowing asking for more was counterproductive.

~ Thirty ~

That it took a week to find Caleb only convinced Kyra that he was to blame. Seeing him bruised, hanging limply between two of his brethren, went a small way to repaying the debt he had created between Kyra and Mary's memory. His confession would do more.

"Take him to the shed," Kyra ordered curtly. If the other vampires had any qualms in taking Caleb to what would no doubt be his demise, they didn't voice them. Loyalty to The Rose was valued above all else; anyone who called it home knew that in their very bones. Mary had never been one of their own, not like Wendy or even Leah, but her death was a threat that couldn't be ignored. Regardless of Kyra's personal feelings, Mary had died under the express protection of The Rose, and the unvoiced challenge could not go unpunished.

Caleb was dragged from the room, his legs failing to keep him up, let alone carry his weight. Kyra watched him from behind an impassive mask, silently stoking the fires of her fury by reminding herself of every painful detail Wendy had shared. Images played in her mind—Mary's torn body, the screams she would have had ripped from her throat.

Kyra counted slowly to a hundred, breathing deeply around each number as it whistled low between her teeth. The screams ringing in her ears had deepened, the blood splashed in her mind's eye brightening into something fresh and flowing. Kyra rose to follow Caleb's limp form.

"I'm going to go deal with something," Kyra spoke to the wall over Wendy's shoulder, uninterested in facing the judgement in her eyes. Wendy would want revenge too, but she no doubt felt Kyra was being too rash. "Don't tell Damian." It was hard to ensure Wendy would follow the last order, but not saying anything would have only guaranteed her calling him as soon as she was out of earshot.

Long strides took Kyra through the belly of The Rose, out the kitchen, and into the night air. The memory of her last trip out here, the night she met Leah, rose unbidden and threatened to dislodge her rage and replace it with sorrow. Kyra forced away the memory and the flood of emotions it brought. She didn't have time for this now. The heavy door before her and the person it concealed were all she could afford to think about now.

As expected, Caleb's hulking form was tightly bound to a chair, chains snaking around limbs and torso to hold him firm. His head was lolled forward, chin resting against his chest. That wouldn't do.

Kyra crossed the space quickly, reaching out to weave her fingers through his hair. She gripped the short strands roughly and jerked his head back. His bloodshot eyes widened as he groaned around the sharp pain, his gaze weaving back and forth. How many glaring demons could he see, she wondered faintly. A bruise, dark and livid, worked to swell his left eye shut, but the right shone with hatred once it finally managed to fix itself on her. The chains rattled as he pulled against them, exercising inhuman strength that was no match to the thick metal binding him. His struggles only brought a smile to Kyra's lips.

"I didn't kill the bitch," he spat before Kyra could speak.

"Then why did you run? Why not come back and tell us that?" She spoke slowly, voice low and gentle. The fingers in his hair loosened, shifting from punishing to run across his scalp in soothing strokes.

"I knew you wouldn't believe me." His tone turned cautious, though the hatred in his eyes was still strong. He was smart enough to sense the trap but unsure enough to attempt bargaining. "I was afraid, so I ran. I would never have hurt her."

"Really? Not even if you were hungry? Not even in the grips of blood lust?"

"I wasn't." He tried to shake his head. Kyra's fingers kept him still, tightening painfully around the motion. Caleb stiffened immediately, and Kyra rewarded his compliance by resuming her gentle patting. "I didn't."

"The thing is..." His hair was soft under her fingers, the short strands tickling her skin. "I don't think I believe you." She shed her glamour between one breath and the next, and her fingers became claws, drawing blood as they pressed hard enough to tear the fragile layer of skin at the base of his skull. Caleb grunted against the pain, jerking feebly in the chair but held tight by the chains. Kyra bared her teeth in a parody of a smile.

Releasing him as quickly as she had scored his flesh, Kyra turned on her heel to examine the tools lining the walls. She could feel his eyes on her back, could feel the weight of his growing unease as she made a show of selecting his doom. Caleb's harsh breathing was loud in the room, each painful drag of air sending shockwaves through her body as the anticipation built.

Her fingers trembled as she reached for a pair of pliers, large enough to feel heavy in her hand but small enough to suit her purpose. The metal was sharply cold against the angry flush of her skin. It did nothing to dampen the fire burning low and hot in her gut. Yes, they would be perfect.

Caleb's eyes locked onto the tool in her hand the moment she turned, his already pale features going entirely bloodless. He began struggling again despite the futility, shaking his head in abortive movements while his fingers curled to hide beneath his palms. Taking her time to return to him, caressing the cool weight of the metal, Kyra ensured the pliers were large in his vision. It was all part of the show, foreplay to the main event.

Even on the cusp of violence, Kyra couldn't help an edge of seduction leaking into her movements. She draped herself over Caleb, her bosom pressing against his shoulder as she brought the pliers up to run down his cheek. He flinched away from the cold metal, though it only pushed him closer to her. Fleeing the press of her naked skin forced the pliers into the soft flesh of his face. A small whimper, barely loud enough to be heard, escaped the confines of his throat, and Kyra drank it in greedily.

A strip of leather hung from the back of the chair, bolted slightly to the right of centre. Kyra caught it with her free hand and wrapped it across Caleb's forehead, feeding it through the buckle screwed to the left of centre. Secured to the chair, his head was held fast, and his neck stretched uncomfortably. Caleb's face was parallel to the ground, eyes darting from the ceiling to Kyra and back again. Fear spread with the blood leaking into his sclera.

Slowly, drawing out the moment as much as possible, Kyra ran a thumb over his lower lip. The muscles in his jaw stood tight and bulged under his skin. She could feel the tension, the determination, holding his teeth clenched. It was a fragile stubbornness, broken by the audible creak of his jaw.

Kyra shifted her grip to cradle his face. She pressed her claws into the sparse flesh of his jaw, sharp tips breaking skin to draw blood. A full body shuddered ripped through him, the creaking of his jaw drowned by the creaking of the chair as his fingers scrambled to ground him, his own blunt nails biting into unforgiving wood.

Kyra pressed harder, feeling the skin give way and bunch under her nails as she gouged lines in his cheeks. She stepped closer, filling his vision entirely, making sure all he saw was the white heat of her rage.

A strangled gasp signalled her victory, and the pliers were between his lips in a flash. She didn't try to line them up, made no move to grip with them, just let the sharp tang of metal sit in his mouth. Abject fear had entered his gaze now, but it wasn't enough.

She released her grip on his jaw, and he drew air through his nose in great lungfuls, the sound whistling and satisfying.

"You should never have come here." Kyra shifted the pliers, careful not to take them out completely. The long nose of the tool settled on his left canine, the grooves helping the metal grip the tooth. She pulled down slowly, applying deliberate and controlled strength. "Erik should have drained you dry." The tooth resisted, root dug deep.

His breathing sped into panting as he began to struggle anew. Kyra didn't loosen her grip, didn't slow the inexorable force. Just as it seemed she would have to apply more strength, the tooth popped free with a crunch. Caleb howled his pain around the blood flooding his mouth, around the pliers still holding his jaw wide.

Kyra let the tooth go. She didn't care if it dropped to the floor or into his mouth; she was already reaching for the next one. Caleb made an attempt at words, garbled begging or prayers to a god he didn't believe in. It didn't matter. Nothing mattered. Leaning back in, Kyra shifted her grip for better leverage. How many teeth could she take before he died?

The blood on Kyra's skin itched under her glamour, but that wasn't important. Just another annoyance to ignore.

Wendy had been waiting at the door when Kyra was done, and though her eyes flashed with something too close to judgement for Kyra's liking, she didn't mention the body Kyra was leaving behind.

"Buddug called. She'd like a word," she said instead, delivering the message in a tone completely devoid of emotion.

Kyra didn't want nor need Wendy's castigation. Mary's killer was dead; that was all that mattered. Justice had been served. And yet her stomach still churned with guilt, and the ever-present burning of tears lingered at the corners of her eyes. The bloody mess she was walking away from wouldn't leave her mind, and no matter how she tried to justify it, the image sickened her. Without the buffer of rage, her guilt was free to raise bile in her throat.

Unable to acknowledge the woman, Kyra simply walked towards The Rose as though she hadn't spoken at all. Wendy would deal with the mess, regardless of how she felt about it.

Kyra kept her mind on putting one foot in front of the other, climbing the well-worn path of the stairs to her room. Her thoughts threatened to spiral out of the iron grip she had on them, wanting to dance to Mary, to Caleb, to Leah, to whatever Buddug needed, to the inevitable bad news she would bring. So many strands to keep in her hands, so many things to go wrong. Too many things to go wrong.

She was painfully aware of her heartbeat, the way it rattled in her chest, an uneven tempo that couldn't settle into a consistent rhythm. Her bedroom door was a beacon in the dark, calling her to safety. It was a relief to slip into the quiet of her room, her furniture vague shapes in the shadows of the night. Moving to her altar, Kyra knew the space well enough to forgo the light switch on the wall. She did grope for the lamp, though, knowing Buddug wouldn't be impressed with trying to read her features in the dark. It would be read as sulking, or worse, an attempt to avoid Buddug's gaze. It didn't matter that both were bordering on the truth; the subsequent questions and thinly veiled accusations weren't worth it. Kyra knew, distantly, that it all came from a place of caring, but Buddug's brand of affection didn't always translate well.

Kyra blinked rapidly against the sudden bloom of light, trying to ignore the dots swimming in her vision as she shifted the items of her altar. The scrying bowl and tools were placed into perfect alignment, hands moving without thought. Once content with the placement of elements to compass points, the flame of her candle pitiful in the artificial light of the lamp, Kyra focused her mind and magic.

"Buddug," she called over the wide expanse of space, allowing her voice to fill every breath of wind between them. Her magic sang along every vibration of her voice, lacing it with power that would call to her mentor. It would settle in her veins and hum along her nerves, an itch beyond her body that could only be scratched by answering the call.

"Kyranthine." Buddug's face materialised in the smooth surface of water in the bowl, her answering magic tangling with Kyra's to solidify the connection.

"Wendy said you called."

"Yes." Buddug pressed her lips together into a thin line, considering her words carefully. If Kyra didn't know her so well, she would have said the older woman was afraid. "There have been some disturbing reports from other sanctuaries."

"What do you mean?"

"There have been attacks. More than normal, in greater numbers." Though she could only see Buddug's head, Kyra got the sense she had folded her arms across her chest. Whether in anger or an attempt to comfort herself, it was impossible to tell. "We have lost contact with Jamal's sanctuary."

Jamal was on the other side of the world, the threat was hardly close, but Kyra's heart stuttered in her chest. Sometimes sanctuaries went silent; sometimes, the risk of discovery by humans, by the Church, was too great for communication. Kyra's mind scrambled to cling to possible explanations, but the sinking feeling in her gut told her all she needed to know. "Has anyone confirmed the loss?"

Jamal was a member of the Council—the most minor member true, but a member, nonetheless. How many sanctuaries were plunged into panic? How many demons eyed darkened windows and bustling streets wearily, acutely aware that their death could be the next human they see.

"No one is willing to risk it when they're effectively under siege."

"We've had nothing here. I'll send someone." It was the least she could do, and it was far too easy for Kyra to tell herself it was enough.

"Thank you. I will let the others know." Buddug sighed, but the tension around her eyes didn't fade. "Are you sure you're safe?"

"Yes. We haven't had any Hunters since..." Since the one Leah let go. Buddug couldn't know about that. "It's been quiet here since we killed the last one."

"I don't like it." Buddug's frown pulled her whole face down, her eyebrows drawn tight. "Please don't let your guard down."

"We're careful here." Kyra waved away Buddug's concern, mind already ticking over who would be best to visit Jamal. Erik couldn't be trusted, not so soon after losing his fledgling. Maybe Andy.

"Kyranthine." The weight of her tone brought Kyra's head up. "Please, be safe."

Kyra nodded solemnly in the face of Buddug's open fear. She had seen her mentor angry, worried, and concerned, but this naked fear was new, and it terrified Kyra. Buddug wasn't meant to be afraid; Buddug was the epitome of strength and determination. She had seen Buddug prepare to lead vampires against Hunters, had watched her tend to bloody gashes in her own flesh like they were nothing. Fear was not something to ever be associated with Buddug. The growing sense of everything slipping out of her control was made all the worse by Buddug's expression.

"You too," Kyra murmured into the dark, Buddug's face already fading. Staring into the clear water once more, Kyra wished that she could find the answers in its shallow depths. All she saw was the soft grain of the wood. If her bowl held any secrets, it wasn't giving them up tonight.

~ Thirty-One ~

Under other circumstances, Kyra may have been suspicious of the timing of Mary's death, a new reporter, police, increased Hunter activity, and a dead vampire so close together. But given the general trajectory of her life recently, she was too tired to consider the coincidences involved. It didn't help that a few days later, when the knowledge could have percolated at the back of her mind before resurfacing in a clearer picture, Wendy barged into her office, newspaper in hand.

Before Kyra could question the move or even finish raising a perfectly shaped brow in mild annoyance, Wendy had tossed the paper on her desk. She flung the offending object as though it burned before turning sharply on her heel to begin pacing the short space between Kyra's book-lined walls. As the human strode first one way and then the other, Kyra shook the paper loose and scanned the first page to identify the cause of her irritation.

It didn't take long to find the culprit. The insipid smiling face that Kyra had recognised some weeks ago, a name nagging at the back of her mind, stared up at her. The headline, splashed large and bold, read 'AN END TO WOMEN OF THE NIGHT'. Reading the opening few paragraphs of the article, Kyra's insides attempted to rearrange themselves under the assault of anger, panic, and fear.

"How?" The word was soft, a pained thing that carried disbelief, though Kyra knew Wendy needed her strength. "Has Damian seen this?" she continued with greater conviction, though the damage had been done. A flash of uncertainty had crossed Wendy's face before hardening into resigned defeat.

"Not yet." Her voice remained even. She would remain by Kyra's side regardless of the face she or The Rose wore.

"Can you get him for me?" Kyra didn't wait for Wendy to nod her assent or even leave the room before pulling her laptop closer. A quick search had the legislation before her. Reading the words, drinking in their meaning, Kyra felt her panic recede in waves.

By the time Damian had strode into her office, concern painted clear on his features, Kyra was chuckling softly to herself. He paused before her desk, the worry changing shape to question the stability of her sanity. She waved him into his usual chair.

"Wendy said there was a problem?"

"No, just more political point scoring." Kyra pushed the now abandoned paper across for Damian to read. His eyes darted over the page in sharp movements, taking in the words without changing the careful set of his jaw.

"Are we sure it's just 'political point scoring'?"

"I've had a quick read over the legislation. We're fine." Kyra closed the laptop softly. "I'm pretty sure they've just put new words on old laws. As long as we maintain our registration and licenses, we'll be fine."

"I'm sick of seeing this name popping up." He threw the paper back down, the shrewd, unscrupulous face of Richard Smith smiling up at them. "How many months until the elections? How long before he's in a position of real power? How long before even our registrations and licenses are not enough?"

"You're overreacting."

"And you're not taking this seriously enough," Damian snapped. "You know he has connections to the Church." The capital was implicit in his tone.

"Who doesn't in that party?" Kyra tried for flippant but fell short. She hadn't known, suspected of course, but having it confirmed wasn't pleasant. "His ideals go against basic human inclinations.

He's trying to outlaw sex, drugs, and rock and roll. When has that ever worked?"

"He may not wipe it out entirely, but he's going to do a lot to make our lives a lot more difficult. Things have been relatively easy the past few decades. I know you don't want to go back to an endless stream of bribes and catering to the needs of corrupt men in power."

"What would you have me do? It's not like I can run for parliament."

"Of course not," he scoffed. "But you could actually admit that the Church is a problem. We have friends who want to do something about them."

"So you'd have me get involved with Buddug's war?" Kyra snapped, tone sneering. "You'd have me welcome the Church's wrath on The Rose? We're not fighters, Damian. Our kind wasn't built for war. We don't have a vampire's strength or a witch's magic."

"We don't have to be," he countered, leaning forward. His eyes burned with a passion that frightened Kyra. He was a man of smiles, not this iron determination. "Warfare like this won't be battles in the streets."

"You want us to fight in the sheets?" Kyra asked archly.

"No." Damian sighed. "I don't know. I just want us to do something."

"'Do something.' How useful."

"At least I'm trying, Kyra. This isn't just Buddug's war, not when they want to wipe us out entirely."

That he had a point was immaterial. There were too many unknowns for Kyra to commit to a course of action. "I can't risk the lives and safety of everyone here on something so vague."

"Can't you see you're risking it anyway by doing nothing?"

This was a pointless argument, one neither of them could truly win. Damian was right, Kyra knew that, but she couldn't act without some form of plan. That she could form one, could open herself to

Buddug's pleadings, was never raised. Damian had made his point; he knew better than to push the matter further. It was just another thing to weigh her down, another concern to wrap around her mind and squeeze. If only she could be given more time to process, to deal with these things. Instead, events were spinning out of her control, circumstances shifting and changing faster than she could keep up with.

"Claire is here to see you." Wendy's voice was flat and near tone-less, the sentence spoken with a complete lack of emotion. Kyra looked up sharply, reply dying in her throat as the named woman pushed her way into the room. Wendy's eyes flashed darkly, reading Kyra's face closely for any sign of direction.

She hesitated. She could let Wendy deal with it. After a long moment of consideration, Kyra shook her head minutely. She tapped the first two fingers of her left hand on her right wrist. One finger would have meant Wendy was to deal with it; two simply meant to summon Damian.

The stern woman crossed the room in clipped strides, taking the seat across from Kyra without invitation or permission. Claire settled herself comfortably, acting all the world like a welcomed friend or as though the office was hers and Kyra the guest. Kyra's eyes flashed with darkening anger, and her lips tightened into a thin line, holding back snarling insults. Maybe she should have let Wendy deal with it after all.

"Do you believe in demons, Ms Clarke?" Claire's voice was as neutral as Wendy's had been. The words were light, as though inconsequential.

"Did you really come all this way to ask me about my religious beliefs?" Kyra was going to have to kill her; she just knew it.

"Should I take that as a no?" She maintained the same neutral, almost flippant tone. Claire made a show of examining the ends of her nails as though they were more important, more interesting, than the conversation at hand. It was designed to disarm, to frustrate Kyra into speaking words she shouldn't. It was amateurish at best and a little insulting.

"Take that as you like." Kyra settled back in her chair, the perfect image of unconcerned boredom with just enough arrogance to suggest she was above all this, was merely gracing Claire with her presence. It was an air she reserved for clients for the most part.

"So, you mean to tell me you're not a demon?" In the small moment Kyra had to affect a natural reaction, she did consider laughing it off, calling the reporter crazy and threatening to call her bosses. If she hadn't established herself as an enemy, if she hadn't accused Kyra of atrocities, if Kyra didn't need the excuse to let off some steam, she might have. Instead, she grinned.

Kyra's smile was all teeth and a sharpness that had Claire pulling back. The reporter recognised her misstep immediately, but it was far too late. Flexing well-worn muscles in the back of her mind, Kyra allowed her glamour to fall in waves of shifting reality. Her skin melted to reveal otherworldly flesh.

Without the cover of her glamour or clothes, sat naked and exposed, Kyra had never felt more powerful than in the fleeting moment in which Claire's eyes widened in unabashed fear. It was sweeter than any lust.

"And if I am?" Kyra crooned.

Claire threw herself backward, nearly tipping the chair in her rush to flee the room. Damian entered the office just as Claire was righting herself, eyes still trained on Kyra as she continued to scramble. He took in Kyra's naked form and Claire's panic with a quick, calculating glance. Whether he agreed with Kyra's tactics didn't matter, he dropped his own glamour just as the petrified woman was turning towards him.

Like Kyra, his skin was a pale purple with dark brown fur around his cloven hooves. His own horns were straight and two hands long, the wicked points designed to tear flesh despite years of evolution. Taller than most men, his lithe body was wrapped in a thin layer of muscle, the well-defined edges clear under the smooth expanses of his skin. A perfect creature that seemed the muse for every Greek hero or Roman god, he was as painfully handsome as Kyra was beautiful. When Claire finally came around to face him, she screamed at the sight and leapt back.

She froze in terror, eyes darting between the demons without looking at them properly, as though she could pretend they weren't real as long as she kept them in her peripheral vision only. Damian rested against the wood of the office door, crossing his arms as he smiled lazily at Kyra. For her part, Kyra rose gracefully, trailing a hand across her desk as she rounded it.

Sensing impending danger, Claire turned to face Kyra, eyes still refusing to rest on her. Every time her gaze came close to Kyra's edges, she jerked it away sharply. For every step Kyra took forward, Claire matched it backwards. A few gliding steps had Claire backed solidly into Damian's waiting chest. She gave a small squeak at the contact, eyes looking up against her better judgement. As far as last looks went, Damian was a better subject than most.

"You." The word trembled, falling from Claire's lips. "You killed Mary."

Lunging forward with a snarl, Kyra wrapped a hand around Claire's throat. Claws bit into skin, drawing blood as her fingers squeezed the air from the human's body. "No, but I will kill you."

Leah's face flashed in her mind, the anger and accusation the Hunter had worn when demanding to know how many Kyra had killed. Shame threatened to eclipse the fire of Kyra's rage, the terror in Claire's eyes heady and pathetic all at once. This was a woman who had accused The Rose of unspeakable acts, had threatened their existence, and would continue to threaten those Kyra loved simply by living. Justifying it to herself was surprisingly easy.

Kyra met Damian's still blandly curious gaze over the cowering woman's shoulder. Claire was held up more by Kyra's hand around her neck than her own legs.

Damian stood perfectly still against the door, making no move to hold up the human between them, acting only as a means of intimidation until Kyra asked him to do more. And he did it all without question or complaint. In that brief moment, in the split second their eyes met, Kyra loved him with all her heart.

"Would you like her?" Kyra offered, watching Claire's eyes roll backwards in fear. Catching sight of the muscled frame she was pressed to, she whimpered. Kyra could only begin to guess what was running through the human's mind, but it was no doubt worse than what they would actually do. That was the beauty of imagination.

"Don't mind if I do." His tone was dark, but Damian was rolling his eyes over Claire's head, safely out of sight. The human near shrieked, attempting to rip herself from Kyra's grip. Damian's arms snaked out, wrapping around Claire's torso in an iron grip, pinning her effectively to his chest.

One arm wrapped tight, gripping her upper arm to keep her still, while the other reached up to press against the side of her face. Claire flinched from his touch, jerking her head away in a pitiful attempt at saving herself. Kyra stepped back to give Damian room to work.

The hand on the reporter's face shifted, fingers seeking to establish as much contact as possible. As soon as his hand had settled flush against her skin, Claire went completely still.

It was over in moments, though it no doubt felt like eternity to the couple, Claire suddenly going limp. Damian let her fall carelessly. Kyra eyed the body with distaste. Technically, she wasn't dead, her chest rising and falling in deep, even breaths that could have been taken for sleep, but she would never wake again. Damian had fed her enough magic, enough lust and pleasure, to overload her brain entirely. Kyra could never decide if it was a good way to go or not.

~ Thirty-Two ~

Kyra was crossing the short space between the back hall and her office door when it happened. The familiar whoosh of the opening door, a small sound she could pick up over a roaring thunderstorm, had her lengthening her stride and keeping her head firmly turned away. She had developed the habit of avoiding clients long before she had taken responsibility for The Rose.

A strangled grunt from Wendy, the brief noise somehow full of surprised anger, pulled Kyra up short. She turned just in time to watch Wendy fly over her desk at reception. Blonde hair streaming like a banner, she was a blur of movement intent on colliding with the two figures entering their door.

In a blink, Wendy had caught the taller person around the middle, bodily swinging them about to knock their partner off track. They crashed to the ground in a tangle of limbs, and Kyra was darting forward before she could think better of it.

She was reaching out with magic even as her eyes strained to confirm either was susceptible. It was a deeper sense that felt him, her eyes jerking from the larger figure to the smaller. He was knocked almost free of Wendy's grip, her focus trained on the body wriggling to throw her off.

A blade of lust was forced into the Hunter's mind, the magic rammed home without any of her usual finesse or care. He shuddered under the assault, lithe body falling slack against the polished floor. Kyra's chest heaved with effort. Adrenaline roiled along her veins, and Kyra was glad for the strength it gave her.

"What-" Kyra barely got the word out before a sickening crunch took her attention from the wide-eyed man gazing up at her with an empty, rapturous expression.

Wendy dropped the other Hunter's head, letting the skull bounce as she turned to the second threat. Her pretty, unassumingly soft face was pulled into harsh lines. The grim set to her mouth was so at odds with her carefully designed features. Kyra tried very hard to keep her gaze on Wendy. She had seen Wendy dispose of numerous threats over the years, but seeing a neck pulled at such a wrong angle made her own skin crawl.

"What," Kyra forced out again, wrenching her eyes back to the Hunter staring up at her. His slavish adoration was more sickening than the sound of his partner's snapping spine, "are you doing here?"

"We came to kill you," he answered immediately. He didn't look to his partner, didn't make any attempt to see if they still lived.

"We need to move," Wendy said. She was already lifting the body, slinging it over her shoulder as though she wasn't half its size.

"Help her," Kyra barked at the Hunter, and he scrambled to comply.

They made a strange procession through The Rose, the body slung between Wendy and the Hunter, and Kyra following a few paces behind. The hall was empty and so was the kitchen, much to Kyra's relief.

The caress of warm sunlight on her skin was a shock as she followed Wendy outside. A crushing emptiness was settling over Kyra's shoulders as the last of her adrenaline leaked out. She felt like hours should have passed since Wendy had first thrown herself over her desk.

It was becoming all too common lately for the passage of time to feel so out of sync with her perception. How many weeks since Leah had left? Since Mary had been murdered? How many days since Claire?

Kyra shook her thoughts loose, dragging her mind back to the here and now in time to dart forward. She shoved the door to the shed open, stepping aside to allow Wendy to drag the body inside. She dropped it unceremoniously in a corner, and the surviving Hunter was pulled off balance by the movement.

Wendy grabbed his shoulder, less to steady him than to propel him further into the room. It didn't matter that he was securely under Kyra's control; Wendy had never taken kindly to threats to her employer.

"We should kill him," She grunted.

"One second." Kyra spoke quickly, frightened that Wendy would wrap her hands around another neck before Kyra could ask the question burning on her tongue. "Where's Leah?"

"I don't know." His brow furrowed, the pulse of magic in his brain making him want to please her above all else. "The General-"

"The General?" Kyra broke in, more incredulous than anything. She had always assumed the Church saw themselves above such militaristic titles, better than that.

"Yeah." He nodded eagerly. "He took her under his personal protection." Kyra tried to tell herself that was a good thing. That it didn't sound as ominous as her mind was trying to make it. "It's an honour to be selected by him, to be one of his favourites."

Panicked rage overwhelmed Kyra, the desire to protect Leah, to hurt anyone that threatened her, welling up in her chest. It blinded her, filled her every sense until she drowned in it. Without thought, without intention, Kyra's magic surged in the Hunter's mind. Lust drenched his every nerve. Between one breath and the next, his mind was destroyed.

Wendy shook her head and sighed to herself as she reached for the Hunter. Kyra had already killed him; Wendy just needed to finish the job.

Spurned by the blood on her hands, by Damian's voice echoing in her mind, by the undeniable growing threat of the Church, Kyra strode into her room and moved straight to her altar. She pulled her scrying bowl into place and tried to quiet the racing thoughts of her mind.

Late afternoon sun played across the wall in front of her as she lit the candle, the small flame adding to the dancing lights of orange and rose.

There was every chance Buddug would be busy, her status and age often making her a preferred font of wisdom and advice. Though the excuse to put off the conversation, maybe even avoid it completely, was one Kyra was sorely tempted to take, she knew she couldn't. She held her resolution close, wrapping it in the layers of determination that had allowed her to turn her back on the danger for so long. Kyra breathed one last uneven sigh before steeling herself.

"Buddug," she called, the word clear and strong despite the misgivings huddled in the back of her mind. Waiting a count of ten, she called again. "Buddug."

The water before her shimmered without breaking the surface, the depths roiling gently as Buddug's face formed. Concern had pulled her brows down, her eyes quick to survey Kyra's face to ensure there was no damage, no danger. Without meaning to, without thought, Kyra smiled in relief, the visage of her mentor a source of comfort regardless of the seriousness of the pending discussion.

"What is wrong?" Buddug said immediately, her face barely sharpened in a full connection. "What has happened?"

"Nothing is wrong," Kyra quickly reassured, raising her hands in surrender, though they were beyond Buddug's line of sight. "I've decided I should be helping with the Church, with the war," she continued in a rush, the last word twisting on her lips. It still felt a foreign concept, something made for vampires or witches, not the likes of succubi.

"Why?" Far from overjoyed by this announcement, Buddug eyed Kyra with a level of suspicion she hadn't seen in years. Not since she had declared she would be taking over The Rose.

"Because it's the right thing to do?" Kyra couldn't bite back the snarky tone to her voice. "Because it's what you and Damian have been telling me to do for years? Because I obviously can't keep avoiding it, no matter how much I think getting involved is suicide."

"Are you doing this because you hope it'll kill you?" The softness to Buddug's voice made it no less cutting, drawing Kyra up short.

"No, of course not." Buddug's raised eyebrow said she doubted this. "I'm not ready to die. I know I've been"— sulking, a traitorous voice whispered at the back of her mind— "out of sorts, but that's a small part of it.

"Too many things are happening, too much is going wrong for it to be coincidence." Her legs itched to pace, but that would risk breaking the connection. Instead, she shifted restlessly, leaning on one leg and then the other, energy coursing through her veins with no place to go. "Damian and I had to deal with a reporter." Mentioning the Hunters would only make Buddug worry.

"So soon after Mary?"

"It was less than ideal." Kyra tried for contrite but landed closer to defensive and slightly petulant. "She had already marked herself as dangerous by making unsavoury accusations about my business practises. Then she had the gall to call me a demon. I know she wasn't technically wrong, but she wasn't like Mary. She would have tried to use it against us."

"Are you saying Mary knew?"

Swearing would have meant admitting her mistake, and biting the inside of her cheek seemed less painful than digging that hole any deeper.

"We're getting off-topic," Kyra forced instead. Buddug allowed it, though the look on her face said this was a discussion to be revisited in the future. If Kyra was really lucky, maybe she'd forget. "I'm joining the cause, whatever my motivations, and you're going to give me orders. And when I say that out loud like that, it suddenly sounds like a bad idea."

Buddug chuckled softly at Kyra's outburst. "I will come through once I am done here. We have much to discuss, but I have matters to attend to first."

"And even more to plan, I'm betting." Kyra shifted again, thinking for what was probably the millionth time that she should get a bar stool or something rather than remain on her feet, stationary, for so long.

~ Thirty-Three ~

Kyra paced her room while waiting for Buddug, feet working to wear the carpet bare in a straight line from wall to wall. Her mind was already whirling with thoughts and questions. Would they discuss strategy? Was she expected to understand tactics? She couldn't even win a game of chess. It was hard not to dwell on what her place would be and the many weaknesses that she had. It hadn't been fear that had kept her from this for so long, though it played a larger part than she cared to admit. Her distaste for fighting came down to a simple truth: it wasn't what she was made for.

It was impossible to focus, not with her mind dancing between the countless ways this was going to kill her. She wondered briefly if Hannah could arrange a protection spell of some sort, or maybe there were ways to adopt other forms of magic. Possibilities she had never even thought to consider began to blossom in her mind. Other avenues of power, other means to gain strength, were raised, explored, and discarded in a rapid procession. Kyra didn't know if half of what she imagined was possible, let alone the prices she would have to pay, but the slightest hint of hope was heady.

The dying light on her wall filtered through yellows and oranges to pinks and reds until the flame from her candle cast more of a shadow than the disappearing sun. In a few minutes, at most, Buddug would be crossing with her battle plans and orders for Kyra.

The sound of her door opening was a welcome if unexpected distraction. Damian barely entered the room, closing the door as though afraid to let the outside world in. There was a tightness to his eyes, a sense of urgency and energy to his stance that put Kyra immediately on edge. "It's Leah," he breathed as though he couldn't believe what he was saying, couldn't believe the situation. "She's here."

The words struck Kyra, landing a harsh blow to her chest, somewhere between her heart and her stomach. For a moment, she couldn't breathe, panic and concern and hope and disbelief warring to be at the front of her mind. Without allowing her the time to process, without offering more information, Damian stepped aside and propped the door open.

All the air rushed out of Kyra as her eyes fell on Leah. The familiar tilt to her head, the gentle smile that Kyra swore was only for her. Her pale features seemed to glow in the falling light of day, the last of the sun catching on the blond of her hair as though she was haloed in light. In that single second of perfection, the past few months ceased to exist. Every wrong turn, every mistake, every misstep since that fateful kiss evaporated in the stretch of air between them.

Leah was here; she was real and warm and would stay. Kyra's heart seemed to swell beneath her breast, pressing against skin and bones. It struggled to break free and land pathetically at Leah's feet, a feeble offering from a filthy demon.

Kyra couldn't remember grabbing the edges of her altar, but she knew without a doubt she would fall if she let go. Her knees had lost their strength as she swayed gently on the breeze caused by the door. How long had they been staring at each other? An hour? A second? It was too long, much too long, but Kyra couldn't find the strength, the coordination, to cross the space between them.

As though sensing her distress, Leah entered the room with long strides. Her steps carried more purpose than Kyra had ever seen her display, as though the gentle, curious woman she had fallen in love with was momentarily possessed by a lady of determination. Still, it was hard to focus on the strangeness when caught up in the warmth of Leah's arms. Wrapped softly around her waist, it felt only natural to shift her balance, raise her own arms, and place them gently around Leah's neck.

Kyra's eyes fluttered closed of their own accord, plunging the world into darkness as she lay her head closer to Leah's hair. The Hunter smelled of sunshine and summer, of something warm and bright, something on the edge of sharpness but still delicate. Leah's breath trailed across Kyra's neck, the heat sending chills down her spine. Air fought to fill her lungs, her muscles still seized by shock and an underlying fear that this wasn't real. That the illusion would burst with a wrong move.

If Damian spoke, his words fell on deaf ears. She wouldn't have even noticed Buddug entering the room or the telltale flood of ozone in the air. The sum of Kyra's focus, of her life, had narrowed into the woman caught in her arms, into the breath against her neck, the heartbeat so close to her own. It was in the softness of Leah's skin, the way her flesh gave way slightly when Kyra tightened her grip without thinking. Leah shifted in her embrace, arms falling down as though to come away. Kyra's own grip tightened again, unwilling to let go so soon. They could be caught up together for a lifetime, a demon's lifetime, and it still wouldn't be enough.

Laughing almost imperceptibly against Kyra's shoulder, Leah simply readjusted her arms to be lower around the demon's waist, settling across her hips for a moment before shifting again. Her hands moved constantly, fingers skimming over Kyra's back in a barely there kiss of flesh. Shivers of pleased anticipation followed Leah's touch, rising Kyra's skin in goosebumps.

Kyra wanted to mirror Leah's movements but couldn't focus beyond the changing pressure on her flesh as Leah gripped her hips. Was the human as desperate to feel the reality beneath her fingers as Kyra was?

At some point, she had begun breathing again, taking great lungfuls of air that tasted of Leah, the Hunter's scent coating her tongue. Kyra's skin tingled with emotion, Leah's touch, and an unreliable oxygen supply.

The whisper of the knife, the slide of blade between muscles and through flesh, was a shock. It took some seconds for Kyra to process the sound and then the pain as it blossomed from between her bottom two ribs to envelop her torso. As quickly as she had arrived, Leah was gone. Gone from her arms, gone from the room, leaving Kyra weak and falling as the remainder of her strength flowed from her on thickly pumped waves of blood.

Shaking hands moved to cup the knife, still stuck deep, probably lodged in something vital. Damian's voice was a wordless roar, his form melting into demonic panic as he flung himself forward to catch Kyra before she could fall. His fingers pressed automatically at the edges of the wound, as though he could hold the blood in, as though he could stop the bleeding with his bare hands and indomitable will.

Kyra thought, rather distantly, that it didn't seem to hurt nearly as much as it should have. A dull ache was beginning to spread from the wound in her side, but even that seemed numbed at the edges, almost as though it was happening to someone else. There was no sharpness to it, nothing biting about it.

Damian lowered Kyra slowly to the ground, voice still loud and distant. There seemed a flurry of movement around her as voices rose and fell on the waves of her consciousness. Damian called for Wendy as Buddug called for Hannah, their voices strained with panic and fighting to be heard over the blood pounding in Kyra's ears.

Darkness began to encroach on her sight, on her thoughts. That too moved in waves, gently lapping at her until there was nothing left beyond the comfortable oblivion of unconsciousness.

~ Thirty-Four ~

Consciousness was slow in returning, bringing with it a pounding headache and roaring pain that left none of her body bereft of its touch. If it were at all possible, Kyra would have happily fallen into the blackness of sleep. Unfortunately, her body had other ideas, awareness of her physical form coming in waves until all she felt was pain everywhere. A dull throbbing had taken residence up behind her eyes while her ribs burned around her wound.

Her wound. She had been stabbed.

Where the pain came in waves, the memories hit her like a full-armed swing. Leah, their embrace, the cold blade. Her stomach churned and tightened, nausea rising on bile to coat her throat in acid. Struggling to roll from the centre of her nest, Kyra tried to at least get her head over the floor before her body rebelled entirely.

Damian started forward at the sound of Kyra stirring but quickly shied away as the first retch spasmed audibly through her. He darted immediately for the door, no doubt to find something to clean the mess with. Kyra was glad for the privacy as her muscles clenched and forced her stomach up and out.

Each heave brought fresh waves of pain, which in turn fed the roiling boil of her insides. Damian returned soon after to find Kyra still half thrown off her bed, head hanging dangerously close to the meagre mess she had left. At least she hadn't eaten much lately, though the taste of pure bile on the back of her tongue made her question her gratefulness.

Wordlessly, Damian lifted her back into the centre of her bed, placing a warmed, damp cloth first to her forehead. A second cloth was used to gently wipe her mouth and hands. The naked concern in his eyes threatened to turn Kyra's stomach once more, her heart clenching at his pain.

Wendy slipped into the room, followed closely by Buddug and Raquel. The first two women immediately crossed the room to stand by Kyra's side, avoiding the mess without openly acknowledging it. Raquel threw one questioning look to Kyra, brief and full of worry, before turning her attention to ridding the room of the rapidly spreading smell of vomit.

"Are you okay? Do you need me to call Hannah?" Damian spoke softly, damp cloth lying forgotten on Kyra's bed beside her. She was momentarily distracted by the spreading damp spot seeping into her sheets. Damian's hand ran over her hair, stroking it to comfort her, to comfort himself.

"I can send for Healers," Buddug added, voice equally gentle. Kyra felt as though she were on her death bed, and they were gathering the strength to say goodbye for the final time.

Turning resolutely to Wendy, trusting the ever-pragmatic woman to not treat her like a child, Kyra asked blankly in a voice rasped raw, "Am I dying?" Wendy merely shook her head, fighting back a smile at Kyra's impertinence and Damian's barely muffled grunt of surprised horror. Buddug's eyes tightened, the only sign of her disapproval, but the movement screamed at Kyra in the silence, admonishing her. "How long until I can be on my feet again?"

Damian glanced at Raquel, still silently cleaning, before answering, "A week at most. Hannah will visit every day to ensure you're healing properly."

"What's that costing us?"

"That's not-" Damian began.

"What's it costing us?" Kyra repeated firmly. Raquel, probably sensing a conversation she had no wish to be caught in or around, hurried to complete her task. She paused only long enough to throw open the window before fleeing.

"Three months' supply," Wendy finally spoke up. Damian shot her a look of dark betrayal, hands darting out to hold Kyra down as she began to push herself up once more.

"Three months?" The question was spat, her eyes dark with anger at Damian's steely grip on her shoulders, keeping her firmly against the mattress. "Anything else I should know about?"

Kyra meant the question to be rhetorical for the most part. That didn't stop Buddug from replying anyway. "Leah got away." Her voice was calm, her tone even, as though discussing the weather.

Relief flooded Kyra's system, chased by a shot of fear, her insides seeming to turn to liquid at the words. Leaning back into her mattress more completely, her eyes slipped shut in a moment of selfish, stupid relief. It was momentary and fleeting, images of Leah again in the hands of the Church coming to mind. How long until she outlived her usefulness? They couldn't expect her to be allowed in again.

"She'll be dealt with," Damian assured with such solemnity Kyra half expected Leah to drop dead at the assertion alone.

"I think," Buddug began carefully, gaze sweeping between Damian's hard-set anger and Kyra's resigned defeat, "we may not want to take such drastic actions just yet."

Given the people in the room with her, Kyra would have placed Buddug last to suggest a peaceful resolution where Hunters were involved. Even speaking the words seemed to pain her, her eyes tight and mouth twitching down in a frown.

"Why?" Damian voiced the question, though it was no doubt shared by Wendy and Kyra as well. Buddug levelled a weighted look at him, whether for questioning her or for not immediately sharing her knowledge, it was hard to say.

"I know I only met her once, but she smelt wrong. She smelt of magic, strong enough that even Kyra should have noticed it." The admonition was clear, though gentle. "I don't think she chose to attack us of her own free will."

"How?" Kyra asked sharply. Under other circumstances, her tone would have resulted in a rebuke. "Humans can't-"

"It wasn't done by a human."

"Correct me if I'm wrong," Wendy broke in when it became clear her bosses had been shocked into silence, "but I thought humans can't do magic? And I can hardly imagine a demon willingly helping the Church. Or the Church using demon magic. Don't they think it's all evil?"

"That's what I thought," Kyra agreed, turning to Buddug.

"Humans can't do magic," she agreed.

"Are you saying demons are working with the Church? Or have they really gone so far as to hold our kind prisoner?" Damian asked, incredulous. Kyra couldn't help but mirror his disturbed shock. It wasn't a pleasant thought to contemplate.

Buddug shook her head. "No, I don't believe so."

"Are you going to tell us what you do believe? Or do we have to keep guessing?" Kyra would later blame the pain in her side for her tone. Whether Buddug would forgive her was another matter entirely.

"I think they have their own source. It didn't feel like any magic I know."

The silence that followed Buddug's statement, delivered on a resigned sigh, seemed so complete, Kyra was sure she had gone deaf. It couldn't be possible; it shouldn't be possible. It felt like everything she had known, everything she had long accepted as hard fact and had come to take for granted, was suddenly, painfully wrong. The way Damian's eyes widened, the way the whites seemed to have grown, suggested he was experiencing the same crisis.

"Well, shit," Wendy breathed into the silence. "What do we do now?"

~ Thirty-Five ~

It took Kyra less than two days to cause enough trouble for Damian and frustration for Wendy to be allowed back into her office, though she did require assistance to make it from her bed to her desk. She even deigned to use the elevator, though Wendy had to ensure it was empty before she would do so. Buddug had returned to her own small home, knowing a longer stay would only raise unwanted questions and place a target on The Rose. Despite her connections and numerous attempts to stay out of conflict, Kyra had gained enemies on all sides and would be attractive prey in such a weakened condition. As far as the outside world was concerned, Kyra was as strong as ever.

She was thankful to be at her desk, tapping ineffectually at the keys of her laptop, pretending to be thinking about anything other than Leah. Her eyes soaked in numbers and reports, signing off on expenses and approving purchases as though her side wasn't throbbing fitfully and her mind wasn't simultaneously focused on and avoiding a pale-eyed Hunter. Whatever lay before her, regardless of its importance, it never quite pierced the fog that had taken residence behind her eyes.

Sat in her throne, safely behind her desk, wrapped in her favourite glamour of powerful businesswoman, Kyra appeared completely in control. Damian could have questioned her on the Church having access to magic, could have told her a Hunter was knocking at their door, and she would have met it with calm certainty. The detectives could have returned with more questions or even accusations regarding Claire, and she would have dealt with them with quiet confidence. Buddug herself could have returned with news that all the other demon factions had joined the Church and they were focused solely on the destruction of their race, and she would have taken it in stride.

Buried beneath layers of careful control, her heart rallied against the walls of her chest. It raced and skipped and thudded roughly, beating on her ribs, demanding to be heard, to be felt. It reminded her of Leah and all the things that had gone wrong. It ensured Kyra would not forget, would not know a moment of peace, even as she pretended to be so entirely in control.

Kyra shoved at her laptop with impotent and directionless anger, the sudden movement sending piles of paperwork tilting alarmingly. Her fingers tightened around the hard edges of the machine, arms rising in a sweep of rage. The laptop stalled above her head, Kyra's movements abortive as she stopped short of throwing it across the room.

She itched to clear her desk in a violent sweep of her arm; her hands wanted to grab and throw and destroy. There was too much going on inside her head, inside her chest. It all boiled and grew, pressing against her edges and wanting to burst free in sharp movements of rage.

With forced calm, she put the laptop back down. Her fingers shook as she took her head in hand, trembles running through her frame as she fought to control the energy raging just below the surface. Tears stung at the corner of her eyes, just another outlet that refused to be ignored or suppressed. She was coming apart at the seams and couldn't possibly hold it all in. But she had to; there was no other choice.

Breathing slowly, counting the seconds between each inhale and exhale, Kyra wrapped her emotions in blankets of control. She lined up every thought, every feeling, and bundled each so tight they became indecipherable. They were nothing more than vague lumps of control. Strange shapes that may have once been feelings were now just another small annoyance to be ignored.

Kyra reached out blindly, pressing a button more out of habit than thought. She barely waited for the click that said Wendy had picked up the line before speaking. "Call Hannah."

"Are you in pain?"

"No, I need to make an appointment." Kyra hung up the line before Wendy could question any further.

Enthroned behind the power and prestige of her desk, Kyra felt caught in a limbo that went far beyond simply waiting for Wendy to confirm Hannah's availability. She could very easily make this her life.

She could use the excuse of Leah's betrayal and whatever magic the Church had used to orchestrate it to renege on her offer to Buddug. She could point to the obvious risks, to her own fragility, and claim it all too much. The flimsy excuses could be packed into something dense enough to hide behind. She could return to the easy normalcy she had created at The Rose.

The reasoning was sound; she was too injured to enter the fight as she had promised, too heartbroken to ever face the Church head on. With her carefully swaddled fears and heartbreak, she could live out the next few centuries as though the past few months had been nothing.

A few months ago, that was exactly what she would have done. Instead, Kyra pulled her laptop close once more and began drawing up a rough agreement for Hannah. It would be a large purchase, if it were possible, and would require some planning.

Her meeting with Hannah had been relatively quick, the witch understanding almost immediately what Kyra was after. Most of their time had been spent ironing out little details Kyra hadn't even known to think of, adding to and adjusting the rough agreement until they were both happy. The cost was high, but Kyra was more than willing to pay it. Before folding reality in that small way only a witch could, Hannah suggested Kyra eat sooner rather than later, her body needing more to recover effectively.

It was this advice in mind that Kyra asked Wendy to find a suitable meal within the day's appointments. Rather than Wendy sending a short email with her selected candidate, Damian strode into her office with a printed file in hand. He threw it down as he collapsed into his usual sprawl. For a second, Kyra could tell herself it was any other day, though the throbbing in her side was quick to dissuade that thought.

"Are you sure you're ready?"

"Hannah suggested it," she said.

"Why was Hannah here?" He lent forward in concern. "Are you okay? Does it hurt?"

"Only when I breathe." Kyra waved off his worry with a wry chuckle. "I just had some business to discuss with her, nothing to concern yourself with." Damian made a show of relaxing back into his chair, but his eyes remained sharp, and the tight line of his lips wouldn't ease. "As she was leaving, she suggested feeding would help me heal quicker."

"Maybe if you weren't pushing yourself so hard."

Kyra scoffed. "As if you wouldn't do the same. You're always telling me The Rose needs me, so I'm attending my duties." Kyra watched him carefully, watched the flash of angry hurt cross his features, watched him push it away roughly. "Have we heard from the detectives again?"

"No," he replied slowly, sensing a trap but unable to see it just yet. "Erik is thorough; they won't know to come here."

"Even if the Church were to give them a nudge?"

"They don't want you arrested any more than I do. They'd much rather deal with you themselves."

"I suppose," Kyra conceded. She cast her eyes around the room, looking for something, anything to stoke the fire she knew would be just below his surface. Kyra told herself she wanted to ensure he wouldn't treat her any differently following the fiasco that was Leah, but really, she was searching for some level of normalcy. Their fights were legendary, started at the smallest provocation, but today, she could think of nothing. "Has Buddug checked in?"

"Only to ask after how you're healing."

"And what did you tell her?" Kyra dragged herself to her feet, restless despite the way the movement pulled at the healing edges of her wound. Hannah had packed it with a mixture of strange plants pounded into a paste. It left an atrocious smell that not even Kyra's glamour could completely hide, but it seemed to help.

"That you were too stubborn to rest but seemed to be doing better." He watched her move slowly, each step carefully considered before being taken. Kyra wondered if he wanted to rise, wanted to help her with a gentle arm around her waist, wanted to admonish her with soft words. "She agrees that sleep would be the best course of action."

"And if I don't agree?" It took more energy than she would have liked to cross to the closest bookshelf, but she refused to let him see her stumble. If he knew she used the shelf to hold herself up under the guise of picking a tome, then so be it. When no answer came, she threw a questioning look over her shoulder, still full of stubborn attitude, daring him to ask if she needed help.

Instead, he shrugged, the move resigned and almost dismissive. "Is that all?" she continued to bait, turning herself to lean against the shelves, arms crossed beneath her breasts to hide the way her hands shook slightly. "Are you going soft in your old age?" She laughed, not cruelly but still with an air of teeth.

"Because I won't take your bait?" Even his retort was calm, sad, defeated. "Because I won't give in to your childishness? Tell me, Kyra, what could I possibly say or do that is going to cut any deeper than that?" He gestured vaguely to her side, eyes not leaving her own. Despite the soft tone, the near emotionless voice, his eyes burned. Kyra could read anger, unfettered rage, with a mix of sadness and disgust. "What's the point? I can't do any worse than you've done to yourself."

The words had barely registered, Kyra's mind caught in trying to decode the rush of emotions in his gaze, before he was gone. Even his movements had been strange, caught between slow defeat and quicksilver rage. He had risen jerkily, but his steps to the door had been measured. Kyra couldn't decide if he had been giving her time to call him back or demonstrating how little he cared if she did.

Walking carefully back to her desk, hands reaching out to grip the edge before she had drawn level with it, Kyra played the non-argument back in her head. Even in the moment, she knew he was right; she was being childish. And probably reckless and a million other little things she should have grown out of some decades ago. She just didn't know how to articulate to him that she was lost and confused and falling apart.

How was she meant to say how afraid she was? What words could she use to describe how much she wished none of this had happened? She wanted so badly to say she wished she had killed Leah, had never let the Hunter live. But even if she could find the words to voice such a thought, they'd both know it to be a lie. Even with her wound radiating muted pain, even with her heartache and listless, unfathomable future, Kyra could never wish Leah harm. And didn't that just suck?

~ Thirty-Six ~

That Buddug insisted on speaking with Kyra directly every day hadn't been a surprise. That Kyra had successfully negotiated it down to every other day had been the shock. Sure, it had taken more stubbornness than should have existed in the world, from both sides, but the agreement had been made. Kyra would call Buddug every second day until such a time as she was fully healed. Who would decide what "fully healed" meant was an argument for another day.

Kyra's arms took the lion's share of her weight as she stood over her scrying bowl. Her legs trembled with the effort despite being seated most of the day. Where she found the energy to ignore the waves of exhaustion, she couldn't say, but she still managed to call Buddug's name half-heartedly.

It was enough to form the connection, Buddug lending more power than strictly necessary to hold the line open between them. Kyra was quietly thankful for the additional support but voicing that thanks would be too much like admitting weakness. Even wounded, Kyra couldn't admit that.

"How are you healing?" Buddug asked immediately, eyes scanning what she could see of Kyra's face and shoulders.

"Hannah suggests I feed more regularly, at least until the wound has closed entirely."

"How often?"

"Once a week should suffice."

"Make it every five days," she ordered.

"Yes, Buddug." If it came out on a sigh, Kyra couldn't help that.

"If you had just killed that Hunter, like you should have-" Buddug began, but Kyra cut her off, surprising them both.

"Leah," she said forcefully. "Her name is Leah, not 'that Hunter,' not 'that woman,' not 'that human.' Leah." Buddug's reflection, shining up from the depths of the scrying bowl, registered shock and no small amount of anger as she quirked an eyebrow at Kyra's strong tone. "Her name is Leah, and I will not have her disrespected."

"She stabbed you," Buddug pointed out, tone flat though it should have been spiked with anger or darkened by disapproval.

"She loved me." Kyra's heart twisted, the words something she hadn't even dared to think, to hope were true. Yet she knew them to be correct, knew it in the same way that she knew Leah yet lived. Leah was alive and under the influence of magic even Buddug didn't recognise. Leah was alive and in danger as long as she was under the Church's sway. And Kyra was the only one who could save her.

The only one who would save her.

"And I love her. I wish I didn't, I wish I could stop, but I can't. I love her, and I think..." Kyra drew a deep breath, steeling herself against the words she had to say, against the truth that she could no longer deny. "I think I'm going to have to save her."

If the silence with Damian had been hard, the quiet way Buddug gazed up at her was torture. Unlike Damian, not even her eyes gave an indication of her thoughts. To see her face shift, to even see her blink, would have been a relief. Buddug's face seemed frozen; the only thing telling Kyra the connection was still strong was the buzz of Buddug's magic beneath her skin and behind her eyes.

"Whether or not you support me in this, I know it's the right thing to do," Kyra continued, needing to fill the silence. "I know she's a human and a Hunter and everything you've taught me to hate, but I can't. I just can't hate her."

Buddug's impassive face stirred fear in Kyra's breast. Every old fear of disappointing her mentor, of not being enough, came rushing to the surface. It warred against her love for Leah and the certainty of her knowledge that Leah would die without her help.

In the face of Buddug's silent judgement, her mind whirled. What if she was wrong? What if Leah didn't love her? What if her feelings weren't returned? Panic rose in crushing waves, flooding her mind even as it twisted her stomach into hard knots. Her already shaking hands, weakened by the wound that seemed to scream Leah's hatred, gripped the altar in a fight to keep Kyra balanced.

"Even if I'm wrong," the words tumbled out without thought, half muttered under her breath as she tried to convince herself, "even if she doesn't love me, even if she never wants to see me again. I have to try. I have to save her."

Tears ran down her cheeks, the sensation distant as Kyra forced herself to meet Buddug's impassive gaze. She wanted to flinch back, to scrub the signs of weakness from her eyes. Mostly, she wanted to feel the warmth of Leah in her arms again, wanted to taste her lips and know she was safe from a world full of threats. The tears continued to roll down her face, and for once in Kyra's life, she wore them as badges of pride and pain.

Standing there, barely propped up against the altar, staring her mentor down from the bottom of a scrying bowl, Kyra felt naked and unmasked. There was nothing left to say, nothing left between herself and the world. There was only her and her heart, still beating, still aching, wanting nothing more than to run out the door and find Leah. It was exhilarating and terrifying all at once.

"If that's what you must do, then that is what you will do," Buddug finally spoke, face still solemn but tone soft. "But Kyra..." She paused, ensuring her protege was completely focused on her next words. "Know that this will make you the most hated person, for both demons and the Church. If you do this, there is no turning back. You will have placed yourself at the centre of my war, whether you like it or not, and I can't promise we will always be fighting on the same side."

"I know." Though Kyra knew there were threats Buddug was alluding to that she didn't yet know or understand, she could grasp the seriousness of her decision. "Whatever side we end up on, I hope I will do you proud."

"You always have." Buddug smiled then. It was small and wry, twisted in sadness that would no doubt blanket their relationship. Kyra could hope it wouldn't all come to that, but it was hard to picture a future with Leah at her side that didn't involve constant risk.

With her mind so firmly made up, Kyra half hoped a fully formed plan would just fall into place with it. That this wasn't the case was both disappointing and disheartening. Lying in the well-worn grooves of her nest, mind toying with sleep, Kyra struggled to focus on potential avenues of attack. In the darkness of night, made all the deeper by her tightly drawn curtains and eyes squeezed shut, it was increasingly difficult to think of anything that wasn't Leah in danger, Leah in pain, Leah on the edge of death.

The cold corners of her mind threw up images of Leah's pale face, the remaining colour drained to be painted across her chest in crimson swaths of blood. Would she arrive just in time to watch the bright, ever curious light fade from her eyes?

Alone in the dark, it was hard not to question her choice, harder to not be swallowed whole by her rising panic. Doubt thrived in the fertile soil of her thoughts, finding every crack and crevice to bloom into something darker. Kyra rolled gently to her other side, keeping her wings carefully folded through the movement. She fought to keep her breathing from speeding further, to keep her mind focused solely on the passage of air through her lungs in measured breaths.

The burn of air lessened gradually, but Kyra refused to relinquish the tight control over her thoughts. Not until her heart stopped racing, not until her stomach stopped churning. Her fingertips tingled as they spasmed against her chest, clutched tight and close within the folds of her wings.

Rationally, she knew blind panic would help no one and nothing. Rationally, she knew sleep was the best course of action for the moment. Rationally, she knew she was better help to Leah well rested and coherent, not caught in spiralling concern in the dead of night. Rationally, she knew a great many things. Unfortunately, rationality seemed to be as attainable as Leah was, so far out of reach it was hard to even picture.

Despite her best efforts, dawn greeted a bleary eyed and vaguely grouching Kyra. Sleep had been slow in coming and fitful, broken by nightmares of Leah and the Church and dark-eyed Hunters making tiny cuts on pale flesh. Rolling from the comforting hold of her nest, Kyra forced herself to move the stiffness from her muscles. Her side throbbed with each step she took, but it was a minor thing. It seemed so distant compared to the pounding of her temples.

Her steps wavered, no matter how closely she focused on placing each foot solidly on the ground as she stumbled to the bathroom. The first splash of cold water on her face did well to mute the still ringing screams in her ears. The second rush, drank directly from the tap, washed the sleep from her mouth and brain. Brushing her teeth and drawing a glamour around her shoulders pushed the last of her fatigue to the back of her mind, burying it deep enough that she could pretend successfully that it didn't exist at all.

The wound in her side was beginning to itch. Kyra resisted the urge to scratch but couldn't help but finger the edges of Hannah's tightly packed mixture through the magic of her glamour. Itching was good; itching meant healing. Itching also gave a point of focus, of distraction, something to hone in on when the thoughts became too much. Kyra used that point of focus as she steeled herself for her greatest challenge since being stabbed; the back stairs.

Though she was breathing harder than she would have liked when she plopped into her chair, accomplishment still buoyed her heart. She cradled the feeling tightly, taking strength in the knowledge she was getting better, was healing. With that strength, Kyra turned her mind back to the decision from the previous night. She was going to do this. She was going to save Leah. The how still alluded her.

Organising her thoughts, or at least forcing them into a semblance of a useful order, Kyra tried to ignore the apparent enormity of the task ahead. Bite-sized chunks, she chanted to herself. Manageable pieces. First, to find Leah. She had options there, various favours to call in or promise. That was possible. A fraction of her panic subsided.

Getting to Leah would be harder and completely dependent on where she was. That she was still in the city was something Kyra was taking for granted. Even if she couldn't safely return to The Rose, Leah was still most useful where she could do the most damage to Kyra.

That Leah wasn't yet dead was something else Kyra was taking for granted. There would be use left in Leah yet, probably still some knowledge to gain, some secret left to learn. That Kyra had so willingly answered Leah's questions, had given the Hunter knowledge, was still a source of guilt Kyra tried very hard to ignore. The risks she had taken, the threats she had created, because she'd been entranced by pale eyes and burning curiosity.

Kyra pushed the guilt aside and forced herself to focus. There was nothing to do for it now but mitigate the damage. The siren call of her spiralling thoughts was alluring, but this was too important to fall into old habits. Her hand moved automatically to her phone to call Wendy. Kyra pulled herself up short, plagued by a new doubt.

Pushing herself forward, she pressed the button resolutely. "Wendy?" she asked after the telltale click. "Can you come in here a minute?" The other woman didn't answer, the line simply going dead. Kyra didn't even have enough time to question the wisdom of her decision before Wendy was entering the room.

"What do you need?" It was hard not to feel a sense of calm confidence in Wendy's presence. The pragmatic woman may not have been such a permanent fixture as Buddug or Damian to The Rose and Kyra's life, but her company was no less soothing.

"If I told you I was going to get Leah back, would you be willing to help?" Kyra tried not to let trepidation enter her voice, tried not to let her doubt show.

"When do we leave?"

It was harder to hold back her relieved smile. That part was dealt with, at least.

"As soon as I can find her."

~ Thirty-Seven ~

Before she could even begin the search, Kyra knew she had a few more difficult conversations ahead of her. She waited an hour to give her aching muscles time to rest before pushing them to their limits by climbing the stairs. Wendy had offered to ensure the elevator was clear, but she wasn't going to prove she could get Leah back if she couldn't even master a set of stairs.

The wood of Damian's door felt darker than its identical mate on either side, and she couldn't tell if the tremble in her limbs was from the walk or the deeply ingrained fear that he would turn her away. Despite his unwavering loyalty over the years, she knew he was far more angry, far more disappointed, than he had ever been before. Kyra lifted her hand, curled into a loose fist, and knocked.

The shock of knuckles against wood did nothing to reduce the flutter of anxiety in her middle. In the seconds it took him to move loud enough to be heard, Kyra had managed to convince herself he had either retreated to his office or left The Rose for good. Both situations involved him not speaking to Kyra again.

"What do you want?" he asked in way of greeting, voice rough with sleep. Apparently, she hadn't been the only one to have a restless night. This did nothing to ease the monster-sized butterflies swarming her stomach.

"Can I come in?" She was proud of herself for keeping her voice calm and even. Rather than respond, Damian stood aside and waved her in dismissively.

His room was dim, curtains pulled tight and bed a mess of tangled blankets. Tucked in the corner was his own altar, though smaller than Kyra's, with its own bowl, candle, and mound of dirt. Beside it was a modest desk flush with the wall, despite him having his own office. Kyra walked with forced stability, knowing any sign of weakness would be noted and catalogued for later. For this conversation to be successful, he couldn't suspect the effort it took her. That didn't stop her from taking the chair at his desk without being offered. Kyra waited for Damian to settle himself on the edge of his bed before speaking.

"I wanted to apologise," she began. It was hard not to be slightly insulted by the open surprise on his face, but drawing attention to it would have only shown he was right in calling her childish. "Not just for the other day. Not just for the whole Leah situation, for everything.

"I know I'm not the easiest person to work for, work with," she quickly corrected at a raised brow. "I know I'm an even harder person to be friends with. I'm dismissive and vindictive and far too much of a coward to claim to be any kind of leader. More than that, I pretend I know better than everyone else when the truth is I have no idea what I'm doing.

"I pick stupid fights and constantly hurt you because I'm afraid. I'm afraid I'm doing the wrong things. I'm afraid I'm leading everyone down the wrong path. I'm afraid I'm going to get people killed. I'm afraid I'm going to get you killed." Kyra let her words rush without filter, without thought, and Damian seemed content to simply listen. "I'm constantly swinging between wanting to keep you close because I have no idea what to do without you and wanting to push you away because I know I can only get you hurt. I know we're demons; I know risk comes with the territory. Hell, I know I've created a massive target for our backs simply by running The Rose, but I don't know how else to keep everyone safe."

Damian barked a mirthless laugh, effectively silencing Kyra with the cutting sound. "Do you think we can't protect ourselves?"

"Of course not." Leaning forward, tone near pleading, Kyra didn't know if the words existed to make him understand. "I know you can, but you shouldn't have to. Everyone here is counting on me to protect them, to look after them. They follow my rules, work these halls, because they know it's what's required to receive that protection."

"Half the people here don't give a shit about your protection." Damian snapped, causing Kyra to pull back sharply. "We're not here just because you can keep us safe from the Church. This isn't just a case of safety in numbers; we're here because we care for you and believe in you. You've made The Rose a home. You've made us a family, and that's more important than a few charms."

"It's more than a few charms," she muttered petulantly, drawing a flash of a smile from Damian. They both sobered at her next words. "Regardless of why they are here, regardless of what keeps them, I have failed them. I've failed you." Kyra forced herself to her feet, allowing Damian to see the effort it took. "I am not strong. I am not heartless. I fell in love with a Hunter, someone who has pretty actively tried to kill me, and I'm going to save her."

Damian considered her words, considered her as she forced her knees straight. "You haven't failed anyone." Damian rose slowly, arm out to offer support. He waited for Kyra to step forward, more a stumble than anything, before wrapping a strong arm beneath her shoulder to hook at her uninjured side. "How are we going to get her back?"

Turning in his grasp, Kyra pulled Damian into a tight hug, ignoring the way her side throbbed uncomfortably against the pressure. They rarely embraced, but that didn't stop him from returning the hug with feeling. "Thank you," she breathed into his hair. She hadn't realised how much she had needed his support until she had it. If he had refused her apology, refused to help, she would have found a way forward anyway, but having him by her side was a greater comfort than she had anticipated. "Can you gather everyone not currently working? Staff meeting in the kitchen, in about ten minutes?"

He nodded his assent, gently extracting himself. Damian eyed Kyra closely to ensure she could comfortably stand without support before leaving the room.

Even with her head start on everyone else, Kyra was still one of the last ones to make it to the kitchen. She had been determined to brave the stairs once more, though she was more than glad when Sam offered her his seat.

Kyra settled herself at the table, watching the final few stragglers find spaces around the edges of the room. Wendy hovered in the doorway, attention split between Kyra and the front of house.

"Thanks," Kyra began awkwardly, smiling around at the faces she knew so well. Most wore expressions of vague curiosity with a tinge of concern, though some were struggling to hide boredom and impatience. "I know I usually leave this kind of thing to Damian, but I thought it was important you heard this from me directly.

"I know Leah's appearance and subsequent stay with us caused a bit of stir. And I know her departure was a shock too." Kyra took a fortifying breath, forcing herself to meet the eyes of those around her. "She came back a few nights ago and stabbed me." A shocked murmur ran through their ranks, though no one spoke loud enough to stop Kyra from continuing. "She didn't do this of her own free will; she was possessed. We don't know how the Church managed it, and while finding out is definitely a priority moving forward, I'm going to do everything I can to save her.

"I don't expect any of you to help, and I wouldn't blame anyone who wanted to leave, but this is something I have to do." She cast another look around the room, surprised to see so many faces set in determination. There was no fear, no hatred, not a hint of question.

"What do you need from us?" Wendy asked from the doorway, still keeping half an ear out for any visitors.

"Nothing," Kyra breathed on a sigh of relief. "I just need you all to know that this is what I'm doing. It's going to put us in more danger, if that's possible, and it'd be unfair if you didn't know."

"Leah's family." Bell's voice carried from the corner of the room. Various voices raised themselves in agreement, with more than one suggesting the ways in which they could help save the Hunter. It felt surreal, sitting in the middle of a group of demons, planning how best to save someone trained in killing them. Kyra didn't expect the surge of warmth, of pure love, that came over her. For a moment, she was ashamed for ever doubting them, but a knowing look from Damian, delivered with a gentle smile, banished that too.

With the support of The Rose behind her, Kyra knew there was one last person she needed to talk to. Though Buddug knew vaguely of her plans, it felt important to voice them clearly. Proving to Damian that she had learnt was one thing; proving to Buddug that she had the strength to undertake something so dangerous was another matter entirely. Giving in to the pressures of her body and the looks from Wendy and Damian, Kyra took the elevator to get back to her room.

Kyra considered the empty depths of her scrying bowl at length. Her chair was abandoned to the side of her altar, the shivers of effort confined to her legs for now.

There was every chance Buddug wouldn't answer. She was a busy woman and couldn't be expected to be available at Kyra's beck and call. While a part of Kyra wanted badly to put it off or avoid it altogether, she knew that if she didn't have this conversation now, she probably never would. At this point, the worst Buddug could do was say no. With that in mind, Kyra steeled herself to ask for a favour that was very likely to be denied and called for her mentor.

"What's wrong?" Buddug's borderline fear made Kyra miss the days of being greeted with a grave 'Kyranthine.'

"Nothing." For a moment she considered not asking, considered making a barely plausible excuse and chalking the whole thing up to pain delirium. "I need your help." The words were out before she could stop them, for better or worse.

"Of course." The solemnity had returned, though the concern was never far from the surface.

"I need your help finding Leah. I'm going to do this with or without you, but I would rather have you at my side."

Buddug's face twitched, though whether in shock or anger, Kyra couldn't say. That she had let any emotion show at all spoke volumes. Before Kyra could plead her case or even find the words to do so, Buddug's face disappeared from beneath the water's surface. A step, the smell of ozone, and then Buddug was beside her. Her scowl was frightening, to say the least, but that she had made the trip at all bode well.

"I'll need something of hers." Buddug's tone was matter of fact. There were things to do, and wasting time was antithesis to her.

~ Thirty-Eight ~

Kyra walked the few doors down to Leah's room. It didn't matter that the Hunter had been gone for some months, and no one had made any effort to claim or reclaim the space. Whether it was because it was Leah's room and would remain as such or because they feared Kyra's wrath, she wasn't sure.

The room tasted of stale air and smelt of disuse. It was hard to move through the space without being reminded of Leah's bright smile, endless curiosity, and strange ability to disarm everyone she met.

Kyra moved quickly, more to save herself any additional pain than to get the ritual underway. She made short work of scouring the room. Very little had been left behind, the only thing close enough to what Buddug needed being a hairbrush. A few strands, near translucent in their paleness, were caught amongst the bristles.

"Will this do?" Kyra waved the brush towards Buddug as she pushed her way back into her own room. Buddug took the proffered item without comment, carefully pulling the stray hairs from the bristles before throwing the brush aside. The hairs were dropped in Kyra's scrying bowl, the usually clear water clouded with a selection of herbs collected from the kitchen, and a drop of Kyra's own blood.

Buddug chanted over the concoction in a low voice, the words harsh and guttural. The demon tongue sounded foreign in the air, as though they pushed against the very fabric of reality in an attempt to break free. The words bled together, becoming indistinguishable, a droning sound carried on the waves of a halting melody. Buddug's voice managed to carry layers of harmony, magic overlapping and echoing in every note.

Kyra hovered awkwardly in the corner as she tried to both stay out of the way and watch Buddug work. It was mildly fascinating to watch the way in which Buddug drew on the power of their magic, the connection of Leah's hair, and the love of Kyra's blood. The throb of power was familiar, but the shape Buddug was creating with it was closer to something a witch would do. For all her brute strength and fine control, Kyra had no hope of emulating the way Buddug was weaving their power into a fine fabric of magic. All Kyra knew was the bite of sharp edges and blunt force pleasure.

Buddug's chanting sped gradually, gaining in volume and tempo in equal measure until it seemed she was near screaming an endless stream of sounds. The air became charged with magic, electricity dancing between every atom, every molecule carrying a current as they collided into one another, filling the space with minuscule explosions of power.

Buddug threw her head back, spine arching as the current of magic ran through her body. The chanting didn't falter; Buddug didn't falter. Kyra ached to reach out and take some of the pain coursing through her mentor's body. To call on the powers Buddug danced with would cause untold pain.

With her eyes screwed shut tight against the agonised fire in her veins, Buddug didn't slow. Kyra could feel the crescendo build, could feel the impending crest as the surge of power threatened to consume everything.

At the peak, where Buddug could chant no faster, raise her voice no higher, she cut off into silence. The transition from chanting to silence, power to stillness, was stark. Kyra felt like she had walked from a fire just to be thrown into an icy pool, and her body didn't know how to adjust to the drastic change.

"I know where she is," Buddug croaked.

Buddug helped Kyra into her office without obviously appearing to do so, their arms linked like old friends to hide the way in which Kyra lent on her so heavily for support. Damian and Wendy were already waiting in the room, sat beside the desk as though this were any other day, as though they weren't all about to risk their lives for Kyra's heart.

"She's in a safe house on the other side of the city," Kyra announced as they entered the room, not wanting to waste another second. "I can be there and back in a few hours."

"You're not going alone." Damian half rose to help Buddug with Kyra, but their mentor waved him away.

"As the only one here able to actually hold their own in a physical fight, I think I should go." Wendy watched impassively as Buddug deposited Kyra in her chair, standing beside the heavy monstrosity like a silent guard.

"I have to go," Kyra shook her head. "This is my fight."

"Our fight." Damian corrected. His mouth was set hard, prepared to argue Kyra into a grudging submission.

"We all go." Three sets of eyes turned to Buddug with open confusion. "Kyra is right. This is her fight, and she must go. Where she goes, Damian goes. Wendy will protect us."

"And you?" Kyra was glad for the support, but she needed to know her mentor's motivations. The fact that they still may end up enemies weighed heavily on her.

"I will continue to maintain a connection with her in case she runs."

That it was so easily decided should have made Kyra suspicious, but instead, it was gratitude that flooded her system as everyone nodded their assent. Once they were decided, it seemed laughably easy to coordinate their next steps. Sam was left with strict instructions to ensure operations ran as though nothing were amiss, with Erik being ordered to remain on site until their return. Even slime ball protection was better than nothing.

Wendy picked the least conspicuous car from their small fleet, a white monstrosity that Kyra affectionately referred to as a soccer mum car. Buddug helped Kyra settle into the back seat with her while Damian rode shotgun. Kyra tried to ignore the periodical concerned glances he sent her way, instead practising what she'd say to Leah when they found her. The sickening smell of plastic and upholstery assaulted her, the scent sharp and overpowering in the small space. She hated the smell of new car, of cars in general. They had always felt so pointless when you could slice holes in reality with magic.

The drive felt both painfully short and to drag on forever. Kyra found she had no idea what she would say to Leah. Any potential declarations of love or apologies or odes to her eyes were driven from her mind as they pulled up outside a disappointingly average house. Nestled in a quiet neighbourhood in the heart of the suburbs, leafy trees lined the road while raining foliage on the parked cars crowding the already painfully narrow street.

The fact that it was so picturesque, yet so decidedly dull, made it the perfect place for a safe house. The small brick home was a near carbon copy of the buildings on either side and across the street. Even the well-kept lawn with a few rose bushes seemed to blend in with its surrounds.

Lights were barely visible, shinning at the edges of closed curtains. Up and down the street, people were succumbing to the growing dark, windows glowing in an attempt to banish the coming night. The last edges of the sun had sunken below the horizon, taking with it the sharp reds, pinks, and oranges that had bathed the world. Despite the greyness of the non-light that filled the space between dusk and night, there was still a sense of greenery and life to the street.

Kyra watched as another light was turned on within the house that was their target. She couldn't help but wonder if that was the room Leah was in. Did she flick the switch? Or was it turned on in a moment of harsh reality, pulling her from a tortured stupor in preparation for more questions?

Wendy cut the ignition with a flick of her wrist, though none of them made any move to leave the vehicle. Buddug's brow was furrowed in concentration beside Kyra, but that was far from her mind. The knowledge that Leah was in there, potentially hurt, maybe being tortured, made her fingers itch. Her leg had started jumping with barely repressed energy at some point, and now she couldn't stop it, even if she tried.

"I'll go first." Wendy spoke with such conviction, not even Kyra was going to argue with her. "Once I signal it's all clear, Damian follows."

"No," Kyra interjected. "I need to see her first."

"We'll both go," he soothed, anxious to get the whole mess dealt with. Wendy threw him a look that said she was less than impressed with his concession but said nothing more.

Instead, she simply undid her seatbelt and slid out of the car. She crossed the street in long strides, barely glancing to check for oncoming traffic. Bypassing the front door, she disappeared down the side of the house into what Kyra assumed was the backyard.

The proceeding five minutes were hell, for all they felt like an hour. In the closed space of the car interior, all Kyra could hear was the echoing sounds of their breathing. Buddug's was sharp and shallow, her mind still submerged in magic. Damian's was deeper, as though he was forcing himself to remain calm, forcing his breathing into a regimented pattern. Kyra's own fought to synchronise with both of them at once, slipping from near panicked panting to forced meditation with every passing moment. It was a relief to see Wendy return, this time from the front door, her slim body appearing long enough to wave them inside.

Kyra beat Damian to the door by a few steps, despite the way her side was beginning to ache with renewed vigour. Wendy's face appeared briefly in the small window beside the door, gesturing for them to get inside. It was hard not to glance guiltily around, but that would have only made it all the more obvious that they didn't belong there.

They had adopted glamours as plain as their nature would allow, wearing masks of average height and build. They were still unfairly attractive; Kyra with her lightly tanned skin, chestnut hair, eyes of clear skies, and Damian a darker and broader copy of her features. Kyra took comfort in their familial appearances.

Steeling herself, for what she didn't know, Kyra opened the door with forced calm. Damian followed on her heels while still appearing to be sauntering without care. Once the door was safely closed behind them, they dropped the act and their glamours, casting fervent eyes around the entryway.

The doorway to her left, spilling light into the unlit hall, revealed an empty lounge room. The furniture was clean, made of simple lines and affordable materials. Everything seemed perfectly placed, down to a blanket draped just so over the arm of the couch. It looked like it belonged in a catalogue or brochure, something selling homes at reasonable prices, displaying all the best of middle-class dreams.

A sound from deeper in the house, presumably the kitchen, drew them down the hall. Bedroom doors stood ajar on the left, and Kyra glanced into each to ensure their dark maws were truly empty.

Like the lounge, the kitchen was well lit. Wendy stood over the sink, washing her hands perfunctorily. A man sat at the table, carefully bound to a matching wooden chair with the zip ties Wendy favoured. Each limb was tied separately, his ankles to a chair leg each and his arms bound to the outer horizontal slats of the chair back. Wendy had ensured he had little hope of freedom.

The man eyed Kyra and Damian as they entered, mouth drawn into a tight line that suggested he wouldn't be sharing anything useful any time soon.

~ Thirty-Nine ~

Kyra would have said she took a chair opposite the bound Hunter as a power move, allowing Damian to stand behind her as silent guardian. Damian probably would have said it was because she had pushed herself too hard all day and needed the rest. Wendy took her designated space over Kyra's other shoulder, forming a united front.

"Where is Leah?" Kyra forced her tone into calm confidence, knowing that showing even a hint of concern would be used against her. She made a show of examining the curved cruelty of her claw-like nails, his answer unimportant, his cooperation a given.

"I won't tell you anything," the Hunter spat. Usually, Kyra was happy to drag things out, play the long game, as it were. There was danger in appearing too eager, but there was a risk in taking her time too. It was a careful line to walk, and she wasn't sure if she had the patience for it today.

Kyra leaned forward with smooth purpose, allowing her bare breasts to rest against her arms folded on the table. She reached out with senses beyond her body, flexing muscles that seemed to exist both outside of her and throughout her entire form. They wrapped around him, reading his desires and tasting his lust.

She wasn't his first succubus, though she was probably the strongest he'd ever faced. The way he held his lust tightly controlled, buried under layers of denial, he managed to hold it both extremely close and entirely separate all at once. It felt as though he had built walls around his desires, carving any sense of sexual want from himself, almost like cleaving his own heart from his breast. Kyra was impressed, though hardly deterred.

Fingers of magic pressed harder at the edges as Kyra explored his carefully crafted walls with the hands of her mind. They were smooth as glass, cold as ice, and stronger than any metal she had ever felt. She traced every inch, pressed hard, touched fleetingly, barely brushed the surface, and threw her strength against it. A smirk pulled at the Hunter's mouth as though he could feel her presence, could guess her intentions, and knew her to be failing.

From every possible angle, she examined the fortress that was his lust. She would have been impressed, grudgingly so, if it weren't for the inconvenience of it all. She had to find Leah; she had to know where she had gone. Where she had been taken. This man was standing in her way. Kyra cultivated her frustration, her rage, drew it close, and used it to fuel her power.

She focused on Leah, hurt and alone. She focused on the pain in her side. She focused on Buddug, on the war that was threatening to define them, no matter how hard she had avoided it. She focused on Damian, the risks he was taking for her.

There it was: a crack. The smallest sliver of weakness. A tiny fracture, barely perceptible and easily overlooked. Kyra honed her anger, her power, into the thinnest blade. She forged it into a trickle of air, let it press into the fracture, let it flow into the crack. Her magic wormed into the breach, filling it, expanding it. As a chest expands with breath, she filled the space until it lengthened, forcing it to deepen. A crunch, heard without making a sound, and the crack split enough for her power to touch his lust. Greedily, her magic surged forward, tearing at the hole to make it larger, exposing more desire to her influence.

The surge of Kyra's triumph was fleeting. The Hunter's smirk twisted darkly, the vicious cast to his eyes sending a thrill of unease through Kyra.

Something sharp, carrying the weight of a mountain, sliced through her power. Cut so close to the source, her magic whipped back at her like a physical blow, leaving her momentarily stunned. The world was silent as her ears rang with the force of it, her eyes trying desperately to blink away the bright lights of pain. A high-pitched whistle grew in intensity before slowly losing pitch and volume as the world rematerialised around her.

The first thing Kyra noticed was the Hunter laughing manically across from her. Wendy had moved, her presence gone from Kyra's side. Damian was saying something, but Kyra couldn't hear him over the laughter, over the whistle still dying in her ears. The sharp sound of an open-handed slap cut all other noises short, Wendy standing over the Hunter with an unreadable face.

"What happened?" Damian demanded again, the hand on Kyra's shoulder drawing more attention than his question had.

"I...I don't know." She raised a hand to her head, surprised when it came away dry. She had expected blood or sweat at the least. The pounding that had taken residence behind her eyes was heavy enough to warrant blood, surely. "I don't know what he did." Forcing herself to think past the pain, Kyra tried to take stock. Something was wrong, she knew it, but it was hard to identify when the ringing in her ears seemed to have migrated to her brain. Other than the throbbing of her knife wound and pounding of her head, she was physically fine. But she wasn't. If only her mind would clear long enough to think.

She turned back to the Hunter, thankfully quiet for now, and tried reaching out with her power once more. It was like reaching out into nothing. There was no Hunter, no desire. Like waking in pitch black, unable to see her own arm before her, she couldn't even find herself in the darkness that enveloped her mind. For a horrible moment, she wondered if she even existed, the whole world having disappeared from around her.

"What did you do?" She hissed, unable to stop the fear leaking into her voice. She had never been cut off from her power. She couldn't even feel the barest hint of magic. There was a hole in her mind, a hole in her. The vast emptiness she had felt watching Leah leave was nothing compared to this. Leah had left jagged edges, scar tissue, and things to heal. There was nothing, no clean edges, no hint of wound, just a crushing void. The Hunter only began laughing again.

Wendy delivered a sharp jab to his solar plexus. He was knocked momentarily breathless, though his pathetic wheezes for air still seemed to carry laughter. Damian looked from the Hunter to Kyra and back again, trying to understand.

"What's wrong?"

"He..." How to describe it? How to put something so horrifying? "He cut me off."

"Cut you off? What do you mean?"

"I can't feel it. I can't feel my power." There was no masking the terror, as though putting it into words made it more real. "I can't feel him. I can't feel anything."

~ Forty ~

The words had barely left Kyra before the Hunter was laughing again. The sound was cut short when Wendy unceremoniously forced a dishcloth into his mouth. Kyra hoped distantly it wasn't clean. Without needing any further words or explanation, Damian laid his hands on Kyra's head. His fingers found her temples, his large frame warm and comforting behind her.

She felt his presence in her mind weakly, the sensation dull and distant when it should have burned brightly. He pressed along the edges of where her magic should have been, his touch light and gentle. It took all of Kyra's will not to pull away, physically and mentally. Neither of them were healers, and this wasn't something that should be possible. But still, he felt around the corners of her pain, searching for a spark of life.

He was clumsy in his rush, his touch too light in his attempts to avoid doing further damage. Kyra wanted so badly to take over, to do it herself, as though such a thing were possible.

She fought against her every instinct and remained perfectly still as Damian worked. Fear was rapidly replacing the shock in her system, and Kyra had to focus on the touch of Damian's skin, of Damian's magic, to avoid succumbing to the urge to hyperventilate or vomit.

The fingers of Damian's magic gripped the edges of the gaping maw in Kyra, trying to push them together to close over the empty expanse where her power should have been. When that didn't work, he pushed his own magic into the depths, trying to fill a void with an energy that didn't belong there. Though the power had come from her in a distant sense, it was too far changed to fit, too different to do anything other than disappear into the hungry depths.

Kyra could feel Damian tiring, could feel the strain in his magic as he forced it into unnatural poses. It wasn't made for this; he wasn't made for this. The situation shouldn't have been possible in the first place.

"Don't," she breathed, wanting to save him from himself. "You can't."

"I can," he said, pressing harder with his magic. Kyra gasped against the pain but didn't try to speak again.

Damian flexed and pushed, muscles bunching and stretching beyond their usual reach. He clawed at the barrier between the world and the burning purity of magic, tearing into it with the fingers of his mind. Kyra couldn't fight the shudder that ran through her body, feeling the veil tear, even so slightly, set her teeth on edge. It was wrong, the pain of it slicing into her mind, though it was nothing compared to the emptiness of her magic.

It had to have been burning him; it had to be torture. Pained grunts fell from Damian's lips, but they went unnoticed compared to the way he screamed in Kyra's mind. With one hand curled protectively over the space where her magic belonged, the other tangled in pure power that should have been beyond his reach, and Damian forced the two together.

Where it caused him pain, it was like ecstasy for Kyra. The wash of magic, a light too white to be visible, a dark too deep to compare. It surrounded her; it filled her every atom. Crystalline energy flowed into the hole in her mind, filling it, over filling it, until it washed over and flooded her.

Damian's hands fell away, both in her mind and at her body, but she didn't notice, couldn't feel it over the surge of power. Every nerve was alive with magic, pulsing with raw strength. Her body was swollen with it, waves of pleasure cresting but never allowing her release. Her every nerve was alight with it, bathed in a fire of pleasure.

It was the rush of lust caught in a permanent feedback loop, when it was held at the perfect moment of not being too much, of not being enough. It was the height of an earth-shattering orgasm shared with the perfect soul. It was everything beautiful about her power, everything she had ever refused herself, every perfect possibility she had scorned in favour of those she judged to be evil, those she felt deserved to be fed from.

Tears ran unbidden down her cheeks, the pleasure never growing to pain, even as it devoured her. It drove everything from her mind; she didn't know her own name, didn't know if she even existed physically beyond the ecstasy of magic. There was nothing except the taste of power, the burn of magic. There was nothing but the need to consume.

Turning her attention to the still bound Hunter, he wasn't laughing any longer. Had he been laughing at all? Had anything existed before this surge of power? It didn't matter. Kyra stood slowly, crossing around the table to caress his cheek. He tried to flinch back but was easily caught in the grip of her taloned fingers. The sharp points of her nails broke his skin, blood trickling down to stain her palm. She swooped down without thought, her tongue tasting the cooper of his blood as her magic screamed to taste his life.

Without pulling away, Kyra trailed her lips across his cheek. Her other hand darted out to remove the cloth pressed into his mouth, and he barely had a moment to suck in a greedy lungful of air before his mouth was covered by the press of her lips.

Fangs pressed at the soft flesh of his lips, threatening to break the skin. A groan bubbled up his chest, catching at the back of his throat. Kyra wouldn't let it go further, wouldn't let him breathe, wouldn't let him be anything beyond a conduit for the magic calling for his life.

Power pulsed from her, enveloping the Hunter in light and bathing him in pleasure. He could feel her touch all over, like licks of flame across his skin and breaths of ice across his mind. His blood sung with pleasure, so pure it ached. And still, she kissed him. The nails on his cheek bit deeper, but the pain was distant, a counterpoint to the way his body begged for more.

The flood of power continued through the tear Damian had created. It was consuming Kyra, consuming the Hunter. It was too much. She couldn't stop it, couldn't control it. It would swallow her whole.

"Kyra." The word didn't fully pierce the roar of magic around her. "Kyra!" Damian yelled, but it wasn't enough. Pain drunk and sluggish from the damage done to his own magic reserves, Damian used the table to prop himself up. Kyra was only a step away, barely out of his reach. Damian threw himself forward in a lurching movement, grasping for Kyra's hand.

Kyra felt the contact of his skin distantly, but the press of his magic against the torrent in her was impossible to ignore. She could feel him being buffeted by it as his magic flowed upstream to the wound he had caused.

She was cleaved in two. A strange after vision of herself was drinking from the Hunter while Damian wrapped himself around her physically and magically. Kyra could feel the tension in him, could feel the effort it took him. His arms tightened around her and pulled her bodily away from the tear he had created. Or as bodily as possible when discussing their metaphysical attachment to the source of their demonic magic.

Kyra gasped at the sudden loss. The world had dulled around her, every sensation washed out and watered down without the surge of magic to make everything sharp. Damian stumbled away, flung back by the whiplash of released power. They were both panting, Kyra still shuddering with the aftershocks of orgasmic feeding.

Wendy moved forward cautiously, stopping beside the Hunter to feel perfunctorily at his neck. The movement was more for show than real need, given a thin stream of blood leaking from the corner of his mouth. His body was slumped forward; the only thing keeping him from the floor was the zip ties still binding him to the chair.

Kyra hadn't meant to kill him, hadn't meant even meant to feed from him. The surge of power had been like a drug, a burning hunger that demanded male energy. She couldn't feel sorry for it, though it would have been better to have learnt something from him first.

"Are you alright?" Wendy's question drew Kyra's attention to Damian. He was leaning heavily on the table, panting to get his breathing under control.

Kyra moved automatically to flank Damian with Wendy, both women slipping under an arm each. The demons assumed glamours without direction from Wendy as they approached the threshold, the women supporting more of Damian's weight than not. There was no way to get him back to the car inconspicuously, so they made the trip as quickly as possible.

Buddug raised a questioning eyebrow as Damian was deposited beside her, but she held her peace until Wendy and Kyra had settled in the car as well. Kyra took a moment to collect her thoughts and take stock of herself. The throbbing in her side had reduced to nothing, and she couldn't help but finger the wound through the magic of her glamour. Finding clear, unblemished skin, she bit back a gasp.

"What happened?" Buddug demanded.

"We killed a Hunter," Wendy supplied tonelessly.

"He cut me off from my power," Kyra added.

"I fixed it," Damian explained on a sigh, voice weak and thready as consciousness threatened to slip away entirely.

"You can say that again," Kyra laughed.

"Where's Leah?" Buddug's tone showed she was less than impressed by the flippancy of her cohorts.

"We don't know." Damian was starting to slur his words, falling asleep in the back seat. Buddug grunted sourly, momentarily

252 ～ BRONWEN WRITE

turning her focus inwards, searching for something only she could sense.

"She's not far." Buddug lowered her voice, positioning herself so that Damian's head could rest on her shoulder. His glamour flickered before melting away completely. "A few streets north, I'd say."

Wendy started the car without a word. The vehicle purred to life beneath them, Wendy pulling away smoothly to reduce the risk of waking Damian. The sound of his breathing was loud in the relative silence of the car interior, each woman caught in her own thoughts.

~ Forty-One ~

"Is nobody going to tell me what happened?" Buddug hissed, voice low to avoid waking Damian. "Left here," she murmured to Wendy, barely glancing away from her fixed glare on Kyra.

"I'm not entirely sure, to be honest." Kyra sighed, running a hand over her face, realising for the first time she still hadn't raised a new glamour. Even with the heavily tinted windows of the car, it wasn't safe to be so bare-faced.

She reached for her magic, and it jumped erratically over her skin as she wrapped herself in a new face. Her glamour formed without visible struggle, but she was far more aware of the coating of magic on her skin than she had ever been before. Magic crackled across her flesh, overcharged and full of a life she hadn't given it.

"The Hunter...he was a trap." Buddug scoffed but didn't say anything. "I wasn't his first succubus; he had his lust wrapped pretty tight. I don't know how he did it, but when I got through, he..." Kyra searched for the right words. "He cut me off from my magic." Her eyes were trained on her trembling fingers, pressed flat against her lap in a vain attempt to hide the shaking. She tried to pretend her voice wasn't as unsteady as her hands. "It was like there was a gaping hole where it used to be."

"And Damian?"

"He forced it back. He tore something, and it flooded back in." The trembles were spreading now, turning into a full-body shiver as her mind replayed the intoxicating feeling of fullness. "He did something, and it all came back, and there was too much-"

"Right here," Buddug ordered Wendy softly, the whisper barely breaking the flow of Kyra's voice.

"-way too much magic, and it had to go somewhere, so I went for the Hunter, and it was so good, so perfect, and it hurt." Kyra couldn't stress that last word enough, curling her hands into fists against the memory. "It was terrifying."

Silence stretched after Kyra's whispered admission. Even Damian's soft snoring had eased into deep breathing. Wendy's eyes were trained on the road, regardless of how empty the streets were around them, her grip nearing white-knuckled, but her worries always remained her own. If Buddug had any theories about what happened, she wasn't prepared to share them. Or she was simply focused on finding Leah. Either way, Kyra was glad to slip into her own thoughts, chaotic though they were.

"Here," Buddug announced less than a minute later, pointing to another house that could have easily been the twin of the first. The same perfect façade, the same trim garden, facing another leafy street bordered by clean, affordable cars.

Wendy shut the car off but made no other move. The silence between them had grown oppressive, broken only by the deep breaths of Damian's sleep.

Kyra knew instinctively she had to go on alone. Damian was too weakened, Buddug unwilling to align herself further with Kyra's idiocy. Wendy would have to stay to protect them. She knew all this, but it did nothing to make the next decision any easier.

Again, Kyra considered retreating, pretending nothing had changed since Leah had so rudely interrupted the calm of her life. There was safety at The Rose and numerous reasons to return now, empty-handed but physically whole. The wellbeing of her people should have been paramount, not some Hunter she had a crush on. She had already risked so much, and for what? A woman who had tried to kill her?

She couldn't even begin to convince herself, let alone those who had willingly risked themselves to help her. The whole situation felt increasingly unfair, and she felt more and more powerless with every passing moment. It was overwhelming, the pressure building around her. Her breathing was beginning to speed, racing to catch up with the tempo of her thoughts.

"Tell me I'm making the right choice," Kyra broke the quiet, needing external validation, some kind of sign that she wasn't completely insane. Even as she spoke the words, Kyra knew she couldn't turn back. Wendy could have called her three kinds of stupid, Buddug could have demanded she go home, but she'd still take the chance. Like some lovesick fool.

Kyra's fingers were releasing her seat belt before Wendy could speak.

"You're making the right choice," Wendy drawled. "Now go get your girl."

Kyra launched herself from the car on a surge of determined energy, forcing herself to move before she could question herself any further. The walk to the house felt like crossing a thousand miles, and it was over in the blink of an eye. She assessed her options, standing on the edge of the sidewalk, knowing she would need to move quickly to avoid drawing unwanted attention.

She couldn't go via the backyard like Wendy had; a precision strike was beyond her capabilities. Instead, she strode with confidence she didn't feel to the front door. Knocking smartly, she hoped this guard would be less crafty but equally male. The moment in which the door swung inward, Kyra found herself doubting the wisdom of such a brash action. The first glimpse of a strong, decidedly male, face was enough to pull a smile to her lips.

~ Forty-Two ~

He didn't have the time to register her presence, let alone question it, before he was hit with the full force of her magic. A wordless flex of her power, and he was backing away from the door, granting her entrance as his eyes hungrily drank her in.

She wielded her magic with none of her usual finesse, the lingering rush of pure power turning her fine blade into a wide hammer. This play of lust didn't require words or a carefully crafted fantasy. He received undistilled demon magic, almost as potent as the Hunter at the other house. Another push and he was leading her to a back bedroom, footsteps hurried to collect the pleasure she seemed to be promising.

Kyra saw nothing of the house, nothing of the room the young guard led her to. Her focus tunnelled immediately to the calmly seated Leah, perched on the edge of the bed, hands folded gently in her lap. The sight of her drove the breath from Kyra, shocked by the wholeness of her skin, unmarked and unblemished. Her eyes were equally clear, watching Kyra enter the room with calm indifference. The male Hunter was dismissed with a thought, another small push of power.

As he began to pass her, squeezing to not brush his unworthy form against her own, Kyra thought better of it. With lightning reflexes, she placed a hand on his arm in passing. He froze immediately, halting despite the lightness of her touch. A final thought, a final flex, and he dropped to the floor.

Killing him took more effort, more power, than she would have liked, but it felt necessary. So soon after feeding from the other Hunter, Kyra felt full and sated, almost sleepy as her energy focused on digesting her meal. It was enough for her to lose her glamour, lose the last line of defence she had between herself and Leah's too impassive gaze. She couldn't have risked him leaving the house and harming those waiting in the car, but the small amount she took from him in the act filled her to bursting.

Maybe it should have worried her, being so close to powerless, so close to human, with Leah so far removed from the woman she knew. For several seconds they simply eyed each other, Kyra in the doorway beside a rapidly cooling corpse, and Leah sat on crisp sheets of white. If Leah felt anything for the man, she showed no sign of it. Her eyes had traced his descent briefly before turning back to watching Kyra.

Kyra knew she should break the silence, should say something to gauge Leah's state of mind at least. Finding the words seemed beyond her though, caught speechless for the first time in a long time.

What she didn't expect was to be hit from behind, a sharp blow landing between her shoulder blades. The shock of impact as she landed on hands and knees was dulled by rising panic as Kyra tried desperately to suck air into lungs that refused to cooperate. Heavy footfalls tracked from the doorway into her line of sight, revealing a towering man-shaped wall of muscle.

Kyra couldn't breathe, couldn't move. She had no choice but to watch as he leaned down and tangled thick fingers in her hair. He pulled her head back sharply, the line of her neck straining as she met piercing grey eyes that felt familiar in a distant way. It was a blandly handsome face, the kind that could have graced a magazine but lacked anything truly unique about it. It tickled the back of her mind, but it was difficult to think through the growing haze of pain.

"I wasn't sure if you'd be dumb enough to come for her." His voice was equally bland, near toneless despite the painful way he held her head back. Crouched over Kyra, examining her like a science experiment gone wrong, he remained expressionless. He took no joy in her pain.

The strange Hunter shoved her away, and Kyra had no choice but to fall into a heap in the centre of the room. Air was returning to her lungs slowly, too slowly. Her heart was pushing oxygen around her body, allowing her mind to focus beyond the fissions of terror. Concentrating through the ache in her back, through her throbbing side where she had hit the ground, Kyra took her magic and honed it into the sharpest blade she could wield. She lashed out with deadly accuracy, magic slicing into his mind.

And her magic lashed back, seeming to bounce ineffectively against an invisible barrier. She gripped it all the tighter, heart stopping for the moment it took to reassure herself that it hadn't been torn away from her again. A dark laughter filled the room, deep and rumbling as he stepped forward. His large boot, heavy with the full force of his swing, caught her square in the gut. Any air she had managed to claim was driven out of her by the kick. Gasping harshly, Kyra's gaze searched for Leah, searched for salvation.

Leah watched on impassively, eyes on Kyra but somehow seeing through her. The hands in her lap didn't twitch; she didn't flinch as the sounds of landing blows filled the air. Kyra kept her eyes on Leah, even as the woman became hazy, her form swimming in tears that sprung without permission.

The Hunter was silent as he beat Kyra, blows landing with full strength and delivered with a calmness that chilled Kyra in the few moments she was able to think before the pain became too much. She had curled in after the first kick to her stomach, instinctively moving to protect her middle. But this had left her head bare. A kick to her temple had sent the room spinning, her head splitting in bright flashes of pain and darkness that didn't edge nearly close enough to save her.

Wrapping arms around her head, pulling herself in tighter, did nothing to dissuade him. Thick fingers were back in her hair, yanking her head back, but she refused to loosen her own grip on her skull.

She was pulled up bodily, and Kyra scrambled to get her feet under herself, anything to reduce the painful tearing of hair from her scalp. Cloven hooves had barely gotten their ground before he was driving a fist into her stomach. She wanted to double over, her body bending under the blow, but the hand in her hair made it impossible.

Pain radiated across her body, unmarked skin burning with the same agony as the places where bruises were rapidly forming, her whole form alight with it. Like the magic, it engulfed every nerve, an all-consuming thing that she couldn't possibly ignore, even as her eyes still fought to find Leah. Leah, who was watching with an unseeing gaze. Leah, who was doing nothing to stop it.

After minutes, maybe hours, the blur of pain the only thing Kyra could feel with any clarity, the Hunter let her fall again. Her right eye had swollen shut, but she couldn't remember the punch that had shattered the socket. A red haze covered the left. Blood, her sluggish mind supplied. She was bleeding. She couldn't see through the blood.

His footsteps, still loud, still heavy, tracked towards what Kyra thought was the bed. Towards Leah. Tremors of pain wracked her body, every movement sending fresh flashes of agony. She needed to stop him; she needed to protect Leah.

"Now, my pet..." His voice warmed, the tone twisting Kyra's stomach with a sickness she knew all too well. "Why don't we end this?"

Kyra forced herself to move. She fought the shaking in her fingers to clear her eye, swallowing the nausea from the pain, from the way the room was spinning. A scream clawed at her throat, but Kyra wouldn't give it voice. She'd die first.

Leah stood slowly, eyes still trained on Kyra unflinchingly. A knife appeared in her hand and, rather than feel afraid, Kyra wondered if it was the same one that had so recently threatened her life.

"Before you try using that..." Kyra's voice cracked over the pain, throat raw from swallowed screams, but her tone was steady. Leah halted her advance, and Kyra pushed her advantage, small though it may end up being. "I just need you to know that I'm sorry. I'm sorry for pushing you away. I'm sorry for thinking I knew what was best for you, for us. I'm sorry for not being honest with you, for being too afraid to face our enemies.

"Mostly, I'm sorry for not having the courage to tell you I love you. You deserve to be told every day how important you are, how beautiful and amazing and intelligent you are." Kyra took a deep breath, regretting it immediately. Her ribs were definitely broken.

Something flickered behind the impassive mask over Leah's features. Emboldened, Kyra pushed on. "I still don't know why I didn't kill you that night, but I think about it all the time. Sometimes I wonder what my life would look like if I had killed you. I can't say if it would be easier, but I know it would be darker." Leah took a faltering step forward. The other Hunter shifted, arms crossed over his chest, but he seemed more interested in letting the scene play out than stopping it. "I'd be darker and dumber if that's possible.

"I've been an idiot; I can see that now." Another step, another flash of unnamed emotion. "I can only hope you'll forgive me." The final step and Leah was crouching down, bringing her face in line with the mess that was Kyra's. Still, Kyra didn't move, didn't flinch away, simply waiting with bated breath to see if it would be her last. "Forgive me for being a coward. Forgive me for fearing the hold you have over me. I'm scared of living a long life with you, just to watch you die. I'm afraid of what the Church will do to us, to you.

"Mostly, I'm afraid of going back to The Rose without you. I'm afraid of not knowing what it's like to love you every day and be loved by you."

Leah shifted, the blade shining large and unavoidable in Kyra's line of sight. Where would she plunge it? Through her heart? That would only be fitting. Kyra waited for the sharp sting of the blade, the gentle release of death. Holding herself still, she awaited the killing blow with passive acceptance. Even waiting for the pain, Kyra revelled in the feeling of Leah's presence. It was hard not to take pleasure, or at least comfort, in it.

"I grow tired of waiting," he spoke, real frustration entering his voice.

Leah stirred slightly, moving against Kyra. Kyra continued to wait patiently for Leah to end her suffering, to quiet the tumble of thoughts and emotions. She was in no real rush to greet death, but she couldn't help but think there were worse ways to go. A sliver of sadness tried to intrude, tried to point out Leah's own existence would be short-lived once her body was found, but that was a middling thing.

Leah stirred again, shifting as though uncomfortable, fighting an itch or pulling away from a pain within herself. Maybe she needed a little time to find the right angle, the exact spot to plunge the knife. It would be rude of Kyra to rush her.

Leah lifted her head, gazing at Kyra through blond lashes. They were gossamer, so thin and pale. Kyra was struck again by Leah's beauty. Not the flawless beauty of a demon, or even the poor reflection of human symmetry, but in the fire barely banked in her eyes. The spark of life was undeniable, and Kyra hated herself for the hope it stoked in her chest.

This was better, Kyra mused distantly. She could die looking in Leah's eyes. She only wished that the fire wasn't as muted, that her curiosity and passion were at the forefront.

Raising a hand slowly, gently, not wanting to startle Leah into movement, Kyra ran her hand through the ends of Leah's hair. Her clawed fingers tangled easily in the softness of the ponytail, and she wished that she could have seen it down at least once more. Seeing Leah haloed by curtains of light would have been nice.

Leah shifted again, this time leaning forward to place a gentle kiss on Kyra's lips. It was a fleeting thing, the softest press. It was momentary, but Kyra could feel it in waves of shivers over her skin. Leah seemed equally affected, blinking owlishly down at Kyra.

"Hi," Kyra cooed without thinking, watching Leah wake up entirely before her.

"Hi," she murmured in response, a soft smile splitting her features into the woman Kyra loved so dearly.

"I said, kill her." The Hunter roared.

With lightning quickness, Leah twirled in her crouch, arm lashing out with a fluid movement. The knife left her fingers, flying through the air in a streak of silver precision. The Hunter yelled, twisting from the blade, allowing it to catch him on the shoulder rather than solidly in the chest. A large hand darted up, pressing against rapidly spreading blood. For a moment, Kyra thought he meant to pull the blade free and turn it on them. Instead, he ran from the room, disappearing into the darkened house.

Leah had turned back to Kyra the moment the knife had left her hand, fingers ghosting over Kyra's face, wanting to touch but fearing the pain it would cause. "I need to get you out of here."

"Wendy's out front." Kyra coughed, vaguely aware of the taste of blood on her tongue. "Help me get to the car."

Kyra was glad to be wrapped in the cool night air; the darkness broken by uniformly placed streetlights was comforting after the bland brightness of the house. Even leaning heavily on Leah, her arm a solid weight around Kyra's aching waist, they moved slowly to the waiting car. The Hunter's body heat seeped into her skin, a physical link to a world that threatened to spin away under the multi-layered pain of her body.

Wendy was out of the car the moment movement caught her eye, rushing to Kyra's other side to take a share of her weight. Kyra went from limping to being gently dragged to the car. Buddug's face watched them from the front passenger seat, eyes tight with concern. The short walk from the front door seemed to stretch into oblivion, the space too much for Kyra's aching limbs, her thoughts fading in and out of focus. Succumbing to the pain was so very tempting, no matter how her mind panicked at the prospect. What if she never woke again?

Kyra was only vaguely aware of being pushed and pulled into the backseat, Leah and Wendy trying to be both quick and careful at once. Damian was awake, barely, watching but unable to help beyond weakly wrapping an arm around Kyra's shoulders once she was seated beside him. Leah slid into the seat on Kyra's other side, her touch light as she carefully manoeuvred Kyra's seat belt into place.

"What happened in there?" Buddug's tone was low but insistent. Wendy slid back into the driver's seat, pulling away from the curb silently. The hum of the engine was the only sound for a very long moment.

Nestled between Damian and Leah, both fighting to stay awake but near exhaustion, Kyra considered the question. It was hard to focus, her mind swimming with relief as the adrenaline that had carried her through the night finally left her. She had a vague understanding of what had passed in that room at best, but a niggling thought refused to go unvoiced.

"True love's kiss." She couldn't help the giggle that spilled forth at the thought, at the statement. It still seemed ludicrous, but here they were. Wendy snorted gracelessly, obviously sharing Kyra's feelings on the matter.

Darkness was creeping at the edges of her vision she couldn't fight it any longer.

Buddug only hummed in thought, keeping her own counsel. The silence that followed, though fleeting to Kyra's frayed nerves, was enough for her body to finally give in. Her eyes must have slid shut, her head falling to rest upon Leah's shoulder. Her glamour, held close to allow her to cross to the car, fell almost immediately. Wendy would no doubt ensure Kyra never complained of the cost of tinted windows again.

~ Forty-Three ~

Kyra awoke in the familiar curve of her nest, morning stealing over her in lazy streams of light. Her mind was slow to catch up, the night replaying itself in snippets until she became sure of two things. Leah was back and unharmed and, hopefully, there to stay. And she did not hurt anywhere near as much as she should have. The warmth of the first drove away worries about the cost of the second. She could yell at Buddug and Damian about the exorbitant cost of saving her life later.

For now, she wanted to focus on Leah curled at the edge of the dip of her nest, carefully balanced to ensure she didn't fall onto Kyra while still being close enough to touch. Leah's small, pale hand looked ethereal against the lavender hue of her skin, but it was pleasantly warm and radiated more than simple body heat.

Kyra considered not waking her, considered watching her sleep, but even if the general creepiness of such a sentiment hadn't stopped her, the flutter of Leah's eyelids did. The Hunter graced Kyra with a soft smile, shifting in the space she had made for herself to stretch. Kyra was instantly sad for the loss of contact.

"Morning," she said instead, returning Leah's smile when it turned more solidly to her face.

"Morning."

Carefully, Kyra extracted herself from the bed, not wanting to jostle Leah while trying to keep her movements smooth, a challenge when rolling from the hollowed centre of a nest. Still, she felt she hadn't made a complete fool of herself, and Leah wasn't laughing, so there was that. Her joints ached, and there was a lingering tightness to her ribs, but it felt like the beating had happened to someone else months ago.

"I'm just going to..." Kyra trailed off, gesturing awkwardly to the bathroom. Leah nodded, pretending not to see the way Kyra's cheeks flushed with colour and embarrassment. Doubt returned with a vengeance, reminding her snidely that Leah hadn't actually returned her feelings. Any declarations of love had been entirely one-sided, and while the possession seemed to be removed, there was nothing to say Leah would actually stay.

Kyra had still lied. She had still mistrusted Leah. Yes, she had risked her life and the lives of those who mattered most to her, but that didn't mean she was deserving of Leah's love. Leah didn't owe her anything; there was no debt to be paid, no commitment created. Performing her morning ablutions, it was hard not to convince herself that Leah had stayed out of pity or assumed obligation.

Her thoughts hadn't slowed by the time she returned to the natural light of her room. Leah had opened the curtains further in Kyra's absence, allowing the sun to paint every wall in warmth.

Kyra was forced to wait and think even longer as Leah saw to her own needs, perched on the edge of her bed. Wendy, or maybe Raquel, had left a spare toothbrush for the Hunter. For some reason, the innocuous white and pink tool had warmed Kyra, the implication of permanence feeding the budding hope still alive from the night's chaste kiss.

The tangle of emotions sat heavy in her stomach, nauseating and thick. Hope and doubt warred tirelessly at the back of her mind. And at the forefront. And in every space in between. She couldn't decide if she wanted Leah to hurry out of the bathroom or spend an eternity in there. Too many questions, too many doubts, too many hints, and never enough information. Kyra hated not having enough information.

When Leah did return, Kyra was no closer to knowing her own emotions, let alone those of the Hunter who stood in the doorway of her bathroom, head cocked to the side in a movement Kyra had missed more than she could say. The curiosity was back in Leah's eyes, burning with a spark of something mischievous that made Kyra's stomach turn over not unpleasantly.

"What?" Leah broke the silence that had fallen over them, but Kyra was still unsure if she could find her own voice.

"I love you." There it was. A small, near broken thing, carried on the breath of a sigh, barely loud enough to be heard by the air around them.

The softening smile across Leah's lips said she heard them none-theless. She crossed the room unhurriedly, as though giving Kyra the time she needed to process, to understand what was happening. Kyra would have been grateful for the additional time if Leah's slow steps hadn't ended in the other woman settling herself in Kyra's lap. The warm weight of her was worth the wait, but still something that should have been experienced long ago.

Long, pale arms wrapped themselves around Kyra's shoulders to hook together behind her neck, holding her right where Leah wanted her. "I love you too," she murmured directly against Kyra's lips, brushing them with her own. That was good, direct and infor-mative, something Kyra could work with.

Any other thoughts were driven from her mind as Leah set about kissing her soundly. Kyra wasn't complaining, pulling the Hunter more firmly to her while wrapping arms and wings around her. Safely cocooned in the well of silence made by Kyra's wings, they were finally able to pretend there was no world beyond each other.

Epilogue

It still felt strange and fragile, being out in the world with Leah at her side. That Kyra was a borderline hermit hadn't meant much when she had been focused solely on The Rose, but with Leah smiling so sweetly, it had been hard to refuse going out. Out in public, amongst humans. Out where it was dangerous, and things were beyond Kyra's control. Out where she could watch sunlight dance in Leah's hair and share gentle smiles over cafe tables and coffee that was probably too expensive.

Leah's quiet laughter, an abortive giggle snorted into her mug, warmed Kyra more than the bright sun overhead. People passed them, pressing together to fit between the wall of the cafe and the crowded outdoor tables perched as close to the road as possible. Kyra's chair wobbled on the uneven ground every time she shifted, and the hard wood was doing no favours to her posture, but she would have sat there forever just to hear Leah make that sound again. She would have given the world to crystallise the moment, have it frozen in its perfection for eternity. Was she even allowed to experience so much happiness?

The laughter died, Leah suddenly stiff in her chair, eyes sharp. Her gaze was over Kyra's shoulder, lips pulling down in a frown. Before Kyra could turn to look, an all too familiar voice drifted over her shoulder, dropping a lump of ice into her stomach and dimming the sun.

"Hey, Kyra." The smirk was audible in Elizabeth's voice.

"Fuck."

ACKNOWLEDGEMENTS

Thank you to my amazing partner, better half and wife, Emma; words can't describe what you mean to me and how important having your support is. I'm sorry for all the rambling you've had to put up with and all the rambling you're going to face in future.

Thank you to my friends, Lucy, Kir and Emily for being the best cheerleaders an author can have. Without you, I'd have given up five times over.
Lucy, you are a constant source of motivation, Damian owes his strength to you.
Kir, you've been a voice of reason and enthusiastic sounding board all in one.
Emily, without you I'd still be crying into a half-formed marketing plan questioning every life choice leading to this moment.

Thank you to Charlie Knight, for being an amazing editor and having the patience of a saint. This book would be nothing without your guidance. I wish more people had half your heart, passion and fierceness (as long as it came with your morals and ethics).

Finally, for Cath, the mother who saw a scared little kid and thought "yeah, I'm going to keep that one". You didn't have to be my friend, or my parent, but you did both and I will always be grateful for that.

Bronwen lives in regional Australia with their wife, cats and angry little dog, where they spend most of their time trying to forget that half the native fauna and flora want to kill them. When they're not writing, thinking about writing or crying over writing, they're playing with yarn. The only thing that outnumbers their list of story ideas is their unfinished knitting projects.

www.ingramcontent.com/pod-product-compliance
Lightning Source LLC
Chambersburg PA
CBHW070549120726
47909CB00007B/2296